Time Benders and the Machine

Time Benders and the Machine

JB Yanni

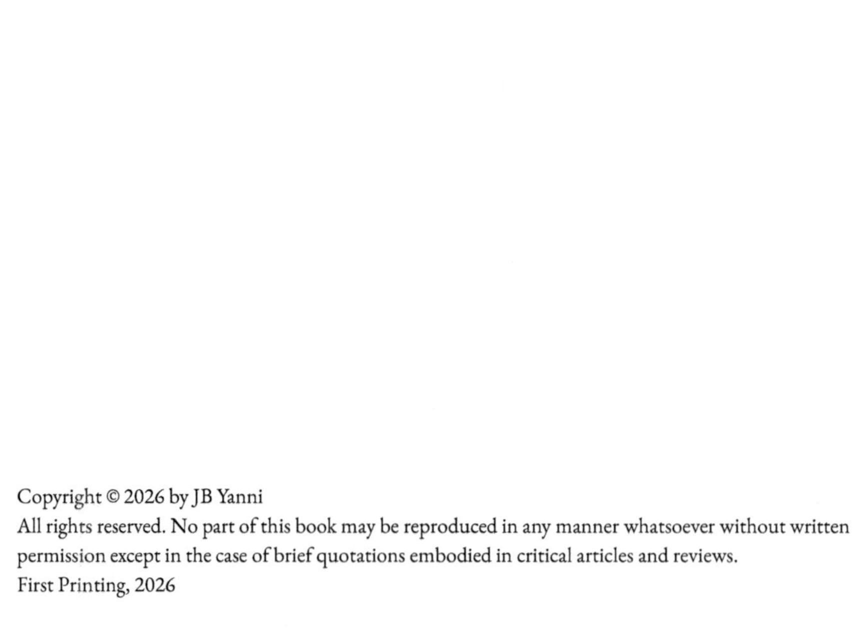

For my three children, who have blessed my life in so many ways, and been the light of my life since the first day. It is for you that I write this book.

Deb's room had walls that were a yellow-like color that had probably once been creamy white. The curtains were grey, the desk old, scratched, and brown. Three or four pictures sitting on the dresser were the only reminder of the life Deb had left behind only a few short weeks ago. As she sat on the bed, with the drab lavender colored bedspread on it, she looked around at the books, one sketch pad and some charcoal sticks, and wondered how it could have changed so quickly for her, her two brothers and her younger sister. She took out a piece of paper and sat at the desk to write her best friend, Denise, a letter. They hadn't seen one another since the funeral and Deb felt terrible about not sending Denise a note to let her know where she was and what was going on.

Five weeks ago, Deb, her brothers Kenneth and Joseph, and younger sister Kimberly were having a great camping trip with their family friends, the Simpsons. Denis Simpson, Deb's best friend, and her two brothers, had lived next door to Deb and her family since they started school. On the camping trip, Deb was getting so bothered by Kim wanting to tag along with her and Denise and now, thinking back, Deb couldn't even remember what Kim did. Whatever it was, it was no longer important. A sheriff's car pulled up near Mr. Simpson's car. The sheriff came over to talk to Mr. and Mrs. Simpson. Mrs. Simpson told the children to take their dog, Heidi, for a walk. When the group of them came back, the sheriff was gone, and the Simpsons were packing the camping gear up. They asked Denise and her two brothers to keep packing and sat Deb, Kim, and their two brothers down at the picnic table.

The news was terrible. Deb's parents had been away that week with their father's business partner, Mr. Davis. Mr. Davis had his own plane, and they flew in it to Colorado to go on a skiing trip with several important clients of theirs. The plane crashed. Everyone had been killed. Now they were heading home to meet Aunt Alicia, who was back at Deb's house. Then there was a funeral. There were hundreds of people there, including the mayor of Cambridge, where they were from, and several people that Aunt Alicia said were from Washington, D.C. The day after the funeral, Aunt Alicia left Ken in charge of the three other kids, and said she had an appointment with the family lawyer. Deb and Ken asked to attend along with Aunt Alicia, but she had said they needed to stay home. Two days after the funeral, Aunt Alicia told the children the news that put Deb in this dorm room. Aunt Alicia had been awarded custody of the four children and she just didn't have a way to keep them in her small apartment in New York City and with her busy schedule as a layout designer for Vogue Magazine, so they were all going to boarding school. It was an excellent school, she said, where their father had gone, and in fact, where President Kennedy had gone, as if that was going to make this gigantic shift in their lives seem like something positive.

The thing was, they didn't have any time to plan, or talk to their friends, as they left the very next morning for Choate Rosemary Hall in Wallingford, Connecticut. It was September twenty-third when they arrived a few weeks ago. The campus looked much like most of Cambridge, with many trees and buildings built and planted when America was a young country. That part was alright with Deb. She liked old buildings and history, American history in particular. And she had always enjoyed reading, especially when she was sitting in the tall chair in her father's office while he worked at his desk at night and on weekends. It was her favorite time. She missed them so much.

Her brothers didn't particularly like it here at all. Ken, the oldest of Deb's brothers, had been on the high school football team in Cambridge and he was both an outstanding athlete and had been being recruited by several colleges. He also had been thinking about going into the Marines, but he told Deb just today that he doubted that was going to happen now, since he had to watch out for all of his younger siblings. And Joe, who was a year younger than Deb, he was something of a math and science genius, so was most frustrated with the loss of access to Harvard's science labs. Since their mother was a professor in the math department, she had access, and Joe was always over there at the lab when she worked in the evenings and weekends. Not that Deb would notice, but the labs at Choate were, according to Joe, so backward, and according to Ken, President Kennedy probably used the equipment when he attended Choate forty years ago. Deb was not sure it was that long ago when John F. Kennedy was a student at Choate, nor did she believe the equipment was purchased forty years ago, but clearly it was older than the equipment at Harvard. Truth be told, Joe was probably saying he hated it here because of the equipment, but Deb knew what was really bothering Joe. He was crushed with grief. Finally, there was Kim, Deb's little sister, who had been so annoying on the camping trip, and was now so despondent over the loss of her parents, home and toys. At ten years old, who could blame her? Her world didn't exist farther than her classroom, her friends, her toy room and the family. Deb wasn't sure if she was glad Kim didn't know much better, or if she wished she were in that same situation.

Here they were, all in different rooms, with the boys in one building, but different floors, and Deb and Kim in another building, all girls; and while Kim was on the first floor with two girls to share a room with, Deb, being older, had her own room. They saw each other every day at morning prayer, meals and during free time. That wasn't so bad, as they spent about that much time together before the accident, but it just felt different and wrong. Clearly it was going to be difficult to write a letter to Denise, thought Deb, in this state of mind.

Just then, someone knocked on Deb's door. When she opened it, there stood Kenny, her older brother, and he was holding Kim's hand. "What is this?" Deb asked.

"I found her wondering around the boys' hall, looking for Joe and me," replied Kenny, "she said she wanted us all to be together again, so I brought her here. I can't find Joe."

"Well, come on in then. Tell me what's bothering you, Kim, please?"

"There was a girl downstairs reading out loud a book to the other girls. It was that favorite book that Mommy and I used to read together. Do you remember?" Kim said as she walked over and sat on Deb's bed.

Deb thought a minute about whether to tell Kim about the things she made sure she snuck out of their house that were not on the list of items they could bring to boarding school, but Deb thought she should take them anyway. Then she said, "Yes, I remember you and Mom used to read that Little House on the Prairie book. Is that what they're reading downstairs?"

Kim said, "Yes, they're reading one of them, but it kept reminding of the nights when Mommy and I read the first two books. I really miss her and Daddy so much." Kenny sat down next to Kim and put his arm around her and pulled her close. Deb decided to go ahead and get out the two things she took from home. She opened her bottom dresser drawer and went under the clothes and pulled out two books. The first was a photo album of their family Christmas celebrations since Kim was born. The second, was the much-worn copy of the Little House on the Prairie book that their mother had first read to Deb when she was Kim's age, and now was reading and promised to give to Kim. Deb held the two books out to Kim. "Which would you like to look at Kim?" asked Deb.

Kim smiled through her tears and pulled the photo album from Deb's hands. Deb sat down on the other side of Kim, and the three of them opened the album rather reverently and started looking through the pictures and sharing their thoughts and memories of these favorite times of their family. The trip to Michigan to enjoy sledding, cross-country skiing and making s'mores by the fireplace, the trip to Key West to enjoy Christmas in the sunshine and go deep sea fishing with their father, and the real favorite, spending Christmas with their family at their grandparents' home. They all cried some as they looked and shared memories, and then Kim leaned into Kenny and fell asleep. Just before the eight o'clock curfew, he carried her down to her room and laid her in bed.

He looked at Deb by the doors to the girls' dorm as he was about to leave to make it back to the boys' dorm before the curfew and said, "I'm so glad you took that photo album, Deb, it was great to look at those pictures, and I'm sure it helped Kim tonight get over her sadness. Thanks for this."

Deb gave Kenny a brief hug and said, "Kenny, we're all in this together. If we make it through this, it'll be because we stick together."

Ken laughed a little, pushed open the door, and looked back and with a small smirk, "Don't call me Kenny, Deb. I'm seventeen and don't need to be called by my little boy nickname."

"Yes, you do, Kenny, it reminds me of better times," Deb yelled back and Ken took off for the boys' dorm.

Walking back up to her room, she wondered what was happening with Joe, as Ken had said he was not in his room tonight. Deb got herself ready for bed and laid down and thought of ways to keep her brothers and little sister together now that their lives had changed forever; the letter to Denise forgotten and unfinished for the time being.

2

About a week later, Deb sat at a small table near the fireplace in the community area of Rosemary Hall, one of the original buildings of the girls' school that was the founding school of this whole campus, studying for a history test that was coming up. Kim sat nearby with a group of girls from her floor, all reading their current books for book reports that were due the week right before the Thanksgiving break. Joe walked up to Deb and slumped down on the sofa near the small table where Deb was reviewing class notes and going through chapters in her history book covering the Kennedy presidency and assassination, the latest unit of her history class. Deb looked up, "Where've you been Joe? We haven't seen you in a few days during free time?"

Joe responded slowly, "I met one of the caretakers here. His name is Mr. Brewster. He lives near campus on a farm, sort of, and we started talking one day last week about the lab that he was working near, when I came out. I've learned he's a really smart man that apparently came here to work after his wife was killed in a car accident. So, he's got a lot in common with us and I kind of wanted to talk to someone."

Deb thought about the best way to respond. "Well, Joe, it's great that you found someone to talk to. You know you can always come to me and Kenny if you need anything or just want to talk."

"Ken told me you had a photo album from home. Can I see it?" Joe worked to change the subject a little since he didn't really want to get all upset again over the loss of his parents.

Deb wondered about why Joe didn't want to talk, but decided to leave that alone. "Sure, I can go get it. Can you sit here with my things for a minute and keep an eye on Kim?"

"Of course, I'll be right here, and on the job," Joe replied, but shut his eyes.

When Deb returned with the photo album, three girls surrounded Joe. Joe not only was the smartest of the four of them, he was very cute. At fourteen years old, he was getting attention from girls. Deb sat back down and continued to study, setting the photo album on the side of the table. She didn't want to barge in on the conversation Joe was having with these three girls. The girls were trying to get his attention by acting like they had no idea about something they were all supposed to be working on in science class.

The clock over the fireplace chimed four thirty. Deb cleaned up her papers and books and prepared to head to the dining hall for dinner. Ken walked into the hall just then and came over to the table where Deb was working.

"What're you studying there, Deb?"

"History exam coming up."

"Joe, you coming with us to the dining hall?" Deb asked as she looked at Joe, holding court on the sofa with the girls.

"Yep. Did you bring the album?"

"It's right here, Joe," Deb indicated by pointing at the book.

Ken then asked as the girls all got up and gave their goodbyes to Joe, "Joe, where have you been hiding lately?"

Deb went over and asked Kim to wrap it up so they could go to dinner, and Kim jumped up and headed over to the sofa where Joe had sat back down.

Joe hugged Kim and answered, "Been talking with a caretaker, Mr. Brewster, for the last few days during break. He worked on testing atomic bombs out west for a company that was working with the government on those bombs. He lost his wife in a car accident about ten years ago and took this job to just get away, he said."

"Wow," it amazed Ken that Joe had talked to anyone since he had been so quiet since they arrived at Choate weeks ago, "So this guy has taken you under his wing, huh?"

The four of them walked to the dining hall and everyone talked about people they had met since arriving here and how that was going. Ken was asking them all kinds of questions to gauge their acceptance of the new circumstances. Deb was sure he was doing this because he felt responsible for them all. As dinner ended, Kim mentioned that one girl had talked last night about one of the classroom buildings that hadn't been used since the early 1900s. They had used it for a while for storage, but the girls all thought it was haunted or something. They all agreed it would be a fun adventure, so they met up after changing out of their school uniforms in front of the boys' dorm. Deb and Ken said they should go check it out during the free time tonight for a fun adventure, so off they went.

The old building was dark, and some windows had wood covering broken pieces of glass from the inside. The four siblings walked up to the front of the building and, of course, found the doors locked. Ken said, "Joe, you go with Deb that way and I will take Kim and we will go this way around. If you find a way in, send Deb around to us, and if I find a way, I will send Kim around."

Joe and Deb started around the right of the building, checking windows and doors to see if anything was unlocked. They had just gotten to the back of the building when Joe saw a few steps down to a door that appeared to go into a basement. He went down to check and found the door unlocked. He called up to Deb, "Go get Ken and Kim. This door is unlocked!"

Deb started back to the front and turned around, saying, "Joe, don't go in without us. I'll be right back." She took off running and found Ken and Kim on the other side of the building, trying to look into a window to see if it was unlocked. When she found them, Ken was lifting Kim up to see if she could fit through a broken section. She called in a loud whisper voice, "Kenny, Joe found an open door around in back."

Ken put Kim down, and they followed Deb back around to the door Joe found. He was standing there in the doorway, with the door open, waiting for them. The four of them went into a room that likely at one point was a boiler room where the heating oil was kept when the building was in use. They wandered around for a bit and found a stairwell. Ken led them up the stairs, which put them in the main hallway of the building. They headed back to the front of the building through the hallway, testing doors. All the doors on the first floor led to old classrooms. There were desks and chalkboards, papers and books, and it looked somewhat spooky with the moonlight streaming in through the windows and the dust on everything, somewhat like class had just been dismissed. There was chalk on the tray of the chalkboard and papers on the teacher's desk. Kim whispered, "This is why people say this building is haunted, cause it seems like a ghost is about to come in and sit down for class. What happened that they just up and abandoned this building like this?"

Joe, who always thought he had the answers to science questions, replied, "Perhaps the building became unsafe, and they immediately had to close it and transfer all these classes to another building."

Deb thought for a minute and countered, "I think they shut it down because of the move of the girls' part of the school way back at the turn of the century. I was reading about the history of Choate Rosemary and there was first a girls' school founded by a woman whose last name was Choate. And then her husband formed the boys' academy, but in nineteen hundred the girls' part of the school moved. Maybe that is why it looks like they just up and left earlier today. Except for all the dust."

Kim whispered in reply, "Someone told me that the upstairs rooms used to be the dorm rooms for the girls, and that's probably where the ghosts go in the evening. "

Ken wrapped his arm around Kim's shoulders and pulled her toward the classroom door. "You don't have to be afraid, Kimmy. We're here with you."

Ken tried to steer them out of the classroom they had entered, "Let's keep moving. Kim mentioned that this was a storage place, so there might be old records somewhere. Let's see if we can find any records of when Dad was a student here."

They all thought that was a great idea, and they headed up the main staircase. They first saw some offices, probably the original teachers' offices at this school. Deb wanted to look around more, and was thumbing through old books when the others headed down the hall to the next rooms. Kim came running back to the room that Deb was in and anxiously called to her, "Deb, come on, Joe and Kenny found a bunch of file cabinets in a room, and they want you to come quick. Kenny said you can come back and dig through dusty old books some other time and take what you like. He's sure no one will miss them. But come quickly!"

Deb grabbed the two books she had found that she wanted to look through and followed Kim down the hall. The room they entered was indeed filled with filing cabinets. They lined the cabinets up in rows, and there were three rows back-to-back in the middle and two rows against the wall. There was a lot of light in this room, thankfully, since no windows were broken, and there was moonlight coming in from a whole side of the room full of windows. Joe and Ken were pulling open some drawers on the first row of file cabinets when Deb and Kim came in.

"There are records of all the students that attended here from the first year of the girls' school, Deb. This entire row of cabinets has years noted on the front of the drawers."

Deb walked over to a drawer marked 1930 to 1935. She opened it and practically screamed, "Look, I found the records of John F. Kennedy. He was a student here. You all know that Dad met his business partner, Mr. Davis, on the day that President Kennedy was assassinated in Dallas, Texas, right? They were both in a bar after the news came out of the death of the President and began talking then. Later, they were sending letters back and forth and came up with the business idea that they started discussing in the letters shortly after Martin Luther King was killed. Both of them were in Memphis when Dr. King was shot, too. They had travelled there, again, to witness history. They share two of the saddest days of American History together."

Kim looked at Deb kind of funny and said, "How did Daddy know the President and the man that did the speech in Washington, this Martin Luther King? I didn't know Martin Luther King was a President or something. I thought it was just a day off from school."

Joe kind of laughed, and Ken stopped him. "Joe, Kim is still pretty little. She hasn't gotten all this in her history classes yet. Kim, Dad didn't know the President, he just really liked him and went there to see him because he thought he could get close to the President, and was trying to do that. Martin Luther King was an important man in American history because he protested the segregation of black people in the south, and did a very important speech in Washington D.C. that everyone remembers. You get that day off from school to honor him."

Deb continued to look through the files that had data on President Kennedy. It was interesting to see comments from his teachers and the staff here. She then closed the file and moved over to the file cabinet where dates matched when her father was here. Finding the drawer with 1950, as that was the year their father graduated from Choate. Thumbing through the files, she found her father's file and called out to her siblings. They all gathered around. There were pictures from each year he was attending, and all the report cards and comments from teachers. He graduated 5th in his class and selected as the student speaker for his graduation. Deb read all of this out and Kim started to cry. Joe turned away from them, and Ken had a grim look on his face, like he now had a goal of being like his father. Kim reached up and pulled the picture from his senior year and took it in her hands.

She said, "I want this picture. Can I have it?"

Ken replied first and said, "Yes, there's one for each of us to have. Joe, which one do you want? Deb?"

Joe said rather sullenly, "I don't want one."

Deb looked at Joe, and then at Ken, and took both of the remaining pictures. She figured Joe might want it later, and she'd just keep it safe until then.

Joe started walking to the door, and looked back at all of them and said, "We should go, it's going to be eight o'clock soon and we need to go back so no one gets into trouble."

"We didn't see a single ghost. Why not? This was no adventure. It was just a bunch of files," Kim lamented as she headed for the door to the file room.

"Oh, Kim, maybe the ghosts will be here the next time we come for a visit," Deb said, trying to console her.

"Can we come back, Ken?" Kim turned to ask.

"Sure, let's come on Halloween."

They all headed back to the dorms. As Deb and Kim were walking back to the girl dorm after leaving Ken and Joe, Kim looked up at Deb and said, "Why doesn't Joe want a picture of Daddy? He misses Daddy and Mommy so much? He seems so angry, and all I want is to see Mommy and Daddy again. If a picture is the only way, I want one and I don't understand why Joe doesn't."

As they entered the girls' dorm, Deb said, "I think Joe is struggling with his feelings over Mom and Dad. He doesn't feel like he can talk about it, but we need to be there for him. That's why I took the picture so he could have it later. Good night, Kim. Sleep well, and love you, my little sister."

Kim hugged Deb and said, "I love you too, and I'm so glad you're here with me."

The next day, during free time, Joe left the hall after classes and headed directly for the building they all went to last night. He carefully went around to the back of the building and looked around to be sure no one saw him, and snuck back into the basement. After seeing no one around, he headed directly to the stairs, down the hall and up the stairs back to the file room they were in last night. Bypassing the file drawers that were noted with years, he quickly went to the files that were not marked on the drawer fronts. He started searching through the drawers and looking for anything related to science or math because he was hoping to find something to take his mind off of his parents, and to bring up with Mr. Brewster since he just knew that Mr. Brewster needed something to occupy his mind in the same way that Joe did. After about an hour, he found a file cabinet against the wall that had many notebooks from students and teachers. He opened one and found something worth the search. It had many pages with calculations on them and diagrams of some mechanical parts of a machine. He found several books from the late 40s as well. Engrossed in the material he found, Joe kept looking, hoping he had discovered some great treasure. He opened another drawer and found an old science book. Grabbing the notebooks, books, and a small prototype of a machine, Joe headed back to his dorm room. He shared a room with another boy from his grade level, but they had little in common and talked very little. He hid all that he brought back to his room under his bed.

Joe was sure he found a treasure trove of materials that had never seen the light of day. He was excited to be the one to look through them and determine if some great science or mathematical discovery was on the way. As he sat contemplating this, he remembered a talk he had with his father on his birthday last year. His father had told him about the increased interest and research to use computers in business. Joe knew computers were going to become a big part of business and society if the people building them could figure out how to reduce the size and allow for more processing of information. They had talked about this, and Joe's father seemed to want to support Joe's ideas about how to accomplish this and wanted him to stay focused and plan for this as he prepared for college in four years.

Joe was constantly looking at mathematical calculations, and mechanical information to see if he could make his ideas possible. He believed that if he could accomplish this, he could make his father proud and now he believed it would make the loss of his parents finally not so painful.

Joe met Ken coming down the stairs. Ken asked, "Where've you been? We're all heading over to the field for a friendly game of football. Thought you would want to join."

Joe looked around to be sure no one was paying attention, as they were in the midst of a crowd of boys headed to the dining hall, and replied, "I went back to the building and was looking around. I figured if there were old school records, maybe there would be old records from the labs and stuff. There were some pretty famous people here, obviously, so I was searching for math and science information."

Ken's response was typical, as these two boys rarely were interested in the same things. "So, let me get this straight, you have two hours in the afternoon and you go looking for old, probably outdated, math and science textbooks and notes? It's probably the last good day of the year to be outside and you want to be digging through dusty books? You're getting as bad as Deb."

Joe smirked at Ken and said, "You can't do everything with muscles, Ken. You need your brain for some things. And to make your brain work, you need books. Not everything comes naturally to everyone. And if I do what I want, maybe it will make this hurt go away."

Ken stopped walking because, clearly, Joe had revealed something important. It wasn't just the muscles and athletic ability Ken had and Joe didn't, and Joe had brains and Ken didn't always get great grades or have an interest in what could be found in books, but because he had just revealed a pain, he hadn't shared with any of them. Ken, on the other hand, didn't have time for the pain, he was too busy feeling guilty about not being able to take care of his brother and two sisters as he wanted, and an immense burden of responsibility to be sure they were ok. Now, hearing this from Joe, Ken felt he had failed again. Joe was struggling with the loss of their parents, and Ken hadn't helped him.

Ken ran to catch up to Joe, and panting a bit said, "Joe, after dinner, in the free time, let's you and me go to my room and have a talk, ok?"

"If you want to. I have a test to study for though, so not long, ok?"

They both went into the dining hall and located Deb and Kim, who had already sat down. The boys joined Deb and Kim and waited for the Reverend to enter and lead the meal prayer. Deb was talking to a girl from her classes who looked at Ken and started giggling. Deb tried to calm her down and looked at Ken, and smiled. Just then, the Reverend walked into the hall and called the dining hall to order. With the prayer over, everyone started talking and eating. Dinner was without a doubt the most relaxed time of the day for all the students. As they began eating, Deb looked up and looked at Ken, "Kenny, this is one of my floor mates, Mary Rollins. Mary, this is my brother Ken. Ken, Mary, just turned sixteen and is from Boston. Here, Mary, why don't you and I switch seats so you and Ken can talk a little?"

With that, Deb got up, slid her plate and waited for Mary to slide over. When Mary moved, Deb sat down and talked with the girls next to her and to Kim, who was across from her at the table.

Mary looked at Ken, and then immediately looked away. "Sorry, I guess Deb is trying to get us to talk. I just noticed you a lot around campus."

Ken thought Mary was cute, with long blond hair and seemed very tall and athletic looking, answered her, "It's cool. I've seen you around, too. So, what classes do you share with Deb? Or is it just that you're on the same floor?"

Mary smiled. "Deb and I have history together. She really likes that class and the other kids in class think that makes her a big drag, but you know, I know better. And, then after class the same guys ask me about her cause they think she's cute. They call her a fox and want me to set them up."

Ken smiled, but looked a little uncomfortable when he said, "I don't think I can handle anyone thinking my sister's a fox, but hey, what can I say?"

Mary blushed. "Maybe it runs in the family?"

Ken smiled at Mary again, and changed the subject, "So where in Boston are you from and what are you doing here at Choate?"

Mary said, "Well, my father is in the House of Representatives and he represents an area in Boston, so we live in Beacon Hill. My mother is very involved with charity fundraising and the Met, so I'm here because they think it is the best preparatory school. My father says it is the 'pathway to the Ivy League'. I hated it when I got here because I had some good friends until then, but now that I've been here for two years, I'm friends with some great people. I'm glad I'm here now. You're in the last year here, right? What are your plans after you finish this year?"

Ken wasn't sure how to answer this, but he did so honestly, "I had planned to go into the Marines, even though my father wanted me to go to some well-known school and play football and then go on to law school or something. I want to be a mechanical engineer. I'm not sure how that would have ended up, but for this accident that brought us all here. Now, I don't know, because who'll look after my brother and two sisters if I go far away? Mr. Knight has been bugging me to fill out applications to colleges, but I'm just not sure right now."

Mary knew about their parents. Deb had told her one night during their first week at the school, "I'm sure it must've been hard, but you know, live your own life, right? You have to live for you. Plus, I hear from Deb that you're about to graduate with some honors so you could go to an Ivy League school and be close by, you know?"

Ken knew he liked Mary, knew it for sure, even though they really just met. She was trying to be so understanding. He just didn't want to put all of his grief and guilt out there, so he changed the subject, "So Mary, are you seeing someone, or have you already been asked to the winter formal?"

Mary was thrilled inside, but maintained a cool composure. "No, I'm not seeing anyone, and yes, it would be totally cool to go with you. If that is what you're asking Ken."

Ken smiled. "Yeah, that's really what I was trying to do. Ask you to the formal."

"Well, then yes, I will go with you."

Deb overheard this and smiled. She was excited for both Ken and Mary. Just then, dinner ended and everyone got up to go back to the hall or dorms or whatever. Deb said, "So, are we all going to the hall for game night?"

Ken got up, smiled at Mary and said, "Nope, Joe and I have some things to talk about, so we're going back to my room. We may be down there soon, but Joe mentioned he has a test coming up, so see ya'll later."

Ken then grabbed Joe and headed for the door. Joe had been quiet during dinner, but Ken thought that might have been because of the conversation on the way over to the dining hall. He asked Joe what was up. Joe responded, "Nothing. I was just giving you space to start this thing with Mary. Good going there, dude, you have a date for formal."

Ken started laughing. Joe continued, "You thinking about not going to college or the Marines now because of us? I agree with Mary. Man, you need to live your own life."

As they got back to the boys' dorm, Ken said, "Joe, I'm the oldest. It's my job to look after you and our sisters. I don't think Aunt Alicia is going to do that, even though she has custody, plus, I'm not sure she was really honest with us since she wouldn't let us go with her to the will reading. Don't tell the girls, but I'm just waiting for my eighteenth birthday to call the lawyer and start asking questions."

Joe closed Ken's room door, and said, "You mean dumping us here while we were still in a tailspin over what happened is not her taking care of us? I figured that was because she doesn't want kids, doesn't like kids, and didn't want to deal with us. Do you think she's up to something?"

Ken didn't want everyone to get suspicious, but he said anyway, "I know all that. I remember how she was when I was younger. She never wanted to do anything with us or barely paid attention to us. But I think this is more than that. Joe, Dad ran a very profitable company with Mr. Davis, and they were worth a huge amount of money. Plus, Mom was a professor at Harvard, and that's a big deal. She has her name in some big journals and publications. Aunt Alicia says the money that was left for us is being used to pay the bills here, but trust me, I think there's way more money than that, and I think that is why we had to get up here in such a hurry and why we couldn't take much with us. But this isn't why I wanted to talk to you. Joe, now that I have been straight with you, it's time for you to be straight with me."

Joe dropped onto Ken's bed and started what he knew was coming. "Ok, so I'd been talking with Dad since this past summer about my ideas on computers. You know that big computer they have at Harvard that Mom let me see, and then the guy that runs the thing let me do some things with it. It was totally cool. The thing is, the computer is the size of a room, well, practically, and it runs on punch cards. Dad suggested I do some research on computers, and I started that with Mom. I went to the Harvard library and came up with a couple of great ideas. I talked to Dad about it and he said the ideas were great for a business; that I should spend the next three years planning it out, and completing research, and doing some prototyping and get ready. He said if I did all that, he and Mr. Davis would probably fund me to do this as a business idea. I finally found my direction. You have football and all the athletics and everything, and I felt like I had nothing."

Ken interrupted, "Joe, are you saying that you were looking at something that made you feel special in the family?"

Joe nodded, "Yeah. You have football, Deb has history and writing, Kim, who knows since she is still too little. So, this was something I shared with Dad and Mom and I was totally psyched to do it. Then they're in that accident. Mr. Davis wrote me a letter right after the accident saying that Dad had talked about my plans, and he said that he was ready to help me out. He said he felt terrible that he wasn't piloting his plane and that he sent some guy he hired to pick up Mom and Dad and those clients. He also told me how thrilled Dad was that I had such an entrepreneurial spirit. So, now I feel like I have to do this, to make Dad proud of me, even though he's gone. I feel like completing this will help me deal with them being gone. Like this will take all the pain away."

Ken went to sit next to Joe and thought for a minute before he answered, "Joe, you're probably the smartest of all of us. You're gifted, and going to make a big difference in the world as you get older, but my brother, doing that may not take away the pain of losing our parents. Dealing with that is dealing with that."

Joe, with some tears in his eyes, said, "It hurts every day, every minute. We don't get to see them again, we don't get to go to Harvard, we don't get to go to the lab, or skiing, or sledding, or celebrating your victories, or birthdays or anything. I just wish we could go back in time and change this."

Ken paced around his room. "That's what I think about, too. All the things we can't do anymore and all the things we might do in the future. But for me, it's how much things have changed for us. I used to be totally bugged by Mom sitting with Kim reading while I was trying to finish homework, but now that will never happen again. Mom and Dad won't see us graduate, won't see you make it big in business, and won't see Deb or Kim get married later. That's what really gets to me."

They both sat silent for a long time. Then Joe said, "Kenny, it helps to know that you're dealing with this too. Thanks for making me talk, but now what?"

Ken checked the clock and noticed that an hour had gone by while they were talking. He then said, "Joe, I'm not sure. I guess we just live one day at a time and hope that it gets easier. Until then, you better get to studying for your test, dude. I'll go check on the girls and give you some space. Is that ok, or do you need to talk more?"

Joe got up and started toward the door. "No man, this was all I could handle tonight."

Joe went downstairs and Ken took off for the main hall to see the girls.

The next day, Joe grabbed the notebooks and prototype and headed to see Mr. Brewster. He met him near the caretaker shed and called out to him as he approached, "Hey Mr. Brewster, I found some materials and I wanted to go through them. Got a place where I can spend some quiet time?"

Mr. Brewster looked around to be sure no one was around and said, "Joe, my place is just over that ridge. Can you see the barn? You can go in there, but make sure you don't miss dinner prayers. I can be over there in about an hour if you need anything."

Joe said he saw the barn and thanked Mr. Brewster, and headed off over the ridge. Mr. Brewster watched him go and thought to himself that this boy was something he wished he and his wife had. Joe was a smart kid and Mr. Brewster missed the intellectual talks with someone who knew math and science.

When Joe got to the barn, he opened the large sliding door and went in. The place was pretty clean, but one entire corner was filled with tools and a large work table and what looked like several attempts to build a machine of some kind. Another corner held a car that was in some stage of rebuilding or restoration. Joe knew that Mr. Brewster had worked as an engineer, but didn't know he was still building things. Joe found another worktable in the center of the large room that had no other work on it and in the light coming in from the door, so he pulled up a stool and laid out the notebooks and prototype he found. He went through the notebook and got engrossed in notes about mathematical equations that took whole pages for a single problem. He jumped when he heard the other sliding door open and looked over to see Mr. Brewster coming in.

Mr. Brewster went to a junction box and flipped a large red lever that lit up the barn. He then went back and closed the two sliding doors. This allowed the barn to warm up a bit because it started to freeze inside the barn. As Mr. Brewster approached the worktable, he said, "Joe, the red lever puts on the barn lights and allows you to turn on the heater over there under the hayloft. That will warm things up in here pretty quick. Once you're warm, hit the green lever over there and that will turn the heater down for you."

"Tell me, what did you find and where was it?" Mr. Brewster asked.

Joe pushed the notebook with the calculation he found over to where Mr. Brewster sat and said, "So, I hope you don't get angry or feel you have to report us Mr. Brewster, but the other day my brother and sisters and I went into the old building that all the kids say is haunted to check it out during free time. We found a door on the back side of the building that was not locked and went in. We were looking through rooms seeing if we could see a ghost, but found a bunch of old records. When I went back yesterday, I found these in a file cabinet that didn't have any markings showing what was in it. See this whole page calculation? It doesn't have any explanation for what it is, and I was going through it trying to figure it out."

Mr. Brewster looked it over and said, "Joe, it would take us a few days to figure this out. There's no solution indicated here and no explanation for what it was trying to solve, so we will have to recreate it from the actual equation. What else did you find?"

Joe replied, "I found some old books and a few other notebooks. There was a bunch of other file cabinets that I hadn't gone through, but I want to. You see, Mr. Brewster, I was working with my mom and dad and a professor at Harvard on this idea for streamlining computers for more business use and even personal use. I think that's the future. Right now, computers are large and fill rooms and only really have scientific uses. I've also been researching Turin. Have you heard of him? He made the first real computer, called the Turin Machine. They used it in the second world war to break the code used by the Germans."

Mr. Brewster, who was thumbing through the notebook, reflected, "I do know about that. We used large computers to calculate the impact of the atomic bombs we were trying to perfect in the western desert. Streamlining would make it much more economical, but Joe, most computers now can only do certain kinds of calculations, and not much else. For business use and personal use, that would have to change."

Joe nodded. "Yeah, that's the point. If they're streamlined, can store more and different data than simply ones and twos, and zeros, then it can do other things. There was also this small machine prototype I found."

Mr. Brewster picked up the prototype and studied it while Joe continued to look through the two notebooks. After another twenty minutes, Mr. Brewster looked at his watch and put the prototype down. "Joe, dinner is in twenty-five minutes. You need to get back to campus. You can leave all this here and pick it up tomorrow."

Joe thanked Mr. Brewster and headed to the door. He looked back, "Mr. Brewster, thank you so much for letting me use the barn and going over this with me. You're such a big help. It's kind of like having my dad around, and I really miss him."

Mr. Brewster called after him, "Joe, you're very welcome. You need to know that having you here is a big help for me, too. I had really gotten to where I was checking out and you have lit up a part of me that had gone out. Have a good night."

Joe made it to the dining hall just in time and found Ken and Deb and sat down just as the Reverend was about to start prayers.

"Where have you been?" Deb asked.

"I was busy working on some math."

"You, you never have math homework, you always finish it in class," laughed Deb.

"Math project, you know, like when I used to go to Harvard with mom," Joe said, eating dinner.

"Where's Kenny?"

"He's over there, eating with Mary."

Later, after dinner, they all went to the hall for some free time, and there was a movie showing. Ken came to where his siblings were sitting and pulled Joe aside. "Where were you today?"

"I took some notebooks and books over to Mr. Brewster to see if he could help me figure out what some of the math is. He told me I could use his barn, which is pretty close to campus, to go over any materials. No actual progress, but I got a look at some notes I found in the cabinets," Joe answered.

"Totally cool. I have some free time tomorrow, so why don't we go get some more of it and take it over there? I'm more than ready to help, Joe," Ken was trying to keep helping him.

"Where's Mary? Thought you two were spending time together?" Joe wanted to change the subject before someone heard about the building they were talking about.

"We are. I just wanted to come and check on you. See you tomorrow then. I'm going to walk Mary back after the movie." Ken turned and walked away.

While the movie played, Kim kept looking back and saw Ken and Mary hold hands and whisper. She kept whispering to Deb and Joe so they knew what was going on.

"They're holding hands and looking at each other more than the movie!" She whispered.

"Now they're whispering to each other!" She reported after only a few minutes.

"Oh, it looks like Ken is smiling now," she said.

Deb finally told Kim to watch the movie and leave Ken and Mary alone. After the movie, Joe, Deb and Kim walked back first to the girls' dorm and then Joe walked back to the boys' dorm and went to bed. They didn't wait for or see Ken and Mary.

The next day, Ken was waiting for Joe in the front hall of the boys' dorm when Joe got out of class. After quickly changing clothes, and gathering up what was left in Joe's room, and they went to the abandoned building, where Joe took Ken to the cabinet he had looked at. They gathered up some more books and notebooks and went on to Mr. Brewster's barn. They put everything on the worktable and started sorting the notebooks, per Joe's instructions. Joe had just finished stacking the books up when Mr. Brewster entered the barn. Joe introduced Ken to Mr. Brewster, and they all started looking through the notebooks. Mr. Brewster had brought in several large chalkboards on wheels, and Joe had Ken writing out some calculations they found on the different boards, based on his and Mr. Brewster's review and categorizing them. The first few Joe dismissed as they were simply math problems from a calculus class or differential equation and finite math classes. The first one that Joe and Mr. Brewster couldn't figure out and several others were still on the board when Joe and Ken had to leave for dinner. Mr. Brewster had been trying to figure out the prototype that Joe brought over, but still had no luck. He indicated he would try to do that over the evening and would find one of them if he had any updates tomorrow.

Ken and Joe found Deb and Kim in the dining hall and sat down to eat with them. Mary came over and sat next to Ken, so Joe started talking to Deb and the girl sitting next to her.

"So, what did you all do with free time today?" Joe asked Deb.

"I was in the library working on my history paper that's due just before winter break. Doing research."

Deb's friend looked at Joe and smiled. Deb saw that and said, "Joe, this is Christy. She lives downstairs from me. She's Kathy's sister from my floor."

Joe looked at Christy and kind of gave her a quirky smile. "I think you're in my English class, aren't you, Christy?"

"Yeah, and music class, but you probably didn't notice that because I play in the orchestra."

Joe thought a minute, "Oh yeah, I remember seeing you when you were moved to first chair violin, right?"

Kim leaned over to whisper to Joe at that moment, "She likes you, Joe. She and her sister asked to sit with us so she could get to know you. Isn't she cute? She has red hair, and she likes math too. You should take her to the dance."

Joe turned red, but then looked at Deb for some help to change the subject. Deb saw and answered his call, "So what were you and Ken up to during free time? Off scheming or something?"

Joe mouthed a thank you to Deb and answered, "Yeah, we're planning to run things in New England, just like the Godfather." They all laughed and started talking about that movie and others that they had seen recently.

Since it was Friday, after dinner there was an extended activity night with everyone congregating in the hall to play foosball, ping-pong and pool. There was a movie on in one big room with bean bag chairs all over the floor, and another room set up with music playing and kids dancing. Deb and Kim and a couple of girls from Deb's floor went to play ping-pong with some of the younger girls that Kim knew. Ken went off with Mary to the room where the dancing was going on with the older kids. Joe looked at Christy and asked if she wanted to go watch the movie. She said that would be great, and they went into that room. Joe kind of wanted to have a quiet moment or two to look at and whisper with Christy. He was excited to know her and decided he liked her. They went into the room just as the lights were going down to start the movie. He found an open spot toward the back of the room and sat down with Christy. By the time the movie was over, they were holding hands.

Ken, having asked Mary to the winter formal, wanted to spend time with her. So, they went and danced with some of their friends and talked. He went, every once in a while, to the open door of that room and checked to see where Deb and Kim were. When he got back one of those times, Mary looked at him with a kind of sad look in her eyes and asked, "What're you checking on? Is there someone out there you're looking at?"

Ken wasn't sure what she was getting at, but then he realized, he reached for Mary and put his arms around her and pulled her toward him as he said, "Mary, I was checking on my two sisters out there, I wasn't looking at any other girl. You're the only girl I want to look at." She smiled up at him, and closed her eyes, and Ken decided that was his chance and he leaned down and kissed her.

At the end of the evening, Ken found Joe and Deb and Kim and started walking behind them, all while holding Mary's hand. He had told Mary that she was his girlfriend after that kiss, and wanted to walk her back to the girls' dorm. Joe, apparently, did that too, as he was holding Christy's hand. Ken commented on it to Mary, and she laughed and said that since they were both only fourteen, it might not last. Ken laughed too as they walked back. Deb and Kim went into the girls' dorm, but Ken stopped them by asking them to wait in the lobby for a minute. Joe said goodnight to Christy, and Ken said goodnight to Mary, and then Ken pulled Deb and Kim outside for a minute.

"So, Joe, are you going to the barn tomorrow?" Ken asked.

"What barn and for what?" asked Deb.

"I'm going on that trip with the girl scouts tomorrow," Kim said. "We leave at nine o'clock just after breakfast, and we won't be back until Sunday. We're going to that camp outside of town."

Ken indicated he had forgotten, but to have fun. Deb was still looking at Joe, waiting for him to answer her question. "I have to work on my paper, and should be at the library all day," Deb replied.

Joe finally answered, "The barn is on Mr. Brewster's property and I have taken some books and things over there that I found in the haunted building," and he laughed a little. "I'm going over there to work on some huge math problems, and to work on a machine prototype I found."

Kim said she wanted to go get packed. They all said goodnight and Kim went inside. Deb said she was going to go too, but asked the boys to please check in with her later tomorrow afternoon. As Joe and Ken walked back to the boys' dorm, Ken said, "I said I would get into a football game tomorrow morning with some guys and then go with Mary into town to get some things at the pharmacy. Did you want to join us, and maybe bring Christy, or are you going ahead with the barn thing?"

Joe smiled at the thought of seeing his new girlfriend, but said, "Christy's parents are coming up for the day to spend with her and her sister Kathy. She told me about it after the movie. Thanks for the invite, but I don't want to get beat up as the scrawny brother on the field or be the third wheel into town."

Ken pulled Joe to a stop and looked kind of angry. "I would never let them rough you up, and you know that, don't you?"

"You're always here to protect me, I know, but remember, I'm just the scrawny one, and you are the muscles."

Ken caught up to Joe again. "My bro, you are the brains of the operations. That is way more important. And, at fourteen, I was scrawny too. Don't be too harsh on yourself. You will probably end up with both brains and muscles in the next few years."

They laughed as they entered the boys' dorm.

The next day, they all went their different ways. Kim left on the Girl Scout trip, Deb went to the library, Joe headed to the barn, and Ken went to the football field. Kim was smiling for the first time since they got to the school and appeared to be having fun as Deb left her to get on the bus with the other girls. Deb was happy that she was finding new friends and appeared to be enjoying herself more. This was playing on her mind as she walked to the library. Deb went into the library and found a table that was unoccupied. She went and looked up the books she was looking for, found them on the shelves, and sat down to read and complete her research. Ken had a great time with the guys on the football field, and it got a little rough, as the touch game turned into a tackle game. Of course, with Ken as quarterback, his team won. As Ken walked off to shower and to meet Mary, he wondered what his life would be like if things had not turned out this way. He scheduled a meeting with his counselor first thing on Monday to talk about college applications, thinking perhaps he could manage to keep an eye on his siblings and go to college at the same time.

Joe went straight to the barn. He and Mr. Brewster worked on the math problem that they had transcribed from the notebook to the chalkboard all morning, and as they did that, it dawned on Joe that what they had was a problem that might solve some sort of time and space calculation. This was something that Einstein had been working on. Joe and Mr. Brewster celebrated at lunchtime with the sandwiches Mr. Brewster made them, as they discovered what the calculation was trying to prove. Now all they had to do was solve it. They knew now that the basis of the formula was Einstein's general relativity, but it took it to a new level with calculations of time and power required to bend time and travel to another time. It had about fifteen parts, and the only one the two of them were sure of was the basis of relativity. By the time it was getting dark and Joe needed to get back for dinner, they had figured out only one other part of the formula.

Ken spent the afternoon with Mary. They walked to town, and she bought some things she needed. As they headed back to campus, Mary told Ken about her childhood and what she wanted to do after she graduated. Mary wanted to be a reporter. She dreamed of working on one of the powerful newspapers and getting credit for a tremendous story. When Ken asked her where she wanted to go to school after she graduated, she answered that she really wanted to go to Wellesley. Ken liked this idea as he was contemplating colleges somewhere between Choate and Boston. He had decided he was ready to work on going to college soon.

Meanwhile, Deb worked in the library. She was making significant progress on her research for the paper that was due after Thanksgiving, but she hated to wait until the last minute to do this kind of research. She got up to return the books she had been looking through and noticed that one boy from her history class was also in the library. He kept looking at her as she walked back and forth to the bookshelves. She thought hard and remembered that his name was Ryan. He played hockey, which was big here at Choate. That and soccer. She looked up from her notes and smiled at Ryan. He smiled back. Early in the afternoon, he got up and brought his books and things to her table. She looked up. "Are you working on the history paper or something else?"

He smiled at her. "Hi, my name is Ryan McDonnell. You're Deborah, right?"

Deb smiled back, "Yeah, call me Deb. Are you working on history or something else?"

Ryan pulled out his book and held it up for Deb. "Nope, studying for the SAT test. I'm taking it in February, but Mr. Longley told me I better study for it cause I need to rock it."

Deb tapped her pencil on the book. "I'm taking it then too, but I haven't started studying for it yet. Should I be worried? I want to rock it too."

Ryan laughed. "I heard you were some sort of Brainiac, so why would you need to study for it?"

"No Brainiac, I just work hard at it. My brother is the Brainiac in my family," Deb said with a quirky smile on her face.

"I heard Ken was a star football quarterback. He's also a Brainiac?" Ryan said.

"Not Ken, I mean Joe, my younger brother. He's fourteen, well until December twelfth, when he turns fifteen. He's the Brainiac in our family," Deb said as she laughed.

"I didn't know you had another brother," Ryan said, looking down at his papers.

Deb wondered what he was looking at, but didn't ask. Then Ryan said, "I was hoping to meet you, and wondered if your brother would like me and accept me, or if he was going to wipe the floor with my behind."

At that point, Ryan noticed Deb looking at him and his fixation on the papers. He felt like such an idiot, but said anyway, "Sorry, I'm not trying to ignore you. I was just trying to work out this math problem that has been plaguing me for the last half hour. It just came to me while you were talking about your brother, Joe."

"Oh, I was wondering what you were doing there."

"Does that happen to you? You struggle with some problem, and then when you stop thinking about it, the answer just comes to you?"

"Sometimes. For me, it is just more like I always have to fight through to the answer."

"So, if I asked you out, would that be a struggle for you that you had to fight through or something you would know the answer to right away?"

"No, that wouldn't be a hard decision for me."

Deb was so excited. She thought Ryan was so cute and tall and dark-haired with bright blue eyes. She couldn't stop looking at those beautiful eyes. They spent the afternoon talking and studying and getting to know one another. She didn't for one minute think of her brothers or sister or even really about the research she was there to complete.

Ken and Mary found Deb and Ryan in the main hall getting ready to join the pizza party, which occurred every Saturday night for dinner. A lot of students went home for the weekend in the fall, and things were much more casual on Saturday night. Joe finally showed up after about twenty minutes, but with Mary and Ryan there, he didn't tell Ken or Deb anything about what he found out this afternoon with Mr. Brewster. Deb noticed Joe appeared to have something to say, but she didn't ask, as she was so engrossed in Ryan that night. The five of them ended up playing Monopoly after dinner, and then they all walked to the girls' dorm to get Mary and Deb back. Ken quizzed Ryan on the way back, and just as they got to the doors of the boys' dorm, Ken said, "Sorry, man, for interrogating you, but she is my sister, and I have to watch out for her."

Ryan laughed. "I get it. I have a younger sister too, and I feel like I need to protect her. You're cool, Ken. I really like Deb. You don't have to worry."

4

For the next few weeks, things went on as had become usual for all four of them. Deb was studying and writing her paper, but spending time with Ryan, Joe was busy at the barn each day working with Mr. Brewster on the formula, and Ken was busy with Mary. Kim was so interested in her new friends that she was busy every day playing and reading and hardly sad looking at all.

As Thanksgiving approached, everyone started making plans to be with their family. Aunt Alicia had telephoned that Sunday after Deb met Ryan and said she was coming up for the weekend of the holiday and would take them to the home of a friend of hers for the weekend. They didn't know who this friend was, but Aunt Alicia wasn't talking much about it. Deb was not looking forward to this at all, and when she mentioned it to Ken, he said he wasn't either. When classes ended on Wednesday before Thanksgiving, Deb was very reluctant to leave. Ryan walked her back from class and sat with her in the lobby of the girls' dorm. He was holding her hand and writing his telephone number for her to call while she was away when Ken walked into the dorm building.

Ken walked up to them. "So, Aunt Alicia just showed up at the boys' dorm. Joe is loading our stuff into her car and she is heading over here. She was a little impatient, so I told her I would get over here and make sure you and Kimmy were ready."

Just then, Kim came out of her room down the hall from the lobby and called to Ken, "Can you help me, Ken? My suitcase is real heavy?"

Ken walked down the hall toward her room, smiling at Kim and picked up her suitcase in one hand and hefted Kim up in the other. "I'm never too busy to help you, Kimmy. And nothing is too heavy for me to lift for you." As they came back, Deb said goodbye to Ryan, and he left the dorm.

Deb headed to the stairs. "I'm all packed, but I have to get my suitcase and stuff. I will be right down."

As Deb returned, Aunt Alicia was out in front of the dorm building with Joe and Ken and Kim waiting for her. She came out and Aunt Alicia did that little kiss thing when she kissed the air near each cheek. Deb hated this. It was so fake. Ken loaded the suitcase into the trunk and they piled into the car. Deb asked, "Aunt Alicia, whose car is this? I thought you drove a different car?"

Aunt Alicia looked around to be sure no other parents were trying to get out onto drive leading out of campus and swerved out onto the drive. She sounded kind of irritated. "Well, I couldn't fit you all in my car at one time, so I borrowed the car of my friend where we are going to be for the weekend."

Ken asked, "Who is this friend? Have we met her?"

"It is not a her, it's a him. His name is Darrick Reynolds. He works for a Wall Street firm. We're going to his house in East Hampton."

Joe said kind of loud, "East Hampton, how are we getting there? That's on Long Island. Are we going to the coast and wading across?"

Aunt Alicia replied curtly, "First, Joe, stop yelling, that is not appropriate behavior, and you should know that. Second, we are not wading across, we are taking a ferry across. It's quicker, and Darrick paid for me to do this."

The four of them all sat quietly for the remainder of the drive from Choate to the coast to meet the ferry. They barely made it to the ferry on time, and this, of course, made Aunt Alicia very irritated. On the ferry, Aunt Alicia said the kids could get out of the car, which they promptly did, and found a place to sit on benches in the upper deck to be away from Aunt Alicia.

They talked about the water and things they saw on this ferry, but then Ken pulled Deb up to the rail, "So, what do you make of this thing with Aunt Alicia and this guy? I was telling Joe a couple of weeks ago that I don't trust Aunt Alicia and think something weird is up with her since we couldn't go to the will reading. And why would she suddenly be in a thing with a Wall Street guy?"

"I was wondering the same thing in the car, like what is up with her going with a Wall Street guy? I used to hear her talking to Mom about guys she was interested in being in the fashion industry because that's what she does. But how can we find out what's up, Kenny?"

"Sometime this week, I'm going to call the lawyer. I have a card from him from the funeral day, and I'm going to ask if he can tell me what's going on. Incidentally, I'm also going to ask if I can have custody of all of you once I'm eighteen years old. That way, I can control what goes on with this family."

"Ken, go to college and start your life. You shouldn't just assume all this responsibility and toss all of your dreams out the window. You do know that, don't you?"

"Parents are somewhere else for all the students at Choate. If they can do it, why can't I?"

"The other parents are much older, Ken. I just want you to think this through. I love the fact that you're here for us all, even though I used to hate the way you over protected me in school before, but you have to have a life too."

"We'll see. I'm still going to figure out what is up with Aunt Alicia and talk to the lawyer."

Kim came over to see what they were doing and leaned over the rail. Ken pulled her back and said they were getting close to the pier, so they should all go find Aunt Alicia. They went down the stairs to find her on the rail, looking at the pier they were approaching. Together, they went and stood by the car until she turned and saw them all there and went to get back into it to be ready to drive off the ferry when it docked. They drove for about fifteen minutes and came to a large house set back from the road. It was overlooking the ocean, with a stairwell leading down to the beach, Deb found out later. The house looked enormous from the drive, and it was all lit up like a party was going on. When they unloaded their suitcases, a man in a uniform came and carried it all inside. He announced himself as Michael, the butler. Deb and Ken looked at each other and tried not to laugh. How pretentious, Deb thought. Like people can't carry their own luggage and get their own things around a house.

They went inside and Michael showed them all upstairs to their rooms. Ken and Joe would be in one room with two beds, and Deb and Kim would be next door in another room with two beds. Deb thought, oh goodie, it's like a sleepover.

As they all walked downstairs, Deb asked, "So, who do you think is going to be making Thanksgiving dinner?"

Someone they didn't know was at the bottom of the stairs and answered, "The cook, of course."

Just as he answered, Aunt Alicia came from another room carrying two drinks and introduced them all to Darrick Reynolds. Aunt Alicia invited them all to come into the dining room for dinner and handed one drink she had been carrying to Darrick. They all sat down and Darrick and Aunt Alicia began talking about people they knew that had also come to the island for the weekend, and totally excluded Deb and her siblings from the conversation. The kids then sat quietly and ate, knowing that they should not speak up since the adults didn't want to have conversations with them. After dinner, Aunt Alicia asked if they wanted to watch some television. Deb answered right away, not wanting to be rude, and said yes, so they went into what appeared to be a family room with a television and Darrick told them to make themselves comfortable. Then both Darrick and Aunt Alicia left the room.

Joe slumped down on the couch. "Wow, why are we here? They sure don't want to talk to us."

Ken walked to the T.V. to turn it on and turned, "Yeah, the house is decent, but really do they have to ignore us throughout dinner?"

Deb returned from grabbing a book from her room and sat in a chair. "She isn't acting any different than she ever did with us around. She'd rather not be bothered with us. I don't know why we are here?"

"We couldn't stay on campus. That's why we're here," Kim announced.

At that moment, as Ken was changing channels trying to find something to watch, Kim flopped down on the floor with a pillow from a nearby chair. "Oh, Wizard of Oz is on. Let's watch that."

Joe shrugged his shoulders and Deb nodded yes, so Ken left it on. He wasn't excited about watching this old movie, but since Kim wanted to, he would. When the movie was over, Deb stood up and turned off the light she had been using to read.

"Come on, Kim, let's get you upstairs for bed. It's getting pretty late."

"Can't we watch more T.V., it's supposed to be vacation."

Ken turned off the T.V. and pulled Kim off the floor. "No television show on after nine o'clock is good for a ten-year-old to be watching."

"You don't have to act like Dad all the time, you know. You're just a kid too," Kim pouted as she followed Deb from the family room.

"We should probably find Aunt Alicia and say goodnight so we don't get yelled at later," Joe said as he took off down the hall to look for her.

They found Aunt Alicia and Darrick on the back screened-in porch. They were all snuggled up on a love seat. Ken called from the doorway, "Good night, Aunt Alicia, and thanks again Mr. Reynolds for letting us stay here."

"Good night children, and we're glad you are with us for this holiday," Mr. Reynolds replied.

Aunt Alicia said nothing.

The next day, the kids all went out onto the beach. They were not dressed for sunning on the beach, with coats and hats and gloves, but they wanted to be out of the house. Aunt Alicia admonished them about the weather, but they said they would bundle up. It was windy, but the water was beautiful crashing on the beach, and the sun was out. The four of them ran and played tag and looked for shells, because Kim wanted to start a collection. It was a great day with all of them together even if they were at some guy's house they didn't know and Aunt Alicia who clearly didn't want to be bothered by them, thought Deb as they walked back to the house for Thanksgiving dinner.

At dinner, when it was quiet, Ken asked, "Aunt Alicia, someone invited Deb to the winter formal that is two weeks after we get back from this break. She will need a dress. Do you think you could help with that? I know you know the best, the coolest, fashion. Wouldn't it be great for Deb to have something spectacular for her first big dance?"

Deb was mortified. First, she had just told Ken earlier while they were at the beach that Ryan had asked her to the formal. She wasn't sure she wanted everyone to know. Then, what if Aunt Alicia made her wear something that differed greatly from the other girls? Then she would be so embarrassed. Still, she looked at Aunt Alicia and smiled.

"Well, of course, dear, we can go shopping tomorrow. I doubt we'll find anything close to the best designers out here, but we'll give it our best effort."

"Thanks Aunt Alicia. I really appreciate you helping me with this."

After that, the kids talked amongst themselves at the end of the table they had been sat at while Aunt Alicia and Darrick whispered to each other at the other end. Naturally, Joe started teasing Deb about having a date for the dance. So, Deb teased Joe about having to wear a suit and dance with a girl. Everything was fine with all of them. Dinner was fine, but not the usual thanksgiving that Deb remembered with her family. She went to bed that night feeling very melancholy.

The next morning, Deb got dressed and was ready to go shopping first thing in the morning. She helped Kim make her bed, and they made their way downstairs. The cook met them in the dining room and asked what they wanted for breakfast. After answering, Deb asked where Aunt Alicia and Mr. Reynolds were. The cook explained that Mr. Reynolds had made several phone calls and then left for a meeting in town and that Alicia had not yet come down from her room. Deb and Kim played cards after breakfast, waiting for Aunt Alicia. The boys came down and had breakfast, and they all sat in the family room together. Joe had brought down a notebook and was going over some math problems that Deb didn't ask about because she was anxiously awaiting a shopping trip with Aunt Alicia. At almost eleven o'clock, Mr. Reynolds arrived home and asked the kids what they were doing.

Deb was quick to answer. "We were waiting for Aunt Alicia to get up so I could go shopping with her, and the boys were just hanging around."

"Mr. Reynolds, do you think I might use the phone to call my girlfriend?" Ken asked tentatively.

"Sure, there is a phone in the other room you can use."

"Well, I wanted to check because she is in Boston for the holiday. It would be a long-distance call."

"That's no problem, Ken, you can go ahead, just try to keep it under twenty minutes, ok?"

"Sure Mr. Reynolds, and thank you."

"Can I maybe call my girlfriend too?" Joe asked.

"Where does she live or where is she for this holiday weekend?"

"She's in New York city for the holiday with her grandparents."

"Well, that's fine. After your brother is done, Joe, go ahead. And, Deb, I will go check on your aunt now and see what's going on."

A few minutes later, Mr. Reynolds returned and told Deb that Aunt Alicia had a terrible headache and could not go shopping today. Deb was very disappointed and didn't know what to do. Just then, Aunt Alicia appeared in the doorway to the family room and said she really didn't want to go shopping this weekend anyway, but she would send something to Deb at school for the dance. She turned then and retreated back upstairs. Ken returned as Deb and Kim started another game of go fish. A few minutes later, Joe returned after calling Christy and was smiling. Deb thought that might have been the first time she had seen Joe smile in a long time. She wanted to tease him about having to check on his girlfriend, but didn't want to spoil the smile. Mr. Reynolds returned and asked Ken if he had his driver's license yet. When Ken replied he hadn't gotten it as it was something he and his father were going to do the week after the accident, Mr. Reynolds said it was time for Ken to practice and asked if Joe wanted to come. Joe was reluctant, but when he found out they would drive Mr. Reynolds' brand new white Trans Am, he jumped on the chance.

As they were preparing to leave, Deb asked Mr. Reynolds if she, too, could make a call to a friend. He indicated that was fine, and then the boys and Mr. Reynolds left to go driving. Deb turned on the T.V. and told Kim to watch for a few minutes while she called Ryan, and went into the library to make the call. She dialed the number Ryan had given her and a woman answered the phone. Deb asked for Ryan after indicating her name to the woman that was likely Ryan's mother. When Ryan got to the phone, Deb said, "Hi, are you busy?"

"No, I was hoping you would call me. I wanted to call you but wasn't sure where you were going for break."

"We are with my Aunt Alicia at this man's house in East Hampton. I think Aunt Alicia might be interested in him or dating him. He's pretty nice and his house is cool."

"How was your Thanksgiving?"

"Weird. Aunt Alicia was busy with Mr. Reynolds and we all sat at the other end of this huge dining room table. Then we watched some television with Kim. How about you?"

"Dinner was excellent. My grandparents are here and that was fun. What else are you all doing out there in the Hamptons?"

"We went to the beach. Aunt Alicia was planning to take me shopping for a dress for the formal, but she had a terrible headache. I told Ken yesterday, and he announced it at dinner. I'm not sure what I'm going to do now."

"I can take you shopping. I mean, I don't know anything about picking out dresses, but I can go with you if you want."

"No way, I don't think I could try on dresses in front of you!"

"Seriously, aren't there doors or curtains in the dressing room? That's not was I was thinking."

Ryan started laughing, and so did Deb. They talked about hockey and Deb told Ryan that she knew little about it, but was looking forward to cheering on her boyfriend. She asked him if that was what he was, and he said yes, that was how he was going to think of himself. The call helped Deb get into a better mood. When she came back to the family room, she asked Kim if she wanted to go back to the beach. Kim jumped up, so Deb took Kim out to the beach and the spent the afternoon building sandcastles. Kim had a lot of fun and ran back to the house to get her little camera to take a picture of their creations. Deb tried to have fun, but all she could think about was not having a dress for the dance, and wishing her mother was here to buy it.

The guys came back and Aunt Alicia came down long enough to get a drink, and find some medicine for her headache and retreat to bed. Dinner was much livelier that night as Mr. Reynolds sat them all together and was talking to them. He seemed like a very nice man. Deb wondered what he was doing with Aunt Alicia, but knew it was not a thing to ask. Ken noticed Deb wasn't very talkative and wondered what was bothering her, but decided to wait until later to ask. They talked about holidays and growing up, and what they all remembered. Mr. Reynolds had very rich parents. He grew up in New York City but said they spent most holidays here in this place. He said that his favorite memory as a child was watching "It's a Wonderful Life" with his nanny. Deb thought it was very sad that he didn't spend time with his parents, but again, didn't feel right about commenting on it. Kim chimed in that she thought it was on T.V. that night because of advertisements she had seen last night while they were watching Wizard of Oz. Mr. Reynolds suggested they get some popcorn and soda and go sit in the family room and watch. Ken thought it was a great idea because he enjoyed talking to Mr. Reynolds. He had gone to Stanford, and had lots of things to say about colleges that Ken was interested in hearing about. It didn't hurt that Mr. Reynolds drove that awesome car and let Ken drive it today, either. So, they all went to the family room to watch the movie. This time, Deb didn't go get a book, but sat curled up in the same chair watching the movie.

Later that night, Ken crept into the room that Deb and Kim shared and tapped Deb on the shoulder. Deb woke up with a start, and Ken tried to hush her so they didn't wake up Kim. He motioned for Deb to come with him. When they got downstairs to the kitchen that was dark except for a light on over the stove, Ken asked her what was going on.

"Well, Aunt Alicia blew me off today, but said she was going to ship me some dresses, and now I won't have any choice but to wear whatever she sends, and what if everything she sends is terrible, what if nothing fits, and what if it is so different from the other girls that everyone laughs at me? I think I should just tell Ryan that I can't go. Although I called him today and he said he would take me shopping. Wasn't that a sweet thing for him to say? He would suffer through that for me and knew it was important."

"Don't be silly. You're going to the dance. It's not cool standing up the first guy that asks you to a dance. Not sure how I feel about him wanting to go dress shopping with you, though. No guy would do that willingly, I think. Besides, I have a secret to tell you. I don't know if maybe Dad knew something might happen, or was just trying to be careful, but he gave me a lot of money before we left on the camping trip with the Simpsons. We'll go into town tomorrow and find you a dress and won't tell anyone about it. We'll get up first thing, and head out and everything will be ok."

Deb was shocked. First that Dad had thought to give Kenny some money before they left. Did he know something might happen? Also, why was Kenny being so nice? He had always hated Deb trying to tag along when she was younger, and said that he ruined it for him because he could never date someone from Deb's class now. Ken, on the other hand, was feeling good for the first time since their parents were in the accident. He finally felt like he was taking care of his siblings the way he knew his father would want him to.

"So, what do you say?" He asked when she didn't respond.

"Sure, let's do it. But, Kenny, how much money did Dad leave with you, and how did you get away with Aunt Alicia not knowing, and how do you have it with you?" Deb rattled off questions at him.

"Ok, so this is the long story. Two days before we left, Dad asked me to come into his office. He sat me down and told me now that I was a senior and getting older, it was time for me to understand the responsibility of being in a family. He said that I was responsible for you three if ever he wasn't around, and I was duty bound to be sure you were always ok. Then he opened the drawer of his desk and took out this envelope and handed it to me. I looked inside and it was full of money. I asked Dad what this was for, and he told me it was in case of an emergency. If I didn't use it because no emergency happened before we were all grown up, then I could decide what to do with the cash. He told me to keep it tucked away, not share that I had it with anyone unless the emergency warranted it. I hid it in my stuff when we went camping, and then hid it in my stuff at home after Aunt Alicia told us we needed to pack up and get ready to go to Choate. It's with me this weekend, because I didn't want to leave it hidden in the dorm, in case someone was doing anything near my room. I didn't want it to accidentally be found."

"This doesn't seem like an emergency to me."

"Deb, no other situation is more an emergency than my sister needing and wanting something that I know Mom and Dad would have been more than happy to make sure you had." Ken smiled, a big smile, like before this all happened and Deb smiled too. She nodded yes and yawned.

"So, let's get to bed, and in the morning, meet me downstairs and we'll walk into town. I'll leave a note with the cook to give to Mr. Reynolds, and we'll find you the best dress we can. But, please, don't tell Joe or Kim about the money, ok?"

"Sure, I'll keep your secret, Kenny."

She wanted to ask if this was why Ken felt so strongly about taking care of them all, but she knew the answer. He had made a solemn promise that day to Dad, never expecting it to become so real so fast, and there was no way Kenny was going to let Dad down. Deb understood that.

The next day, Ken and Deb went to town. They left a note, and Mr. Reynolds simply told Aunt Alicia that Ken and Deb had gotten up early and left the note saying they were going for a walk so the rest of the family could sleep. Aunt Alicia was accepting of this, and Joe and Kim went down to the beach. Aunt Alicia seemed to be feeling better, but Joe didn't want to push his luck without Ken and Deb around to help. Deb and Ken managed to get back into the house and get the dress and shoes upstairs, with no one noticing. As Ken went out to join Joe and Kim, Mr. Reynolds stopped him.

"So, what was so pressing you had to take off first thing for town today? If I am going to be made a co-conspirator, shouldn't I know the truth?"

"Well, Sir, I took Deb to town to find a dress for the dance. She was really upset about it, and I wanted to make sure she got something she liked. That's all. No big deal, but sometimes things we say and do really irritate Aunt Alicia, and we wanted to keep it a secret."

"Your aunt wanted to send Deb a dress from New York, so I won't tell her what you did. Perhaps Deb will like the dress that Alicia sends her. But where did you get the money for this?"

"I had some money saved up, you know from allowance and odd jobs I did for my mom and dad, and things like that." Ken didn't want to look at Mr. Reynolds as he told him this white lie, because he wasn't sure if he should trust him.

"That was big of you, Ken, to spend your money on your sister. How about if you let me reimburse you?"

"Oh, Mr. Reynolds, you don't have to do that. It's real cool of you to offer, but I'm cool here."

"Ok, Ken, I get it. You want to take care of your sister. And, by the way, you don't have to call me Sir or Mr. Reynolds. It makes me feel like I should look around for my father," he laughed as he said that.

"Well, my dad always told me to be respectful of those older than me. I mean nothing else by it."

"Just call me Darrick. It's ok."

"Ok."

Darrick turned at that point and walked to the bottom of the stairs as Aunt Alicia had come out of the bedroom.

"I just heard from Eileen Ford, and she is hosting a wonderful party tonight. She asked that I attend, and I really want to go to this. We have to get back to the city immediately so I can get ready. Darrick, please get ready."

"What about the children, Alicia? They have to get back to the school tomorrow, don't they?"

"Michael can take them, can't he?"

Michael appeared magically when he heard his name being called. Ken couldn't believe that Aunt Alicia would just dump them off on the butler because of a party, but that seemed to be how she operated.

"Well, I can certainly ask Michael, but darling, don't you want to spend time with your nieces and nephews before they have to go back to school?"

"Darrick, this could be the break I have been looking for. You do not pass up an invitation from Eileen Ford. It is just too important. I can be there for the next holiday with them." As she said that, she looked at Ken for confirmation that he was ok with her plan. He nodded in agreement, but said nothing. Darrick looked at Michael and he nodded in agreement as well. So, it was decided.

"Michael said he would be happy to drive the children back, so this is fine, darling." Darrick shook his head as Aunt Alicia ran back to her room to pack.

"Do you want to tell your sisters and brother, or shall I do it?"

"I'll tell them."

"I'll tell cook to order you up some pizza. I think that the new movie, Star Wars, is in the theater in town. How about if I ask Michael to drive you all down there tonight? Would that soften the blow here?"

"That would be great, but you don't need to do this if you don't want to."

"No problem, Ken. I remember what it was like to be left behind for a big social engagement when I was growing up. It wasn't fun. Let me do this for you kids."

"Thanks."

Ken went to inform the others what was going on. No one was overly disappointed to not have to spend an evening and the long drive with Aunt Alicia, so they thought the pizza and movie were a great idea.

Aunt Alicia said goodbye to them all shortly after the announcement, and said she would call next week, and send out a dress or two for Deb, then as well. They all said goodbye and thank you to Mr. Reynolds, and then they were alone in this large house, with the cook and butler. The evening actually was fine. Ken invited the cook and Michael to have pizza with them, which they seemed to appreciate. Then Michael drove them all to see the movie and back to the house afterwards. The next day they all packed, ate breakfast and left with Michael for the ferry and drive back to school. They talked about the movie and the beach and Kim showed them all the shell collections she had acquired over the weekend. When they got back to campus, Kim jumped out of the car and squealed. She had noticed one of her friends getting out of her parent's car and ran toward her. Ken laughed, and he and Joe got the rest of the girls' luggage out and took Kim's bags to her room. Michael then took the boys to the boys' dorm and got them deposited back on campus. Ken thanked Michael for taking care of them.

Joe went in search of Christy, and Mary had come to the boys' dorm to see Ken, and they went on a walk. Kim was busy with her friends, and just as Deb thought she might sit down to read, Ryan showed up and asked if she wanted to go up to the main hall, as there were kids there decorating for Christmas. Ryan asked Deb how her weekend finished up, and Deb recounted the beach trips and the movie they saw, and the cook and butler and told him that Ken had taken her shopping for a dress on Saturday morning, so Ryan was off the hook. Ryan laughed at that and asked about her aunt, as he knew Deb was upset over the dress shopping issue. Deb told him how she had wanted to rush back to New York City on Saturday for a big party. She said she was even happier after Aunt Alicia left, but that Mr. Reynolds had been pretty nice. After she told Ryan all she had thought about that weekend, she added that she didn't understand why Mr. Reynolds was interested in her aunt. Ryan was helpful and listened, and that made Deb feel so much better. After they were done talking about Deb's weekend, Ryan said, "It's official, right? I can call you my girlfriend now?"

Deb replied a bit shyly, "Yes, I guess it is official."

"I think we're supposed to have something to show for this, so will this do?"

At this point, Ryan pulled a box out of his pocket and handed it to Deb. She opened the box, and it was a beautiful locket on a chain. He said it had been his grandmother's when she was little. Deb reverently held the locket and asked Ryan to put it on her. He did, and she knew how much she liked him at that moment.

When Deb got back to her room, she wrote another note to Denise. Deb told her again how much she missed her, and how terrible it had been to leave their house, and how sad she was to not see her best friend every day, but then she shared her news about getting a boyfriend here at Choate and promised to write more later. Deb went to bed feeling better and was strangely thinking of Choate as home.

5

A week later as Deb was contentedly reading the last of her book that she needed to finish for her English paper, but had already completed and turned in her history research paper, Joe came clamoring into the main hall where Deb was sitting with Ryan doing homework.

"Where is Ken, do you know, Deb?"

"He said he was going to be spending time in the library today finishing a paper or project or something with Mary."

"I checked there, and he wasn't there."

Ryan looked up at that point and indicated that he heard Ken talking to some guys about playing football if he got done in time.

"In this weather? It's snowing out there."

"Yeah, isn't it great? Hockey starts Monday."

Ryan played on the hockey team, and he was very excited about the season starting. Deb had promised to come to the games, but wondered how the ice stayed cold while the spectators stayed warm. When she asked Ryan about this earlier in the week, he laughed and said it was the same temp all over the hockey stadium. Spectators had to wear coats and hats during the games. Deb wasn't so sure she wanted to spend a few hours in the cold like that, but she liked Ryan too much to tell him that, and knew she would endure it to watch this boy that she was sure now she loved.

"So, Deb, we need to talk right after dinner tonight, you and me and Ken, ok?"

"Sure Joe, is everything ok?"

"Yeah, I just discovered something monumental, and I need to tell you and Kenny about it."

"What could be monumental to a fourteen-year-old? Do you think Christy broke up with him or something?" Ryan asked as Joe walked away from them.

Deb replied she doubted it was about Christy, but given that Joe was such a math fanatic, it was probably about some breakthrough he thought he made on a big math problem. They both laughed and got back to their homework.

After dinner, Joe and Deb and Ken went into one of the music practice rooms in the basement of the main hall. It was quiet there, and Christy had suggested it when Joe asked where he might go to have a private talk with his brother and sister. They went downstairs and into the quiet room, and both Deb and Ken looked at Joe expectantly.

"So, I have been working with Mr. Brewster on that math calculation, remember? Well, today we had a tremendous breakthrough, and we think we've figured it out. Remember that I said at Thanksgiving break that the basis of the problem was Einstein's theory of relativity. Well, the other parts of the equation are about time and power. The whole thing is a theoretical calculation that shows how to make time bend so you can travel through time. Think about it?"

Ken and Deb were slow to answer. Deb looked at Ken and then back at Joe.

"So, you think you have found a theoretical calculation that would show that time travel is possible? Am I understanding this correctly?"

"Yes, and what's better is that we think the prototype that we found with this notebook is actually a prototype for the machine to time travel."

"Joe, man, that is all science fiction stuff. You can't travel through time. That's a story started by H. G. Wells. Plus, if it's theoretical, how can there be a prototype?"

"I'm not sure, but think about the possibilities? We could go back in time and stop Mom and Dad from getting on that plane."

As Joe looked at the two of them, Deb understood why Joe was so excited about this. She knew how much Joe wanted to change what had happened, even if it meant he wouldn't have met Christy or anything else.

"Joe, let's think about this for a minute. I don't particularly care for science class, but I know this. First, there is no evidence that you can move through time. How do you think this theoretical calculation can make time travel possible? How does a math problem mean you can do this? Also, isn't there a paradox that states that you cannot go back and meet yourself? What does your calculation have to say about that?"

Joe didn't like what Ken was saying. He was way too excited about what he found and what the possibilities were, and he was not ready to give up yet.

"Clearly, there's more to work out, but just think about it. We could solve so many other things too, besides just bringing our parents back from the dead."

"Again, if the calculation is theoretical, how do you get to the practical, Joe?"

"Deb, I'm not sure yet. Can you both at least be a little excited about what we've discovered? Not only did we figure out what the calculation is about, we solved the mathematical problem. Mr. Brewster says if we want to, this can make us famous. We could release it to the scientific community as is, with just a finished calculation, and we would be famous."

"So, you want to be famous, do you?" Ken tried to lighten the mood because he knew how much Joe wanted to find his place in the family with something special, as Joe put it.

Joe frowned at Ken.

"Ok Joe, sorry, it sounds really cool. So how do you verify it, and do you want to release it, or do you want to keep working on it, and see if you can turn into the practical?"

Joe thought for a minute.

"I want to keep it quiet for now, just you two and me and Mr. Brewster, is that ok? I want to see if we can connect the calculation to this prototype, and if the prototype is really the machine before we do anything."

"Sure, so here's what I might do to help. I'm meeting tomorrow with my counselor to finish filling out college applications, and he is really cool. I can ask him on the QT about how someone might get published or get something to some experts to verify or announce to the world or something."

Deb agreed that someone other than Joe should do some poking around, so they decided that was the plan. They also decided they would try to get to the barn the next day for Joe to show them what they found.

As they left the music practice room, Deb asked what they were planning to tell Mary, Christy and Ryan since Christy had helped arrange the practice room for them, Ryan was there when Joe asked for this little meeting, and Mary was sure to know now, since Ken was not in the main hall right after dinner. They decided they would tell them that Joe had discovered some notes from their mother in his old books and was excited about it, as none of them had told their girlfriends or boyfriend about their trip to the haunted building yet.

Later that night, as Deb lay in bed, she was thinking about what Joe said. She was a little worried about lying to Ryan, even though he believed what she said. Knowing it was a little wrong for them to all lie to their girlfriends and boyfriend, she didn't quite know how to tell him about this. She was also mulling over the details of what Joe had told them he had found. Was it really possible to bend time? What if they could do this and save their parents? What about what Kenny said about the paradox if you met yourself in another time? Joe had said they could solve other things. What about that? Could they change the course of history? She drifted off to sleep very troubled that night.

The next day, Ken and Deb went with Joe to the barn to go over what they had found. Mr. Brewster was not there since he had to work that day, but Joe went over everything and why they thought the prototype might be some sort of machine to do the time travel. Joe explained, or tried to explain, the complex math, but really Deb didn't understand how you could go from finite numbers to some theoretical idea. After Joe had gone through the chalkboard for what seemed like a hundred times, he sat both Deb and Ken down at the worktable and tried to connect the pieces for them as he and Mr. Brewster had.

"About a month before the accident, Dad and I were talking about the computer at Harvard after I got home with Mom. I told him I had been going over some calculations with the guys at the lab and how we found some limits on what the computer there could do. Then I told Dad about the research I had done that day in the Harvard library while she was working. I told him about the Turin Machine. That was really the first computer ever developed during World War II. Turin was a guy that had this remarkable brain; he figured out you could set a machine to take in codes, and if you found the key, you could break the code and the machine could read the messages. It was a tremendous breakthrough for programming, which it wasn't called then, and the war actually. So, I was telling Dad that if you can get a computer to understand ones, and twos and zeros, and get it to understand written messages with the right key, why wouldn't a computer do other things, like save written documents, or a series of calculations, like an accounting book. He agreed, but said that the size required to hold a computer was very cost prohibitive to businesses and especially for personal use. I suggested that if you used some of the technology that had been developed by NASA for the Apollo program that was making its way into the public, and all that was learned by the first computers and Turin, I thought you could build a computer that could be programed to do anything. I still think I am right about this, and Dad was very supportive of this, and so is Mr. Davis as he wrote me a letter shortly after the accident telling me if I ever was ready to get into this business, he would support me. So, if I'm right about programming a computer, why then can't this theoretical calculation be turned into some program that is put into a machine that can then bend time and allow time travel?"

Joe continued, "What the theoretical problem shows is that if you apply the correct amount of energy in the form of light to an arrangement of magnets, it would act on this to create a magnetic field. That magnetic field could then be used by the program to move it in isolation along a field, like the theory of relativity, and effectively bend time so that when you slowed down the energy and magnetic field, you could release yourself at that other time in the past or the future."

After Joe had finished retelling his tale of the conversations with their father and connecting it to this calculation and prototype, even Ken believed. As they talked excitedly about all the different possibilities, like changing history, or finding out details like who won the world series and going back to place bets and make a lot of money, to even finding a way to save Mom and Dad, Deb wondered if it might be true.

"So, what does Mr. Brewster say about this, Joe?" Deb asked.

"He thinks it might be possible, and he's pretty excited about seeing it through, but I asked him if he wanted his name on any of this if we went public or if he thought it would be a great idea to go back and stop his wife from being in the car accident she was in, he said no. When I asked him why, he said he was past his time, and just ready for things to wind down. He didn't want to go messing with his past or his future. Like our grandfather, he said that if God had a plan, and it was for him to be alone now, then nothing he could do would change that. He understands our youth's desire to see this through, and he said he would help us, but he didn't want to use the machine to make money or mess too much with history, and if that was what I wanted, maybe it wasn't a great idea to make it work."

"Maybe we should consider what Mr. Brewster said. Should we really be contemplating changing history or trying to stop the accident of our parents? Are we messing with God's plan?" Deb offered.

"What about free will? Don't we all have free will from God?" Ken asked, not ready to publicize his doubts about his religious past.

"Ok, maybe it's just me, but free will probably doesn't include the free will to go back and change something that has already occurred," Deb explained her doubts about Ken's statement.

"If we don't keep learning and exploring science and finding new ways for everything, or even let's imagine we didn't discover all the things we have, we would be in the dark ages still. How is that part of God's plan?" Joe asked.

"What if we time travel, and talk to someone and really change their life without realizing it? Should we be doing that? Isn't that messing with someone else's plan?" Deb asked as her thoughts wandered like they did last night.

"Don't you want our mother and father back?" Joe solemnly asked.

"Joe, that would be great, but not if we hurt someone else. I could turn it back on you. Why do you want to mess with the path of our lives? What if this is supposed to happen so you can make this discovery and become famous? If we do what you're suggesting, and our parents don't die, then how different our lives would be even now. Have you thought about that?" Deb continued to press.

"I think about it every day, Deb. All I can think about is that I'm not sure I will be successful without our parents. I can't believe that God intended for me to go through life, make my dreams happen, without my parents. It can't be the plan, and if it is the plan, it's wrong, and if I have free will and the means, why shouldn't I change it?" Joe countered.

Ken held his hands up to stop Deb and Joe. Emotions were getting pretty heated.

"Ok, you two are both making good points. When we get right down to it, the question is, just because we may have discovered a way to move through time, and try to change history, ours or anyone else's, should we do that? Should we mess with the higher power, God, and the plan that must be directing some part of our lives?" Ken tried to reason with both Joe and Deb.

"I don't want to get hung up on the spiritual side of this. For me, it is a simple question, save our parents or not," Joe said in a somewhat pouty voice.

"I don't think we can decide without considering the bigger picture," Deb said, equally pouty.

"As I see it, we don't have a final decision here. I'm not sure which one of you I agree with, but we have some time right, since Joe hasn't worked this all out," Ken concluded.

They agreed to think it over the rest of this week, and the formal was this weekend, so they all agreed they would discuss it again on Sunday after church service. They walked back and found Kim to go to dinner. That night, they all also agreed that they would figure out a way to tell Mary, Christy and Ryan, as they all thought it was wrong to keep something so monumental from them. They just weren't sure yet how or when was the right time.

No one talked about the discovery Joe made or the big questions brought up in their conversation for the rest of the week. They finished work for class and prepared for the formal that weekend. The campus was doing something special for those students that were too young for the formal this year. They were having a huge slumber party at the main hall. Kim was very excited about it, even though she had been disappointed she couldn't go to the dance with her sister and brothers. Aunt Alicia sent a different dress. It arrived the Saturday after the holiday break week. All the girls on Deb's floor thought it was great, and it was a designer gown, but it was strapless, and Deb was just not sure it was her style, or if such a dress would be appropriate for such a formal. She actually could hear her mother's voice in her ear saying she was still too young for such a dress and she wished all her children could stay young forever. So, Deb opted to wear the dress she had picked out shopping with Ken. It was more her style, simple and what she was sure her mother would call elegant, and for some reason this mattered to Deb; that her mother would approve and that Kenny helped her pick it out. So she went in the coral colored, spaghetti strapped dress, and she and Ryan had so much fun. He was so sweet to her and had purchased, which she didn't know how, the most beautiful corsage. She decided she would press it in a book like her mother used to do to keep it always. Ken and Joe had a good time also, if their smiles were any sign. Deb was glad they were happy too, except when their happiness erupted into teasing Deb about the necklace. Luckily, when Joe noticed it, Ryan was not right there. Ken asked what it meant, and Deb said he asked her to be his girlfriend, which had Joe chanting "Deb has a boyfriend". It was a great night.

Deb received a long, minute by minute detail of the slumber party from Kim the next day as they went to breakfast, and then later that afternoon they all went on to town with several other girls and their younger sisters. It was a wintry day, but the younger girls kept things lively with their talk about Christmas and what they wanted. When they got back, they had dinner, and there was movie night for everyone. The younger group of students watched Benji and the older kids watched Star Wars, which Ken and Deb and Joe saw at Thanksgiving break. None of them minded, as it was a great movie, and they got to sit in the dark with their honeys, as Joe put it.

After church service, Ken and Joe, and Deb sat at a table in the main hall while Kim sat on the floor, working on a puzzle before the walk to town. They talked about what they had all been thinking and asked Joe a lot more questions about the computer idea and how this might all work. Then Ken asked the big question, "If we do this, how far do we take it without telling anyone else? Are we seeing this through and seeing if we can do this? I can see the military wanting to get their hands on this, the government, spies, and, of course, as Joe has pointed out, there are surely some businessmen and some really eccentric rich folks that are sure to want this."

Joe responded first, "Scientific methods dictate we see it through until we have empirical proof that it does what we say it is going to do. Then we go public. We have to be able to repeat the process that got us to the conclusion."

"Is that what they did with the atom bomb? Repeated it until they got it right," Ken jokingly asked.

"If by right," replied Deb, "You mean, after they killed millions of people, I hope that is not what we're planning."

"Deb, don't get on your soapbox. I was trying to make the connection here that what we are talking about doing will probably be as explosive as the atom bomb, not that I wanted to kill a bunch of people," Ken said, trying to calm Deb down.

Joe had been thoughtful through this brief exchange between Ken and Deb, but then he chimed in, "I want to see this through, but only if the goal is to get Mom and Dad back. I don't want to bet on big games or change history or anything."

"What about the question of whether that is the right thing to do? Are we sure we shouldn't document all of this, propose what it can do and not go further, not mess with God's plan?" Deb asked, as the implications of what they were talking about started to really sink in.

"I think for Joe's sake, Deb, because it was his discovery, we have to see it through with him, and for him. I would really like to have Mom and Dad back, and would love to give Joe this opportunity. Plus, I'm not sure I fully buy into the whole idea that God has a plan for each of us. I mean I know that is what Grandpa taught us, but given what has happened, and the idea of each of us having free will, how can it be that we were born with a roadmap already in place," Ken declared his intent to support Joe.

Deb nodded. She agreed with Ken, and Joe smiled. Then Deb said, "Well, then what do we do about this paradox that Kenny mentioned? How do we get Mom and Dad off that plane without meeting up with ourselves?"

The three of them talked through how to research this and how to plan for this for several more minutes, when finally, Kim, who hadn't appeared to be listening added, "Why don't you go back to a time before we were born, and try to stop something else that would lead to the airplane accident?"

That stopped the other three in their tracks. They had not thought about that possibility, and little Kimmy, ten years old, had found a solution. Ken dropped to the floor and hugged his little sister.

"You are the smartest little sister in the world. Someday you will do great things, Kimberly Fitzgerald."

They agreed on a plan which had Joe working on turning the little calculation into a machined program, and Ken helping to turn the little prototype into a life like first run machine, and Deb doing a lot of research on her parents and especially her father's business, to find the one little event that would start this bigger chain of events.

As they were walking back from dinner that evening, Deb told Ken she needed to talk to him. After Ryan left Deb, and Mary and Kim went off to read stories with her friends, and Joe hung out with Christy, Ken and Deb went into a small parlor in the girls' dorms to talk.

"You know Joe's birthday is this Friday, right? And I walked with Kim to town this weekend and she and all her friends were talking about what they wanted for Christmas. How are we going to take care of this, Ken?" she asked.

That she called him Ken instead of Kenny expressed her concern for this situation more than anything else. Ken knew Deb was coming to him for answers. He liked the fact that his siblings looked up to him, and were allowing him to keep his promise to his father, but sometimes it was a heavy load. He thought for a minute about how he could make this work.

"Well, I can ask my counselor if he can help me get approval for us all to go out next week on Sunday together. We can go to that Italian place in town for dinner, and maybe I can get Mary to go with me on Saturday to buy him a gift. Does that sound ok for Joe?"

"Do you think your counselor will help us with this? We aren't supposed to be out on Sunday without a parent or guardian."

"Let me check and I will let you know tomorrow. On the other thing, I'm not sure. Have you heard from Aunt Alicia yet about Christmas break?"

"She called today. She asked what the dates were for the break and said she would call tomorrow night during after dinner free time to discuss a plan. I don't think she's thrilled about the break being two weeks long, but I'm not sure," Deb replied.

"Maybe she will have a headache for two weeks?" Ken said, smiling.

"That's not nice Kenny!"

"Sorry, her disinterest in all of us just bugs me, and I don't trust her."

"I will let you know what she says, and then we can figure out Christmas. If you buy all kinds of things and take them to her house, or wherever we will be for break, she's going to ask where the money came from. I don't want your secret to get out, but this is as big an emergency, if not bigger, than my dress."

"I know. We can't let Kimmy down this first Christmas, so we have to get her everything she wants. You need to help her write her letter to Santa this week, so we know what is on the list. Then, after you talk to Auntie, we can figure things out."

"She actually asked about the dance, if you can believe it. Asked if there were pictures of the dress. I didn't think about that, but I told her I wasn't sure, but all the girls on my floor really loved the dress. She liked that part, and it wasn't a lie."

"If she asks again, just tell her having your picture taken at the formal cost money, and you didn't have any so you didn't get one. That ought to shut her up. We just have to be sure to not get the film developed when we're with her."

"Thanks a lot, make me look like the snot with our snotty aunt. Why don't you?"

"Any time, little sister!"

Aunt Alicia announced to Deb the next day that they were all coming to New York for the Christmas break and staying with Mr. Reynolds in his large central park apartment. Oh, goodie, Deb thought as she got off the phone with their aunt. At least the food would be decent, since surely if Mr. Reynolds had a cook in the Hamptons, he had one in his central park west apartment. Before Deb could tell Ken about the news, he found her in the main hall and told her that Mr. Reynolds had actually just called him.

"What did he want?" Deb asked.

"Come over here, can you?" Ken asked, instead of answering where they were standing with other people around.

Deb got up from the table where she, some girlfriends, and Ryan were sitting finishing up a project due at the end of this week for their science class.

"He told me we're all coming to his apartment in New York for Christmas break and he asked me if I could either mail him a list of what everyone wanted for Christmas, or plan to go out with him as soon as we arrived, so that we could all have a nice Christmas. He's really a good guy. I hope, for Auntie's sake, that he stays with her."

"Our sake too, Ken. This will keep Aunt Alicia from knowing about your little secret."

They walked back over to where Deb had been sitting as everyone was cleaning things up, as it was just about time to make their way to the dining hall. At dinner, Deb told both Joe and Kim to make a list of what they wanted for Christmas. Joe was skeptical, but he only made a face at Deb. Kim was very excited about it, so Joe didn't spoil it for her. Later, he asked Ken about it as they were heading into the boys' dorm, and Ken told him about Mr. Reynolds. Joe thought that was pretty nice of him and went ahead with a list.

During that last week before Christmas break, Deb wrote to Mr. Davis and asked all kinds of questions about the business and their history, saying she was trying to compile some history about her father and mother. Mr. Davis wrote back right away saying he was compiling some documents and information and would be happy to help, and send it to her right away. Joe worked on the calculations, and Mr. Brewster helped as well, and Ken started working to compile the supplies they would need to build a life-size version of the prototype. Ken planned on helping on the building, but as it was approaching the last week of the school for this year, said it would have to wait until after break because Ken and Joe and Deb had finals the last week of school.

That Sunday, Ken got permission for them to go off to town for dinner, and he and Mary found a few things they knew Joe would like to give him as birthday gifts. Ken had decided that this year, for everyone's birthday, he would try for the celebrations to be just the four of them, and he explained this to Mary, Ryan and Christy. So, after Church service and study time, they all went into town to have dinner and celebrate Joe's birthday. Ken had called the restaurant and explained to the manager a little about their situation, and that this was for his brother's birthday. The manager responded with a sumptuous meal and a specially made birthday cake. They gave Joe his gifts of a leather-bound book for him to keep his treasured notes in, a small tape recorder so he could tape notes if he wanted to, and an antique abacus and slide ruler because, as Ken pointed out when Joe opened them, these were really the first computers. Kim made him a new coffee-like mug since Christy had gotten Joe started on drinking tea sometimes. It was green, Joe's favorite color, but there was a design on it that looked like math symbols and the handle was made to look like the curved edge of a protractor. Joe loved all the gifts and asked Deb and Ken on the way back how they managed all this. Ken said he was not giving away his secrets until after they had all had their birthdays that year. Kim was excited about her turn and said the only place she wanted to go was to the bake shop in town, as they had the best cupcakes with the most frosting. Deb again thought about how they had become so close and so different, and as they approached campus in the cold winter Sunday evening, how much like home this was now.

Ken spoke to Mr. Reynolds one other time prior to the start of the Christmas break, and Deb talked to their aunt and got everything all arranged. Mr. Reynolds was going to buy some gifts in advance, but was planning to take Ken out shopping when they arrived in New York City, and he said he would help Ken get his driver's license. On the last day of school, all the kids said tearful goodbyes to friends, and the two boys said goodbye to their girlfriends and Deb said goodbye to Ryan. They got in the car to go to New York City for Christmas. Again, Michael was there to get them, but this time they arrived in style, as he came in a limousine.

The four siblings had been to New York City many times, but usually at the end of summer to go on a massive shopping trip to get clothes for school, and during that long weekend, also visit museums and art galleries, and their father to conduct business. Christmas in New York City was something entirely different. Everything was lit up, the storefronts all had displays, and the park was amazing from the view of the formal living room in Mr. Reynolds' apartment. It amazed Deb at the bustle of the city every time she looked out over the park and the roads surrounding the park. They went on a carriage ride in the park and went to all the shops down Madison Avenue. Deb was enthralled with the windows at Macy's, even more than Kim was. Aunt Alicia tolerated these excursions because they were Mr. Reynolds' idea. He seemed to really want a family-like holiday. Deb didn't really understand what this was about, but Ken said he knew and understood, and for Deb to just relax and enjoy it. Each day, Mary and Christy and Ryan would call them as Mr. Reynolds had agreed they could call the apartment. Mary was up in Boston, but both Christy and Ryan were in the city, so they met them for lunch twice during the break.

Christmas Eve, Aunt Alicia had a big social event. So, of course, she and Mr. Reynolds went out, but before they left, Mr. Reynolds told Deb and Ken where all the gifts were hidden, and asked them to get them all out after Kim and Joe went to bed. He said he had wanted it to be just Ken, but then who would get Ken's gifts out, so he included Deb in this little plan. Aunt Alicia looked almost as surprised as Kim when they all got up on Christmas morning. She was amazed at the gifts, and was pounding Mr. Reynolds with questions until he presented her with a little gift from Tiffany's. Mr. Reynolds had given Aunt Alicia a diamond necklace, so after that, Aunt Alicia didn't care what everyone else received. It ended up being a fun day, even though all four of the kids were thinking about their parents all day. They had talked about that on Christmas Eve, and had laid out a note for their parents, not Santa. The note was not there in the morning when Kim dragged Deb into the family room to see what Santa had brought them. She thought maybe Ken took it, but later, when she asked him, he said he did not have it. It was a mystery that lasted almost a year.

During the break, Joe spent a lot of time going over his calculations and Deb spent time reading, and Ken wrote essays for his college applications. Kim just played around the three of them with her new toys that she got for Christmas. Every once in a while, she would look up at one of them and make some profound statement about missing their parents, or about the plan to finish the time travel experiment. Deb was often surprised at the amount of information that Kim heard and didn't respond to but saved up, and about the insight she sometimes had that was unexpected from someone that was only ten years old. Ryan told her yesterday on the phone that it was probably because she was the youngest and somewhat younger than all of them and was always watching them. His mother was a big psychiatrist here in New York City, and she was always talking about the order of birth and the significance of that for children and their development.

Ryan came over to meet Deb a couple of days after Christmas to take her to lunch. Mr. Reynolds insisted on coming home to be there when Ryan arrived, and to meet him. Ryan handled being questioned pretty well, but sighed heavily as they got into the elevator to go downstairs. At lunch, they exchanged gifts. Ryan gave Deb a first edition copy of two of the archeology books that Deb had commented about in one of their discussions last fall. Deb gave Ryan a jersey from Islander hockey team, and a new watch that Mr. Reynolds helped her pick out. They had a really great lunch and walked through the park to get back to the apartment. Ryan was heading back to campus the next day for hockey, so they wouldn't see each other again until Deb came back to school.

In some ways, Deb was sorry to see the break end because she had really enjoyed being in the city. She now understood a bit about the draw this place had for Aunt Alicia. Aunt Alicia had dragged Deb to her Vogue office one day to see how the fashion industry operated.

Aunt Alicia thought maybe Deb should look into this as a career, but Deb really wanted nothing to do with the superficial world of ultra-skinny models and endless costume changes. Deb really wanted to go into archeology and study history. She was more the academic type, like her mother had been, but she tolerated the day downtown and had enjoyed trying on clothing, and Aunt Alicia had sent her back to the apartment in a taxi loaded down with cool clothing for Deb to have. That part she liked. Deb was ashamed to admit that although she was an academic by nature, she had a slightly girly and frivolous side that made having great clothes and great hair fun to have. She knew the other girls on her floor would be just a little jealous of all the clothing, and she hoped Ryan would enjoy seeing her in it.

New Year's Eve was a bit dull. Naturally, Aunt Alicia and Mr. Reynolds went to some huge social event party, while the four of them were left at home. The cook at the apartment was different, but she suggested a fondue party, which the kids really enjoyed, and then they played games until the stroke of midnight. Deb wished she could see Ryan, but it was fun to be with her brothers and sister, anyway. All too soon, it was time to head back to school.

Unfortunately, the rules at Choate would not allow them to take all the toys and things back to campus, so Mr. Reynolds said they could store things in the rooms they stayed in here in New York City. He seemed to act like they would be back, so that was ok with Kim. Most of the gifts the other three received were clothes and books and records and things that could be brought to campus, but they all left a few things so Kim would not be upset and prepared to head back to campus. Mr. Reynolds insisted that this time, Aunt Alicia should take the kids back, but he joined on the trip to see what all the fuss was about with this school. As they drove through town and arrived at campus, Mr. Reynolds said he thought it was a great place, way better than his boarding school. Aunt Alicia pointed out that they shouldn't be upset about being there, since all the best adults went to boarding school, just like Mr. Reynolds. She seemed very intent on this trip to getting the kids to like Mr. Reynolds. Deb was not sure why, but Ken was forming a theory about all this. He couldn't wait until February when he was eighteen and could find out the details on everything Aunt Alicia kept from them.

6

January in Wallingford, Connecticut, was filled mostly with snow and cold temperatures in 1975. However, it went unnoticed by Deb, Joe and Ken as they each did their work on the time traveling project. Ken assisted Mr. Brewster in trying to replicate the prototype in a lifelike version, Joe continued working on proving his calculations and trying to turn them into some sort of means to make the machine work, and Deb was tasked with doing research on their father's business to find a way to reverse the accident.

Deb had written back and forth with Mr. Davis multiple times during January so far, and he had been very helpful with the responses, but was starting to wonder what all the questions were really about. Deb was worried that she might lose her source of information if she asked too many questions, but kept taking notes and trying to compile a picture of the start of their business. Late in January, she was going over the latest correspondence from Mr. Davis when Ryan came into the main hall after hockey practice and found Deb. She stopped to talk with him, and when they were finished discussing hockey, classes and everything, Ryan asked Deb what she was working on. Deb knew that if she answered this, it might be time to tell Ryan everything, but she just couldn't keep it from him any longer.

"I've been writing back and forth with my father's former business partner, Mr. Davis. I was asking him questions about the business and when and how and where they met and started this business and things."

"I know it must be hard, Deb, dealing with the loss of your parents, but is this really how you are trying to deal with it?"

As he said that, Ryan reached out and held Deb's hand, that had been resting on the table. After a minute, Deb began to tear up, and Ryan got up and moved closer to Deb so he could wrap his arm around her shoulder. That didn't seem to help, and he was wondering what to do.

"Do you want to go somewhere and talk?"

"That would probably be good before I totally embarrass myself. People will be staring at us soon."

Ryan stood and led her downstairs to the music practice rooms. Everyone knew they were quiet places that were not supervised diligently by the school staff, so you could have some time alone there. He found a room that was empty and pulled Deb inside and sat on the piano bench. Deb sat down next to him. He waited, hoping she would just start telling him what was making her so upset.

"We found out about my parents' accident while we were on a camping trip with my best friend and her parents. It was so unreal, like from a movie or something. A Sherriff was there, and we packed up really fast, and Mr. Simpson drove like a madman to get us home that day. Aunt Alicia was at the house when we got home. She was talking to the Reverend from our church. It all went so fast. She took us shopping the next day for clothing to wear and then left us with Kenny to go finish arrangements. Then she had some assistant from her office come out and help her make calls. They spent the whole next day making phone calls. We were kind of left all alone. Kimmy cried all the time, and Joe got really sullen, and Kenny and I just tried to help them. We had no time to even think about what was happening. Then the next day was the wake, and then the funeral. Two days after that, Aunt Alicia dropped us off here. So, in five days, we messed up that great camping trip, lost our parents, sat through all that, weren't told anything, then packed up and got deposited here because Aunt Alicia didn't have room for us in her New York apartment and lifestyle."

Deb took a breath and looked at Ryan. He looked a little surprised, but only rubbed her back.

"Everything changed in an instant, and then we got here and Joe found some things, see Kimmy had told us some kids told her that old building across from the administrative building was haunted. You know the one that used to be for storage, and has broken windows and looks like no one had been in it for ages? Well, Ken was worried she would be afraid her whole life, so last fall in the evening, we all went over there and found a way in through the basement and walked around. We didn't find any ghosts, but we found all kinds of old files. Did you know my father went here?"

"No, my father went here too. Maybe they knew each other?"

"Wouldn't that be funny?"

They smiled. Deb went on.

"Hey, I also found old files of John F. Kennedy. Did you know he went here?"

"Yeah, that was something my father used to convince me this was an excellent school. Like one President went here. I was thinking, so what at the time? But it's kind of cool."

"Well, Joe found some files from some old students and teachers that were all filled with complex math problems. And you know he is really into that. Well, he took them and started working on trying to figure out what they were and to solve them. You may not know, but Joe really wants to go into some math or science field and he has this dream of turning computers into something everyone uses, like in business, and even for everyday use. He had talked to our father about it, and Dad was trying to support him in this. Part of the reason I think Joe is doing this is to be closer to Dad, or deal with his grief or something. Anyway, you remember the night that Joe came running into the main hall and wanted to talk to Ken and I?"

Ryan nodded he remembered, but stayed silent to hear her out.

"Well, that day he had figured the big math problem out, and he told us it was a calculation based on the theory of relativity and included parts that would show how to manipulate some power and bend time so you could time travel. Well, so we're working together on this now.

Joe is working on how to prove the calculations, Ken is working with Mr. Brewster, the caretaker that hardly ever talks to anyone, to build this prototype machine and I'm trying to research a place in time for us to go and change things so our parents are not in the accident. That is why I am writing to Mr. Davis."

Deb sat quietly now, allowing Ryan to digest all she had just revealed to him and was now pretty sure he was going to announce he didn't want a crazy girl or girl with a crazy family to be his girlfriend.

Ryan spent that time wondering what to say.

"So why is it important to find a time to go back and change things? Why don't you just go back to the day they left and ask them not to go?"

"Joe and Ken say there is some paradox in time that will not allow you to meet yourself in the past or the future. I don't know, science isn't really my thing."

"Science is my thing, but not time travel. That's really classified as science fiction."

When he said it, he was trying to act as understanding as he could. Deb saw it and looked down.

"You think I'm crazy, don't you?"

"Baby, I think you're fun, beautiful, smart and going through a hard time. And if this helps you, regardless of whether I think it might be a little crazy or not, I'll help you if I can."

Deb got a little tearful again, and then Ryan kissed her. They sat there on the piano bench for some time, kissing and talking. Ryan then just held her.

Deb pulled away a bit and got up.

"Are you ok, baby?"

"Yes, I just realized I left all that paperwork on the table upstairs is all."

They went back upstairs and retrieved all Deb's things, and then prepared to head to the dining hall. Kim found Deb to help her with her coat and hat and things for the walk, and asked where she'd been. Deb replied that she and Ryan had some things to talk about. Kim started laughing, and then started chanting, "Kim and Ryan sitting in a tree, K-I-S-S-I-N-G..." Deb covered her mouth with the scarf as Ryan walked up. He grabbed Kim and lifted her up.

"You just wait. We'll be ready and waiting to tease you in a few years when you have your first boyfriend, little one!"

Deb was thrilled to see Kim hug Ryan, and the two of them getting along so well.

At dinner, Deb told Ken and Joe that she needed to talk to them a few minutes. Ryan said he had to go study because of his busy hockey schedule and gave Deb a kiss as he headed out. Mary and Christy also had projects to work on, so they left right after dinner to go to work. So, they all bundled up and headed back to the main hall.

Kim said she wanted to do homework with a friend, so she found a table and they started working. Deb and Joe, and Ken sat down at another table and talked softly so people around them couldn't hear.

"So today I was working on going over the mail from Mr. Davis and was getting a little frustrated and worried, and Ryan came in. He questioned me, and I told him all about what we're doing."

"What did he say?" Joe asked.

"Joe, what do you think he said? He said what we're doing wasn't science, it was science fiction. That was his first reaction, anyway. Then, when I asked him if he thought I was crazy, he said no, and if I or we believed, then he would trust us, and help in any way we needed him to."

"Joe, that means you should probably tell Christy, and I'm going to need to tell Mary. Deb, do you think Ryan will hold off saying anything in front of them until we tell the girls?" Ken suggested.

"I'm sure he will if I ask him to," Deb answered.

"Tomorrow is that big hockey game, right? Tim is on the team, so a bunch of us are planning to go to the game if we don't get buried with work from chemistry class. You probably won't be able to talk to him much before then, though," Ken thought out loud.

"I have a class with him right before lunch. We usually walk to the dining hall together after class. I know the game will distract him, but I'll ask him."

"That would be great, because I'm not sure how I'm going to explain this to Mary. She thinks I'm so level-headed. She told her girlfriend that yesterday, I heard her."

"I'm just going to tell Christy we're working on some math project that I found. She hates both math and science, so she likely won't ask any other questions. She has been asking where I have been lately, so this will probably help," Joe said.

"I'm sorry guys, I didn't mean to do this before we were ready, but Ryan has been so good to me, I couldn't keep it from him any longer," Deb said. "Joe, I thought Christy liked math? Are you guys ok?"

"Yeah, I thought she liked math, too. I don't know. We have fun, but I just don't feel like sharing this with her," Joe said.

"No problem, sis," Ken added, giving Joe a thoughtful look.

"By the way, Kenny, did you finish your college applications and get them all out in the mail?"

"Yeah, Mr. Richards wrote the recommendation I needed for Harvard, and Mr. Davis wrote a letter too, and sent me a copy that I got yesterday. In it, he reminded the Harvard admissions office that my mother was a professor there until recently because of a terrible accident. We'll see."

"I'm sure they will accept you wherever you apply," Deb said, trying to be assuring.

"I don't think Harvard has a football team, Ken." Joe said this looking a little skeptically at Ken.

"I haven't played since last fall before the accident. I'm not sure anyone wants to take me on now. Besides, I have other priorities now."

"Your priorities wouldn't have long blond hair, and be planning on going to Wellesley, would they?" Joe asked.

Joe was laughing, and they got shushed from a table of very stern-looking girls at the next table.

"Like you aren't already thinking about where you want to go to school?" Ken said, leaning down to not be too loud.

"Man, I already have written a letter to the math professor at Harvard and the computer professor there to ask them to help. I want to go to Harvard. That is the only place I intend to apply to in a year or whatever it is."

"I think Mom would like that, Joe." Deb said it without thinking, and they all got quiet for a minute.

Joe got up first and said he had to go finish some homework. Ken then said he was going to head back to his room to finish working on a paper due tomorrow. Deb admonished them as they walked away for waiting until the last minute. She then sat down to study for the SAT while Kim worked on her homework. The two girls walked back a little later to the girls' dorm played in the snow for a little break.

"Deb, I want to go with you when you try to make this machine work. Can I?" Kim asked as they finished playing and headed to the dorm.

Deb thought a minute, and then, "Kim, we're all together in this. If Joe and Kenny and I go, you're going with us."

Kim smiled, and they went into the dorm.

"Goodnight, Deb."

"Goodnight, Kimmy. Sleep tight, and don't let the bedbugs bite!"

Kim laughed as she went down the hall and Deb went up the stairs.

Deb asked Ryan to keep what she told him to himself the next day on the way to lunch. He said he would, but was distracted talking about, and thinking about, the hockey game. Deb went to the arena after class and found a seat, remembering to bring a blanket to sit on so she would not freeze like at the last two games. She totally didn't understand what was going on in this game, but Ryan was out there, so she went and watched him. It was amazing how fast he could skate, and still control a stick and puck. She had learned the correct name for the equipment, at least. Ken sat with his friends, and joked around and watched their friend Tim, who was the goalie for the team. Ryan scored two goals and got to hit someone, which apparently was also a cool part of the game she had learned, at least for the players and the male spectators. Maybe Ryan would let Deb nurse his black eye if he got one from the fight he had. She laughed as she walked back to the girls' dorm after the game with someone from her floor that apparently was now dating one of the other hockey players.

The next day was Friday. Last one in January and Deb was more than glad to see January go. Hopefully, it would warm up soon. She was tired of being cold. She got a letter from Denise that day. Deb was very glad they were writing now. She missed her friend, but as she reflected later that night in bed, she hadn't thought about their old home once this whole week. Maybe it was true, time healed all wounds.

Friday it warmed up a bit, and with Ken off with Mary and Joe off with Christy, but Ryan having a practice that afternoon and a game on Saturday, Deb decided to walk into town with Kim. She had asked Ken for some money so she could buy Kim one of the other books in the series that she had been reading with Mom and now was reading on her own. They had fun and stopped at the hamburger joint just inside of town for burgers for dinner. Then on Saturday, Kim had another Girl Scout event. They were doing some community service project, so she would be gone all day. Deb went to the hockey game with Sue, the girl from her floor that was dating one player, and they sat together for the game. Afterward, Deb sat in her room to study for the SAT test that was now in two weeks.

Just before dinnertime, one of the girls knocked on Deb's door and said that Ryan was downstairs asking for her. Deb went down and Ryan smiled, and indeed had a black eye now because of another game, another goal and another fight on the ice.

"What you doin?"

"I was studying for the SAT and hoping my boyfriend would come find me."

She smiled, and he grabbed her in a big bear hug, lifting her up.

"Well, he's here. Go get your coat, I'm taking you out, and dress warm. I have a surprise for you."

Deb ran upstairs, checked her hair and put on some makeup, hoping Ryan hadn't noticed she didn't have any on, and went back downstairs carrying her heavy parka, gloves, hat and scarf. They walked into town and had dinner at the Italian place Ken had taken them all for Joe's to for his birthday in December. Then they walked back toward campus, but Ryan diverted them toward the arena.

"Why are we headed to the arena?"

"That is where the surprise is."

"What surprise? You have another game tonight? Shouldn't you have had a lighter dinner if you were going to play tonight?"

Deb laughed as Ryan tried to push out his stomach like he was a fat guy or something. They walked into the arena that was suspiciously unlocked, and toward the bullpen door. Ryan opened the door and on the bench were two sets of skates. His and a white pair. Deb smiled because she thought she had discovered the surprise, but the surprise was going to be on Ryan because she thought he must think she couldn't skate. He had never asked her, but she had commented after the first game that they skated so fast in hockey.

She let him help her put on the skates, like maybe she didn't know how, and smiled as sweetly as she could to hide the fact that she thought the surprise would be on Ryan. He glided out onto the ice and then turned and put out his hand and motioned with his finger for her to come out on the ice. She tentatively went onto the ice rink but then glided off and skated backwards, then did the little turn that her mother had taught her years ago when they were in Michigan for Christmas break. Ryan skated after her, "You sneak. You know how to skate, and well, at that." He was laughing as he caught her and lifted her off the ice. She laughed and told him she had ice skated and roller skated before. She just didn't know how they skated so fast. They spent the next couple of hours laughing and skating. Ryan taught her how to hold the stick and Deb finally asked him how to play the game of hockey. Ryan tried to teach her, but she kept getting confused about fast breaks, and the lines on the ice and rules. It was a fun night.

On the way back, Ryan told Deb that he talked to his father about how to research a company, and his dad had given him several ideas on where to write to get details about a company and how to research them at the library. Ryan said he wanted to help Deb, and they agreed after the SAT tests they would work on researching Mr. Fitzgerald's company.

For the next two weeks, Deb concentrated on studying for the SAT. She and Ryan sat quietly at the library most of the time they were free to do this studying. While that was going on, Joe kept up on his work on the calculations and trying to put that into mechanical use, and Ken and Mr. Brewster finished the life-size prototype of the machine. A week went by, and then Deb realized that Ken's birthday was the Sunday after the SAT test. She found Mary and asked if she wanted to help her plan something. Mary really wanted to do something special for Ken, and they started the planning. When Deb mentioned this to Ryan, he said that he had heard in the boys' dorm that Ken was talking about wanting to try his hand at a little hockey. He suggested they have a little party at the arena. Deb said that might be good, and Ryan asked his coach, who said it was fine. So, they started planning. Deb arranged to have pizza delivered to the arena on Sunday, and she Ryan and Mary went downtown with Kim for a short period the Saturday before the birthday, but after Deb and Ryan had finished studying for their SAT test, and found a bakery and ordered a cake. Mary disappeared into a jewelry store, saying she was getting something for Ken, and then they got back to campus. Ryan had two games the week before the party and SAT test, but he helped them get ready for the party as well. Deb was worried about what to get Ken when he mentioned that he really wanted this stereo he had seen advertised in town. Deb convinced Ken that she needed some money for something, and he gave her some, and she went downtown on Friday before the big test and purchased the stereo he wanted.

She was so excited about this. Kim and Mary and Christy wrapped the stereo box, and Joe said he would carry it to the arena on Sunday.

All the plans were in place, and Deb was very excited when she headed into the building for the SAT exam that Saturday morning. She and Ryan and Mary were all taking the exam that day. It was a long day, but she was so glad when it was over, and so were Ryan and Mary. They all went to meet the others at the main hall for the usual Saturday night event there. They played pool, foosball, ping-pong and watched a movie that night. Kim had to play with her friends that night so she would not be around Ken because she was bursting with excitement for the party the next day, and she was afraid she would spoil the surprise.

Sunday after church service, Joe took Ken over to the barn to look at the now completed programs for the machine that was ready to be combined, while the girls and Ryan set up the arena for the party. All of Ken's friends were there, and they got everything ready. There were a ton of balloons that the guys and Kim blew up and put all over the skating rink. The pizza arrived, the cake had been picked up by Joe and Christy yesterday while the others were taking the test, and Mary had snuck off to pick up her gift from the jewelry store after the SAT exam.

Joe brought Ken over to the arena on the pretext that Ryan was there and wanted to show them something. It really surprised Ken when the lights came on and all of his friends were on the skating rink, half the hockey team was there, and they had a great time playing hockey and eating a ton of pizza. Deb was so happy they had surprised him.

After everyone was exhausted from skating, they went into the team room and Ken saw the gifts and cake. He was so happy that his sister had set this up for his big birthday. He was now eighteen years old. He loved the stereo and pulled Deb aside a bit and whispered to her she had spent the money on him, and he was very glad and furious she did that. Kimmy had made Ken a plaque in her ceramics class that read to the best brother in the whole wide world. It was gold edged and had the colors of his former football team on it. Ken hugged her and thanked her when he opened it. The guys from his floor had all given him gag gifts since it was his eighteenth birthday. The entire group went to clean up and found Mr. Brewster in the rink cleaning up the balloons and food and things. Joe and Deb went and thanked him for doing this and for being there. They brought him a piece of cake, and Mr. Brewster acted like it was the best cake he had ever had. He then gave Ken a very fancy leather note pad holder and said that he might need it for his future career. Then they all finished up, and Mary took Ken aside to give him his special gift.

Mary had found the pocket watch that had been Ken's grandfather's and that their father had told Ken he would one day be given. Aunt Alicia had given it to Ken when she returned from the lawyer's office to read the will, but it had not worked in ages. It was engraved from their grandmother and had been given to their grandfather on their wedding day in 1934. It may have been older, but no one knew. Mary had taken it to the jewelry store and had it repaired, so it worked now, and had an engraving put on the back of it. It said, 'To Kenneth on his 18th birthday as a special gift from his father and grandfather and with all the love inside from Mary.'

Ken was awestruck when he opened the box and read the back at Mary's instance. He was so touched by her thoughts and her support for the grief that he still felt almost every day. He told her as much and she hugged him. She told him she was sorry she didn't have the money to get a chain for it, but Ken assured her he would take care of that. It was a great day.

Later that night, Mr. Reynolds called Ken and was so apologetic. He said he had just found out from Aunt Alicia that they had totally missed Joe's birthday in December, and that he found this out when he noticed the date in Aunt Alicia's calendar that day, that they had also just missed Ken's birthday. Ken told him not to worry, and told him about the party that his sisters and brother and his girlfriend had set up, and the special little gift his youngest sister had made him. Mr. Reynolds said then he was bringing Aunt Alicia up the next weekend so they could take them all out for dinner and was bringing them gifts for the missed birthdays.

Ken said he didn't need to do that, but Mr. Reynolds again said he remembered a time when the only person who remembered his birthday was his nanny and the butler, and he didn't want these kids to feel that way. Ken thanked him and said he would tell the others.

The next week, they went to the same Italian place they had taken Joe to for dinner. Mr. Reynolds presented Joe with a new bicycle and, amazingly, he gave Ken the keys to his Trans Am and said it was Ken's now. Aunt Alicia gave them both cards with $100 in them. Later that next week, Ken started receiving acceptance letters from the schools he had applied to. It wasn't until the first of March that he received the one he wanted from Harvard, but it did finally come. By the first of March, Mary, Deb, and Ryan had received their results from the SAT exam in February. A perfect score was 1600. That included 800 on verbal and 800 on math. All three of them scored above 1400, so they were all thrilled with their scores. Mary was accepted into Wellesley on an early application program, which is where she wanted to go. Deb and Ryan were not yet sure where they wanted to go, but their scores, according to their counselors, assured their acceptance. Since they were in their junior year, they had time to decide, so neither was worried, but secretly, Deb wanted to see where Ryan wanted to go before she decided.

While all this was going on, Joe and Mr. Brewster were hard at work completing the proof of the calculations, and using the research of the Turin project to figure out how to turn the calculations and Joe's program into something they could set in motion in the machine. When things settled down in March, and they all gathered in the barn, Joe explained what they had done, Deb and Ken were shocked to learn all that Joe and Mr. Brewster had accomplished. Joe thought he was only a few short weeks from doing a test with the machine. Ken and Mr. Brewster had just about finished the life-size machine build as well, but were waiting for Joe to complete the inside to accommodate the computer-like parts and the printing machine that Joe wanted to install so that they could print out readings from the machine during the testing. The machine itself looked like two of those photo booths you set inside and get pictures taken. Mr. Brewster said that was what the frame actually was. There was room inside to fit four seats that had been taken from old cars and bolted to the floor. They covered the outside with metal, but had three rows of wide extended trim that Ken said held the powerful magnets that Mr. Brewster had purchased from some old friend he knew from long ago. On top of the machine were four half circles Joe said contained powerful lights, placed on the four corners of the machine. In the center, on the top, was a large cylinder that was about fourteen inches high and about twenty-four inches in diameter. This, according to Mr. Brewster, contained the antennae. On one side was a door that looked like it came from a ship or submarine, and on the side opposite the door, there was a large rectangular box with a trap door on top that Ken said held the power generator for the machine. It looked a little like a junk yard build, but Mr. Brewster said that all mechanical inventions started out this way. As they all stood there looking at the machine, Ken made like he was clinking a bottle on the side and pronounced, "I hereby declare the machine born and christened!" They all cheered.

Deb had been working with Ryan on researching information on the company and had corresponded with Mr. Davis a couple of more times. She said that she thought she had a good idea for the one event that caused the accident later, but had just a few more points to check on. They all agreed that by the next weekend, they should be ready to do a test on the machine and have a plan to discuss. They agreed to meet early next Saturday to go over the plan that Deb had come up with.

Spring had sprung in Wallingford, and everyone was happier that week. Deb had confirmed a couple of details, and in fact had just received a letter from Mr. Davis confirming where and when he met their father. Deb was writing up the plan. She was sitting in her room finishing up some homework and was about to get the plan paper out to finish up when she got a phone call. It was Aunt Alicia, who apparently was shamed by Mr. Reynolds about missing Joe's and Ken's birthdays, and realized that day that Deb's birthday was a little over a week away. She had contacted the school master that day and was telling Deb that she was coming to get her on Saturday morning to bring her back to the city to spend the week with her at Vogue and do some shopping. Deb tried to act excited, but she was not. She really wanted to spend the time with Ryan, and had arranged to go over this plan with Joe and Ken and Mr. Brewster that Saturday. What was she going to do?

She called Aunt Alicia the next day and told her that one of her teachers had indicated that she should not miss the end of the week because of a project due. Aunt Alicia told Deb that she had received a call back from the school about that as well. She was still coming to get her, but was going to come on Sunday, and then bring her back Wednesday night. She also had a commitment that she had forgotten about on Saturday evening, so she was coming Sunday. Deb told Ken and Joe about it the next day in the dining hall, and told them she was finishing up some research and getting ready to finish the plan, and would be ready to go over it with them the next weekend when she got back from New York. Kim was very upset that Deb was going to go to New York, and she wasn't able to go. Deb tried to calm her down by saying she would bring her something special back, and that it probably wouldn't be fun, but nothing would console her. Ken and Joe told Deb later that day on the way to the dining hall for dinner that they were going to do something special for Kim that weekend with Mary and Christy. Deb was glad they were doing this, but was very sorry she was going to miss it all.

A new roller-skating rink had opened in town right next to the bowling alley and the school had arranged for the use of it on Saturday afternoon/evening for the students. Ryan's last hockey game was on Friday for the regular season, so Deb and her friend Sue went to the game, but this time, Joe and Christy, and Mary and Ken, went with her. This prompted Kim to want to go, even after Deb explained that she would have to leave her winter coat on throughout the game, as it was cold in the arena. Ken promised to buy her some treats, so she was fine with that. The game was great. There were two fights, but Ryan was not in either of them. Ryan's team won six to three, so he was thrilled. This meant they were now in the playoffs. Most of the games would be away, so Deb and Sue could not see them. The first one was this next week on Tuesday while Deb was in New York City. She was sorry to be gone, but since Ryan was going to be gone that day too, it made it a little better.

Saturday, the school had a bus to take everyone that wanted to go to the rink. All the younger kids went because this was something they could do, but not all the older kids went. This didn't seem fun to a bunch of the high school aged kids, but Deb, Ryan, Ken, Mary, Joe and Christy all went along. They spent most of the time helping Kim and her friends master the art of roller skating, but it was great fun. Deb and Ryan got to hold hands and skate in the couple's skate. She thought it was funny watching Ryan try to skate at first because he had issues transferring from one skate to four wheels. Deb said that maybe he should skip it so he would not have trouble transferring back for the playoff game, but that might have come off more like a dare, as he then had to skate backwards, and do all kinds of tricks, which thrilled all the young girls that were with Kim. Ken and Ryan and Joe took turns taking the little girls around so they could feel special and get to be out during some of the couple's skates, and of course, Deb, Mary and Christy thought that was sweet.

Sunday, Deb got up and packed before the church service as Aunt Alicia would be there by the time she got back. Ryan walked back with her to the girls' dorm, and they waited for Aunt Alicia to show up. She was not there when they got back, and in fact, was over an hour late. She seemed very flustered when she arrived, but since Deb was ready, it made her feel better. They were back on the road quickly. They went directly to Aunt Alicia's apartment. She had explained that it was closer and easier to get to her office than Mr. Reynolds' apartment on central park, but was perfect for the two of them. That being said, Deb was sleeping on the couch, as there was only one bedroom. They got back, and Deb sat and completed homework and read, while Aunt Alicia finished up some work for the next day.

On Monday morning, when they arrived at the Vogue offices, it surprised Deb at all the activity. There were tall, thin models running around, and all kinds of people. There were people for make-up, hair, clothing, accessories, lighting and even someone that was there just to run around and get Perrier for the models. Deb was enthralled with all excitement and activity. Aunt Alicia said she could watch the photo shoot while she was in a big meeting and Deb found a quiet place to sit and watch. It was amazing. Deb was shocked at the models changing clothes right out in the middle of rooms as if no one else was there, and more than a little shocked at the things they wore. But the clothing was really cool and Deb could tell this is when and how the hippest clothing was determined for the public. It was here in this room. The photographers moved here and there, and got lighting changed and accessories changed, and it seemed to be like a choreographed dance. Two hours flew by, and Aunt Alicia returned and retrieved Deb for her next meeting.

Deb followed Aunt Alicia into a big meeting room with all kinds of boards around the room with things pinned to it, like fabrics, pictures, colors. It seemed like total disarray, but Deb knew there was some method to this. Aunt Alicia put her in a chair right behind where Aunt Alicia sat down. The other adults filed into the room until the last person arrived. It turned out that the last person who entered the room was Grace Mirabella, the editor-in-chief of the magazine. She was very tall and blonde and appeared confident as she walked into the room. Deb felt suddenly small and frumpy. The meeting was to go over the next monthly issue of Vogue and everyone had all their materials ready as Ms. Mirabella went around the room. Aunt Alicia was the editor in charge of picture selection and placement. She laid out an array of pictures on the table.

The meeting was interesting to see how magazines come together, and how a big fashion magazine gets published. Deb really enjoyed the day and told Aunt Alicia that evening that she appreciated the opportunity to see things. The next day, Aunt Alicia said they would go to a photo shoot on location. Deb was excited about this. They had dinner at a fancy restaurant on the way home from Aunt Alicia's office, and then Deb sat down to finish up her research on the time when their father met Mr. Davis.

The photo shoot day was really cool. On Wednesday, they went back to Aunt Alicia's office and spent most of the day looking at the pictures that were taken the day before. Aunt Alicia talked through her process with Deb, and it was fun to see all this. It shocked Deb to see Aunt Alicia so at ease and so ready to share information. She really liked her work. Just after lunch, Aunt Alicia took Deb into this big room with racks and racks of clothing. An older woman walked up to them and smiled at Deb. Aunt Alicia introduced Deb to Miss Wilson. She was going to work with Deb to pick out some new clothing from these racks. Deb looked surprised at Aunt Alicia and asked if she got to keep what they picked out. Aunt Alicia said yes and said she would be back in an hour, and they would then leave to get Deb's things and head back to the campus.

Deb and Miss Wilson worked through the hour selecting clothing that Deb could wear on weekends and during free time as they had uniforms for class, but it was such fun to just look at the clothes and try on and get Miss Wilson's help to pick out the right styles and colors for Deb. Miss Wilson had gone to school to learn how to artistically do this styling, so Deb let her do most of the picking. After about an hour and a half, Miss Wilson packed all the clothing up in two bags that said Vogue and had Deb all ready when Aunt Alicia returned. They left the office and took a cab back to Aunt Alicia's apartment. They gathered up all the rest of Deb's things and got in the car, and met Mr. Reynolds for dinner. He said he wanted to see her before she went back to campus to deliver her birthday gift, as he was going to be in Europe when her birthday occurred during their Easter break. Mr. Reynolds gave Deb a beautiful gold watch. Deb was very surprised at the gift. Aunt Alicia then said that she had given Deb a new wardrobe, compliments of Vogue Magazine for her birthday. They had a nice dinner in a very fancy place, and then Aunt Alicia took Deb on the long ride back to campus. They arrived well after eight o'clock, but Aunt Alicia had informed the girls' dorm supervisor of the timing in advance, so Deb did not get into trouble, but her brothers and sister and Ryan could not be there. It had been a very fun few days, and Deb really saw Aunt Alicia in a different light now, and wondered if they had been wrong about her. She was going to talk to Ken about this tomorrow. Even though it was late, Deb sat down that night and wrote Denise a long note telling her all that happened that week. She so missed her best friend from home.

7 |

Ken had a busy week as well. When they had found out that Deb was going to be with Aunt Alicia that week, Ken had contacted Mr. Reynolds and asked a huge favor, and a second, even bigger favor, to not tell Aunt Alicia about any of this. He had contacted the lawyer that had handled business for his father for years. He asked to come and meet with him and had arranged for a meeting on Tuesday in New York City. Ken had asked Mr. Reynolds to help get Ken back and forth to campus for this meeting, and told him he was meeting the attorney to take care of some business that had been put on hold until Ken was eighteen, which had occurred a month ago now, so he needed to get this straightened out. Mr. Reynolds was happy to help, and sent Ken a ticket on the train, and then arranged for a car to pick up Ken at Grand Central Station when his train got in, and take him to the appointment.

When Ken arrived at the lawyer's office, he was shown into a big office with a large desk and very plush carpeting. There was an entire wall of bookcases filled with leather bound legal books, Ken presumed. Mr. Richards, the attorney Ken had arranged to meet with, entered the office after the secretary had offered Ken coffee or something, and Ken had politely refused.

"So, Ken, you have become a fine young man. Eighteen now? And a bit cryptic about what you required of me at this point. Do sit down and tell me what I can do for you?"

"Mr. Richards, I apologize if I could not fully describe why I wanted to see you today over the phone, but I need your assistance in several matters. First, I would like to read my parents' wills if I might? You see our aunt never included us in this, and I'm more than a bit confused about the details of what happened in those days after the accident, and getting whisked off to boarding school so quickly, but I couldn't address it until now."

"This is most unusual, Ken. I am not at all sure how this happened either, then. You see, you were to become co-executor of your parents' estate upon your eighteenth birthday. I presumed your aunt had informed you of this, and you were simply waiting until after graduation to address your requirements with us. Wait one moment, please."

Mr. Richards used his phone to contact his secretary and asked that she bring the Fitzgerald estate file into his office. When she came in, she was carrying three extensive files and placed them in front of Mr. Richards and left quietly.

"This first file contains the last will and testament of each of your parents. There are the two originals signed by your parents and witnessed, and they have stamps on them, showing we have processed them through the county clerk as necessary upon death. These two copies I am giving you are your copies of these wills. They do not have the stamps of processing, but we witnessed them per the originals. If I might use your father's document to direct you to the salient points and then we can give you some time to read them over in their entirety if you choose. Here on page four is the clause that makes your Aunt Alicia the temporary guardian and executor of the estates if your parents should pass prior to your eighteenth birthday."

Mr. Richards directed Ken to the section, and they went over the terms.

"You see here, upon your reaching legal age, you are to become co-executor of the estate and have all rights to manage the trust activity. You can, should you choose, take custody of your three siblings, but you will see in the letter your father wrote to you that is here, he wanted to encourage you to wait on this until you completed college unencumbered by the responsibility of caring for your siblings so directly."

"Did my aunt read this letter?"

"No, your father gave a letter to each of you children that I was to give you when you reached eighteen and you were to decide when to give them to each of your siblings. There are also letters from your mother. Your aunt did not read them, but Ken, as your parent's attorney, I reviewed them to ensure they had not inadvertently included something that would create conflicts with their wishes committed in the legal document."

"I understand. So why was I, at least, not invited to the will reading?"

"Ken, I pleaded with your aunt when we spoke after that horrible accident that you should be present, and suggested she bring you and all of your siblings. She didn't think it appropriate to bring you, as she thought you were all too young and grieving too much. I could only insist on your being here if this had occurred after your eighteenth birthday."

"Why would she hide all this from me? I had no idea that I was to be a co-executor at all."

"I can only speculate why she did not inform you of this. And, please note in the next clause, the co-executor status between you and your aunt only lasts one year. On your nineteenth birthday, she is no longer a co-executor of the estate. She has certain rights if you leave her as guardian of your siblings until they would each reach their eighteenth birthday, however."

"What rights would she have?"

"She would have the right to request funds from the trust to pay for their care. She would have voting rights of their stock until they came of age in your father's company. Those are the only rights she would retain after your next birthday, again, so long as she remains as the guardian of your siblings."

"I will be out of college long before Kim is eighteen. If I hold off until then, but then get guardianship of Kim, what happens then?"

"Then your aunt would have no further rights to the trust funds at that point and no further voting rights."

"Are there any other important points we need to go over? I would like a minute or two to read all this over if I could?"

"Certainly, the other important details concern the creation of the trust from all the assets sold after your parents' death, and the disbursement process for the trust, and the management of your father's ownership of the business with Mr. Davis."

Mr. Richards pointed out the areas of the document where these three subjects were covered and then told Ken how to get funds from the trust. Then Mr. Richards surprised Ken again by saying that per the terms of his father's will, Ken would have the right to make a decision, and then work out with Mr. Davis his father's ownership, now that he was eighteen. After going over these two points, Mr. Richards took Ken into the next room, which was a small conference room, and sat him down with the two documents and the letters from his parents. The secretary came in and showed Ken how to work the lights if he needed more light to read, to bring him a glass of water, and then she quietly sat down a box of tissues and left the room.

Ken read over the wills and didn't really find anything there that Mr. Richards hadn't gone over that seemed hard to understand. Ken didn't realize that the home they had lived in had been sold already. That was a bit of a blow. He also saw that personal assets such as jewelry, books, papers and memorabilia had been boxed by Mr. Richards and his team and were in storage at this time. Apparently, that was up to Ken and his sisters and brothers to deal with when they were ready.

The letters were another matter. Ken had a hard time reading both letters. His mother spoke of how she hoped he didn't have to read this until all the events she spoke of had occurred, and she had the opportunity to share them. How she was so proud of the young man he had become, and how she was so excited about his going to college, finding a beautiful and smart woman to marry, and then to present her with grandchildren that she would lavish attention on. She said she knew he would go on to do great things, but never would lose his caring heart and love for his family. Ken sat for many minutes after he read his mother's letter and missed her so much. It felt as if she could have written these words just yesterday, but it was now already almost six months since that day. He had never felt the weight of the care of his family more than he did at this moment.

With that, Ken opened his father's letter. He had expected this letter to be all about promises that his father expected him to keep, but it wasn't. It was filled with pride over the first day that Ken walked, the first day he played football, the first day he went to school and all the days that his father said he would treasure about his first-born son. He spoke of responsibility, but then apologized if it had come too soon for Ken because something had forced Ken to read this letter before he had experienced life and finished with most of his firsts. He said he was sure of all his children, he could trust the others in Ken's hands because of his strong will, love of family and maturity that his father had seen in him from a very early age. It also said that his father did not expect Ken to follow in his footsteps, but in fact wished that he would find his own path, and that he hoped Ken would not burden himself with continuing the business unless it was absolutely what Ken wanted.

After Ken finished with the letters, he sat at that table for many minutes thinking about what he was going to do now, how he was going to handle all of this, and if he should change his plans about Harvard. He finally got up, gathered up the papers, and exited the conference room. Mr. Richards' office door was open, and the secretary motioned for Ken to go back in.

"Ah, I see you have finished reading. I know this must still be hard for you, and I realize this meeting may have made it seem harder, but Ken, I am here to help you. What questions do you have?"

"Mr. Richards, I don't think I have many questions. The information you gave me before and reading things over has cleared up a lot of why I came here today."

"Well, good, then let's move on. In order to establish you as the co-executor and allow you to draw funds from the trust fund, and act on voting for the business and other areas related to the business, we are going to need you to sign some papers. Please sit down again, if you will."

Ken sat down and they went over each paper before Mr. Richards had Ken sign them. All the papers that were required were in the second file that the secretary had brought in originally. When they finished going through and signing everything, Ken asked what the third file was about.

"That is an accounting of all activity of the trust fund over the past months since your parents' passing. It contains a copy of every document for you."

"Mr. Richards, I need two other things from you. First, I would like my activities with you related to estate and trust fund kept in confidence. Is that possible? And it would seem we might need to enter into an agreement for you to become my lawyer too, so that I can have representation when I need it. Second, I do not currently have a savings account or a checking account and I think it might be a good idea for me to get one. Can you assist with that as well?"

"Ken, I would be more than happy to continue as your family's representative in legal matters. Where the estate and trust are concerned, so long as your aunt is co-executor, she will receive notices of any activity and updates on the funds activities as you will. What you and I discuss here in my office, however, that is confidential and will not be shared with her. And, yes, I can assist you in establishing accounts with a bank. Would you prefer it be one here or one closer to campus for the next few months?"

"I graduate in May. I'm planning on going to Harvard, so it would be better to establish these accounts with a bank that can transfer me to a branch closer there. Can you help find this bank and arranging it for me?"

"Certainly, however, we will need you to sign a card at the bank in order to conduct business there. Let me locate a bank that might be convenient to both Choate and Harvard, and I will let you know."

"Thank you. And my concern about my aunt knowing things is that I am very concerned about her not telling me any of this. She might be trying to spare me, as you said, but it has been almost six months, and we spent both Thanksgiving and Christmas with her. I do not want her knowing about our conversations or this concern I have over her intentions, if you don't mind."

"Certainly. Now, if you can just wait one minute, I can have all the papers gathered for you and placed in an envelope for you to carry with you."

After Mr. Richards handed Ken the envelope with the letters, the wills, the trust and executor documents and a letter from Mr. Davis that was forwarded to Mr. Richards after the accident and will reading, Ken thanked Mr. Richards for his time and addressing all of his questions. He said he would be in touch about his decision on the guardianship within thirty days, and would be in contact about the business after he had read over Mr. Davis' letter and possibly spoken to Mr. Davis. Ken shook Mr. Richards' hand and left.

Mr. Reynolds met Ken downstairs by the car and offered to buy him lunch. They went to a restaurant nearby that Mr. Reynolds knew and had lunch and talked. Mr. Reynolds asked what the meeting was about and Ken simply indicated that because of his eighteenth birthday, he had to sign some papers related to the business, the stocks, and such. Mr. Reynolds didn't ask further, but said he could help Ken any way he could if he ever had any questions about stock, voting and such. Ken thanked him and again thanked him for helping to work out this travel and such.

As they departed the restaurant, Mr. Reynolds asked when the Easter break was and Ken gave him the dates. Mr. Reynolds left Ken with the car to get back to the station to catch the train and said he would call later in the week. On the long train ride back, Ken was deep in thought about the letters from his parents and what he was going to do now.

As Ken exited the train in Wallingford and prepared for the drive back with the car that Mr. Reynolds had given him, he saw Mary standing by his car. He smiled and crossed the parking area, and gave her a big hug.

"You can't believe how good it is to see you, and how much I needed to see you today, Mary."

"Gee, maybe you should go away for the day more often?"

"Are you ok Ken? Did you get the answers you needed?" She added when he released her from the hug.

"I got more than I bargained for, I think. Let's talk about it over some burgers. I'm starved."

They went to the burger joint just inside of town and then headed back to campus. During all that time, Ken told Mary all he learned from his meeting, and all he was thinking on the way back on the train. Mary was very supportive and listened closely to all that Ken had to say. As they approached campus, she finally spoke, "Ken, I know you want to take care of your sisters and brothers, but I agree with what your father said in the letter, that you should wait until after you finish college. You can't just jump into your father's business role, either. I think you need to spend some time learning things about business before you do that."

"I agree with you, I think, but what if Aunt Alicia goes nuts now that I have the information, and she has to share the control of things with me?"

"She is getting some money in order to care for all of you, but as you said, Mr. Richards said, she can't get money just because, it has to be related to your care. She will not jeopardize that just to spite you. You don't know your aunt's motives. Ken, I think you should talk to her," Mary said supportively.

"I hope you're right. Anyway, I have a little time to think it over before I have to do anything else with Mr. Richards. Thanks for listening and letting me talk your ear off, Mary. You mean the world to me and I wouldn't want to mess that up."

She smiled at him as they walked to the girls' dorm and reached out to hold his hand.

"You aren't going to mess it up, Ken. I'm here for you and want you to be happy all the time. Let's let this go for a few days and talk about it again after you have had some time to let it all sink in. How about that?"

"Sounds great, babe."

They kissed goodnight, and Ken headed back to the boys' dorm. He checked on Joe and then went to finish up some homework.

The next day, Ken had a meeting with his counselor and said he was going to reply to Harvard and accept admission to them for the fall. He forwent going anywhere where he could play football because he wanted time to get out to see his brother and sisters and wanted to make college his priority. His counselor helped him write his response letters and said he would put them in the mail for Ken.

Ken still wasn't sure if he was making the right decision, but Deb was due back the next day, and he decided he would talk this all over with her first.

8

Deb returned to campus late on Wednesday night. Ken had gone looking for her after dinner and found out that she had not returned yet. He left her a message at the dorm, but didn't hear from her before the curfew at eight. The next day, he didn't see her at breakfast, but Sue had told him she was trying to finish up something for class today. Ken finally caught up with Deb after class that day. He saw her leaving one of the buildings and ran over to catch up with her as she headed back to the dorms.

"Deb, wait up!"

Deb turned, saw Ken, and stopped and waited for him to catch up to her on the pathway back to the dorms. The girls Deb had been with waved and kept going while Deb waited for Ken.

"Sorry I didn't get to you last night. I saw your note, but Aunt Alicia didn't get me back here until almost ten o'clock last night. Then this morning I had to finish up some math homework that was due today."

"No problem. Listen, I really need to talk to you tonight. Can we meet in the library right after dinner? I've reserved one of those study rooms. I really need to talk to you."

"Sure, I was going to meet up with Ryan, though. How long do you think you need?"

"Not sure. I actually already talked to Ryan and Mary and told them we needed to talk about some family stuff."

"What's up Kenny? This sounds serious."

"I actually got permission to go on Tuesday to see Mr. Richards, Dad's attorney. Can we sit down and talk about it? I haven't talked to Joe or Kim yet, but figured I should start with you. Listen, I have to run and meet a couple of people from class for a study group for an enormous project we are working on. Can you just meet me, Deb?"

"Sure. I'll head over there right after dinner tonight. Kim has a girl scout meeting so she won't need either of us."

"See you then."

Ken took off toward the main hall to meet with his classmates, and Deb went into the girls' dorm to find Kim to see if she needed any help with homework. Kim said she was fine, but would need help this weekend with a paper. Deb said she would be glad to go over it and then went to her room to finish her homework. Before she could make it all the way to her room, someone yelled up the stairs that she had a visitor. Deb returned to the entry hall and saw Ryan standing there. He had a bag in his hand and motioned for her to join him in the receiving room. Deb said she had her books, and Ryan said to bring them. They went into the hall and sat at a small table. Ryan had already put his books on the table.

"I know you're busy trying to get caught up from being gone this week, and I am, too. I also know you didn't have breakfast, and I didn't see you at lunch either, so I brought you a snack."

At this Ryan produced the bag and in it were some grapes, a banana, some crackers and cheese. Deb gave him a big hug and said she missed him and thanked him for thinking of her. They sat down and snacked for a minute.

"So, tell me about the playoff game. How did you do?"

"You didn't see the posters in the main hall today?"

"I haven't been in the main hall today, but Sue told me you won. She also told me Dave got hurt. Is he going to be ok?"

"It's looking like he broke his collarbone. The doctor is checking him out again tomorrow, but not sure if he is going to be able to play in the next game. The game was fantastic! We really put it to them. The final score was only three to one, but they probably tried to score about fifteen times. The defense was awesome!"

"I'm so happy for you, Ryan. The team is doing so great. Did you score at all?"

"I made two of our goals."

"And no fights?"

"Only one, and I wasn't a part of it. It happened when I was out for a break."

"So, when is the next game?"

"Saturday night. We leave Saturday early morning. Can I take you to the movie night Friday night? Coach said we can go as long as we hit the sack right after the movie."

"That would be great if you're sure you won't be tired for the game the next day."

"I can sleep on the bus. So, I'll pick you up here for dinner? Is that ok?"

"Sure, but you know I will probably have Kim with me."

"No problem. I like your little sister."

"I think she thinks she's going to end up with you, by the way."

They both laughed, finished the snacks and got busy finishing home-work. Kim came down about ten minutes before they had to leave for dinner. She sat on the window seat and read while they finished up. Ryan left his books with Deb, who took all the materials up to her room for dinner. Then they, and a few more of Kim's friends, headed to the dining hall. Joe and Ken were already in the dining hall. Mary and Christy came up to Deb and asked how her trip to New York went. Deb sat down with them and regaled them with stories of the models and the photo shoot and everything, while Ryan gave Ken and Joe an update on the hockey tournament. After dinner, Kim took off right away to go to the Girl Scout meeting, and the rest of them walked back toward the girls' dorm. Ryan waited for Deb to retrieve his books and things, and then walked her to the library where she was meeting Ken.

Deb entered the library and went to the second floor. Along the wall with windows, there were small rooms with tables and chairs for small groups to go to work on projects, or for someone to go to study in a very quiet place. Deb found Ken in one of the rooms and went in and sat down.

"Thanks for doing this, Deb. I wanted to talk to you first about this so you could help me figure out how to tell the others. I think I told you, and I know I told Joe, that I think something is up with Aunt Alicia. The way this all went down since the accident and our getting shipped off here with little warning or time to react bothered me. The way she treated us at Thanksgiving and Christmas worried me, too. What bothered me most is that she said nothing about the reading of Mom and Dad's wills, and so I contacted Mr. Richards, and made an appointment to meet with him."

"But Kenny, isn't Mr. Richards in New York City?"

"He is. I asked Mr. Reynolds for some help, and he helped me get a train ticket, and had a car pick me up at Grand Central and take me to Mr. Richards office, then he met me, we had lunch, and he took me back to Grand Central to get back here on Tuesday, while you were in the city with Aunt Alicia."

"What did you tell him you were doing? Wouldn't he be suspicious or tell Aunt Alicia?"

"I told him I just had to sign some things because I was eighteen now. He thought nothing of it, and frankly, as consumed as Aunt Alicia is with what is going on with Aunt Alicia, I doubt it will come up in conversation. If it does, then hopefully you can help me figure out how to manage it with what I'm about to tell you."

"Ok sure, you know I'll help you."

"The first newsflash is the Mr. Richards was surprised to see me. Said he expected me to come to go over everything after graduation."

"Like he expected you, just not now?"

"Exactly. When I told him I would like to see the wills, he said, of course, he was confused why Aunt Alicia had not gone over them with me. He said he had to defer to her for the official reading, but had all indication from her that she would explain everything to me. "

"She didn't, did she? This is all news to you, right?"

"Right. So, Mr. Richards has his secretary go get the wills, and he goes over them with me. Here's the next round of newsflashes. Aunt Alicia is our guardian, well I should say, now yours and Joe's and Kim's guardians. She stopped being my guardian the day I turned eighteen. They have sold all the tangible assets and put into a trust along with all the savings and investments that Mom and Dad had. That includes life insurance and other things."

"Like our home, right? They've sold the house? We can never go back there, can we?"

Ken moved his chair closer to Deb's and put his arm around her. She was struggling with this little bit of news.

"That's right. I know it hurts to know this."

"There were things there, pictures, Mom's jewelry, Dad's certificates and that really cool stuff in his office that's all gone?"

"No, that stuff is in storage under the direction of Mr. Richards. The wills have terms directing the personal effects have to be held for me to address with all of you after I turn eighteen."

"Wait a minute, you mean Aunt Alicia knew we would get all that stuff, and she didn't tell you and she didn't tell any of us?"

"That's not all. Should I stop now?"

"No, tell me all of it."

"The assets are held in trust to be spent in the care of the four of us. For our living, education, health and well-being, that is a direct quote from the documentation. They are to be dispersed upon request from the executor of the wills for our care. Until Tuesday, the only person who could make those requests was Aunt Alicia. Now I can too."

"You mean you took control from her?"

"No, the wills stipulated I was to become co-executor with Aunt Alicia when I turned eighteen. That is why Mr. Richards expected me at some point, because I had to sign some documents to set that all up. Here is the catch though, once I am eighteen, Aunt Alicia can't simply ask for money for you three, and me, when she makes the request, they will check with me to be sure I know what the money is being spent on, and I get reports every month on disbursements."

"Wow. Do you think she's stealing money from Mom and Dad?"

"No, I've gone over all the transactions and it appears all legit, but why would she not tell us about this? She does have the right to ask for money when she is directly responsible for us. I think that is why we are spending breaks with her, and maybe why she took you to New York this week because there were charges to the trust for those time periods."

"Great, I just had a really great time with her and started seeing her in a different light, and now I find out that was all so she could get some extra cash this month from having me in her apartment for a few days!"

"Mr. Richards thinks it's all a big misunderstanding, and she was probably overwrought about the death of her sister and the sudden responsibility of us four, and that nothing bad is going on, if that helps you. And I don't think this means we shouldn't have a relationship with her. She is our aunt after all, and our mother's sister. It's just that I'll watch more carefully now."

"What else? There's more, right?"

"What isn't in the trust is Dad's interest in the business. That has been given to me with the instructions that I am to do whatever I want with it, and not feel like I have to follow Dad into the business. I am going to be meeting with Mr. Davis over our Easter break to see what he thinks about all this. Also, we all have stock in Dad's company, which, while Aunt Alicia is your guardian, she gets to vote in your place. She can also sell it, but if she does, the money has to go into the trust."

"How much is in this trust? Is it going to cover college for all of us? Will it help make sure Kim is ok? She is so much younger than all of us, or at least it seems that way."

"The trust has a little over two million in it right now. We can all go to college. And even if it wasn't large enough, I would make sure you all were taken care of."

"How can you do that if Aunt Alicia is our guardian? Wait a minute, you are not thinking of what I think you are thinking?"

Deb had stood up and was pacing around the table. Ken waited for her to stop for a minute and then asked her to sit back down. She sat down and he continued.

"I know what you're thinking, that I was going to become all of your guardians and then not go to college. Don't worry, I've decided not to do that. I actually went yesterday to my counselor and accepted at Harvard. So, chill, will you?"

"Thank goodness. I know you feel like you have to be responsible for us all, but that would go way too far, and I think Mom and Dad would agree with me on this, if that matters to you at all."

"Well, they did, as a matter of fact. The last newsflash. Mom and Dad both wrote letters to me that were included in the will. In it they both spoke about the fact that if this happened before I finished school, I should really finish even if I had a strong desire to take care of you all. I would be in a better position to do that with a college degree."

"It's not just that Kenny. I can't let you throw your whole life away for us. You need time to live too, don't you? Don't you deserve that? And with us here at Choate and doing much better now, why would you want to take that on?"

"Mom agrees with you."

Ken smiled at Deb and put his hand over hers. They sat there for a few minutes while Deb absorbed all she had been told here.

"Wait, did Aunt Alicia get to read the letters they wrote you?"

"No, that was stipulated in the will that the letters were for our eyes only."

"What do you mean, our eyes?"

"Deb, they wrote letters to each of us."

"Wow, it's a little creepy, isn't it? Like they knew something was going to happen or something?"

"I think it was more about planning for us. Mr. Richards said they had intended to make periodic updates on these letters over the years. I don't think they expected to go for a long time, but you know Dad, always trying to prepare for what was to come. They set all this up and wrote letters, expecting to update them later."

"Did you read them all?"

"No. I read mine only. I'll share mine with you if you want to see it, but I'm not going to show it to either Joe or Kim. It will upset them too much and given what they wrote to me, I am expecting each of you to be a little upset with whatever they write to you. I don't want to add to that."

"Did you bring mine?"

"I brought all the papers in case you wanted to look at anything. I think you should know what the process is with the trust fund in case something ever happens. The will says that if something happens to me, then you get all this when you are eighteen and on down the line."

"If you're ok with everything you read in the wills and stuff, I don't think I need to read it right now, if that's ok. I'm not sure I am up for that tonight."

"I understand. Just know, Deb, that I would never keep anything related to the wills or trust or our parents' plans from you, and I don't want you to feel you don't have a place in this family to decide with me and for us."

"Kenny, it's a really great thing that you're the oldest. I would pick you anyway to do all this, because you have always taken care of us all. Ever since I was little, I knew I could always count on you. I'm just sorry that you now have to really be the responsible one. Do you think you can ever cut loose and have fun again?"

"I felt like that all the way home on the train. Then Mary met me at the train station, and I felt better. Talking with you makes me feel better, too. I feel bad though. Taking care of my brother and sisters shouldn't feel like a burden, should it?"

"I remember one time I was playing with Denise in the backyard, and she got stung by a bee. Running into the house, I found Mom talking to one of the neighbors. I didn't want to interrupt, so I just stood there and listened. They were talking about that family that lived in the neighborhood. Do you remember the Smiths? They had those two boys that were always running wild in town and never seemed to come home at night, and then one of them got hit by a car. Do you remember?"

"Yes."

"Well, Mom was talking about it to that neighbor, and she said something that stuck with me, and I think it's what being a parent is about. She said, 'If you don't treat it as a blessed burden, you aren't doing it right.'"

"Yeah," Ken said solemnly.

"So, I think it's ok that you consider some of this a burden. It means you're a good older brother, will be a good parent, and apparently, we need that, since Aunt Alicia is clearly hiding things. I want to believe she is not up to something, but she is smart, Kenny, and if Mr. Richards is right, she was just upset about losing her sister. Then what about the last five months? She couldn't come up here and sit us down and explain all of this? She couldn't come to you and go over everything?"

"Let's not convict her until all the evidence is in, ok, and I don't want to alarm Joe and Kim."

They sat silent for a few minutes.

"Do you want to have your letters, Deb?"

"I do, but I don't. Does that make any sense?"

"Totally. It's how I felt as I sat in the conference room at Mr. Richard's office and read mine. Do you want me to be here when you read them, or do you want to read them alone in your room?"

Ken waited for her answer and then looked down and notice the watch that Deb had on.

"Where did you get the fancy watch? I know you have some new clothes care of Vogue. Mary told me."

"Mr. Reynolds gave it to me for my birthday. We met him for an early dinner the day Aunt Alicia brought me back here. It has diamonds around it. Isn't it great?!"

"Yeah, it is beautiful. I bet it cost a fortune. You better be very careful with it."

"Ryan told me today that he thought it might be from Tiffany's. He said it was expensive. I don't think I will wear it every day anymore, but I really wanted to wear it today and show it off."

"So, what's it going to be? Letters here, then I walk you back, or walk you back and hand you the letters?"

"If it's ok with you, Kenny, I think I'd like to read them alone. It might be harder with someone sitting here."

"I'm ok with that. We'd better get going as it is going to be eight o'clock soon."

They walked back to the girls' dorm kind of quietly. Deb told Ken that Ryan was taking her to the movie night tomorrow, and Ken said he and Mary would take the parade of ten-year-olds to the movie so she could have an evening without Kim bugging her. At that, they were at the door of the dorm. Ken reached into the large envelope that he had from Mr. Richards and pulled out two letters and handed them to Deb. Deb looked at them for a minute. Seeing her parent's handwriting was even affecting her. She hugged Ken quickly and went inside.

Upstairs, Deb sat down on the bed and opened the letter from her mother first. Her mother spoke of the day Deb was born, and how beautiful she was and how smart she was becoming. It spoke of how her mother was sad to think about Deb going to her first dance and prom and off to college without her, and all the life events that she would miss sharing if Deb was reading this letter. Her mother scolded her about not getting out more, meeting people and having experiences that were not in the past or contained in print in a book or buried under some dirt and rock. Deb laughed a little then, thinking that at least one thing had changed for the better coming to Choate. She had gotten out more. Deb sat there for a while, tears forming, thinking about the dance, and how she wished her mother had been there to help her with her hair and picking out a dress. At the end of the letter, her mother was hopeful. Hopeful that Deb would continue to excel in school and make something great of herself and doing something great in the world to advance understanding of history. Deb was really crying by the time she finished it. She hugged her pillow and whispered that she missed her and wished she was there.

After a long time, she opened the letter from her father. He always called Deb my angel, and he called Kim my princess. Naturally, he started the letter to My Angel. Like her mother, he, too, spoke of how wonderful he thought his beautiful daughter was becoming. How much he worried about her, but secretly always knew she would be alright. She had her older brother to watch after her. She cried when she read his apology for not being there to question her first love, for not being there to walk her down the aisle at her wedding, for not being there to see Deb graduate and for not being there to lift her daughter the way he had Deb when she was little. He then asked Deb to look after Ken as much as he was sure Ken would look after her. He said he would need her gentle and considered counsel as he made some tough decisions. Deb was really crying when she finished reading her father's letter.

When she calmed down, she wondered if she even wanted to read the letters they wrote to Ken, even though Ken had offered to share them. Of course, she would ask Ken if he wanted to read her letters as well. She wondered what would be in Joe's and Kim's letters and how she and Ken could best help them through this. She was going to need to talk to Ken about this, and soon, before he gave letters to Joe or Kim.

She went to bed with a heavy heart that night. Wishing for her parents and wondering what they should do now. Ken also went to bed with a heavy heart, but mostly because he was concerned about Deb.

The next day, Ken sprinted from his English class to get to the building that Deb was coming out of heading to the dining hall for lunch. He caught her just as she came out the door.

"So, how are you today?"

"Ok, I guess. I really need to talk to you again. Can you find me right after classes today at two thirty? I have a test that hour and we can leave as soon as we're done with the test so I can get out and find you."

"Sure, I'll meet you by Dey Hall, ok?"

"Ok."

They parted, and Deb ate lunch with several of her friends and headed back to class. At two thirty, she met Ken outside Dey Hall. It was a good afternoon in late March, so they sat on a bench near to the doors to Dey Hall.

"Deb, I saw you in the dining hall this morning at breakfast and you looked like you had cried all night long. Are you ok?"

"Yeah, the letters did really get to me. I may have cried myself to sleep last night."

"Deb, I'm so sorry. What can I do?"

"It's ok. It was just hard to read what they had to say. Here, I brought the letters with me for you to read if you want to."

"Let's trade and you can read what they had to say to me, too."

They exchanged letters and read each other's. It was easier reading them today than it was last night, and when Deb finished, she gave the letters back to Ken and sat there looking at him.

"I told you this is what they would want, Kenny. You need to go to college and deal with the guardianship issue after you graduate. Of course, by the time you graduate, both Joe and I will be eighteen, but Kim won't. Maybe you should just wait and see how things go until then, though."

"A big part of me agrees with you. I want to go to Harvard and want to have this time to grow, but I also know that I need to be there for you three. And then there is Mary, and I really like her Deb. I mean, I really like her, and I wouldn't want to change things with her by finishing high school, and then taking you all away from here."

"I was thinking last night after I read my letters, and now after reading your letters, when we first got here, I thought I would never like it here, and never get to know anyone and my life was pretty much over without Denise, but Kenny, some things are better here. We all seem so much closer here, and you found Mary, and Joe found Christy and I found Ryan. My teachers are outstanding, and I feel like I'm learning so much more here. It is tougher, but I kind of like it. Maybe it's not such a bad thing to leave all of this as it is."

"I've been thinking the same things. Kimmy is so excited about the Girl Scout things she is doing and has made so many friends and seems to really be growing up here, and I would hate to take this away from her. Joe, he has finally found something he is excited about and although I seriously doubt Christy is the girl he will end up marrying later, who knows?"

"I have been meaning to talk to you about Joe and this time bending thing too, Kenny. The more I think about it, the more I get a little concerned about it. I was talking to him at the hockey game recently about the things that might go wrong, and I'm a little worried. Plus, again, if we do this, things will instantly change. What if we find a way to stop the accident? We would come back here in that machine and find out that we are not students here, and have to find a way home, wouldn't we?"

"I don't know if that is how it would work. If we stopped the accident, we would never know this place existed. I have asked both Joe and Mr. Brewster about this. If you could go back and change something in history when you got to the moment where the change occurred, you wouldn't even remember that you built the machine and changed things. It seems weird to me too. Like, how do we get back then?"

"I miss Mom and Dad, don't get me wrong, but I'm liking it here. Plus, what if this was always the plan? What if Grandpa was right about everything? That there is a greater plan and we can only tweak it a little as we go, not dramatically alter it. What if we're supposed to be here at Choate and without our parents?"

"I'm still not sure I believe in Grandpa's spiritual stuff, or that God has a plan for all of us and we have free will, but that does not dramatically alter the course."

"The other thing I have been thinking about today is if you give the letters to Joe, it just might drive him forward, not make him stop and consider. Is that really a good idea if you and I are having misgivings?"

They decided to ponder it a bit and talk over their questions with Joe and Mr. Brewster tomorrow at the barn, as they had all arranged. Joe had told them at lunch that he and Mr. Brewster had figured out the last calculations, and they thought they were ready for some testing. They had all agreed to meet at the barn on Saturday afternoon. Deb and Ken walked back toward the dorms and went their separate ways after a quick hug.

Later, they all met at the dining hall and then Kim took off with Ken and Mary and a bunch of the girls from Kim's floor and classes, and Joe and Christy and Deb and Ryan went to find a quieter spot to watch the older kids' movie. Deb and Ryan snuggled on a big bean bag chair together for the movie, and then Ryan walked Deb back to the dorms so he could get back in by the time the coach wanted everybody in that night. Deb kissed him goodbye and told him good luck in the game the next day and went inside.

While in the other room, Mary was getting a little upset at their babysitting duty. She wanted to spend time alone with Ken and he didn't even ask her if she wanted to watch the younger kids. She tried to bring it up with him, but he didn't seem to even notice she was upset. At one point he even shushed her. She was going to have to find a way to talk to him about this, but what would he think? Would he decide she was too demanding? Maybe she would talk to Deb first.

Saturday morning, Deb was up and gathered Kim and some friends to go to breakfast. When breakfast was over, they went back to the girls' dorm and Deb, as promised, went up to Kim's room and went over her paper. She had done a superb job, and Deb told her so. This made Kim very happy. Deb decided this was the right moment to give Kim the books she had bought in town some time ago. Kim was delighted to get the entire collection of the Little House books. She asked Deb if she could bring them to the barn, and Deb suggested she just bring the next in line of order that she had not read yet, and she could sit and read while the others worked if she wanted to.

Deb and Kim headed off to the barn in search of the boys, and found them sitting at the big work table this had all started on. They were speaking about the mechanicals of the computer parts in the machine and Deb didn't really understand, but she sat and listened to the discussion. At some point, Ken pointed out that as a mechanical engineer student to be, this was something he might know more about than Joe, and Mr. Brewster laughed and agreed with Ken. They set about making some adjustments to the machine and while they worked, Deb decided this was a good time to start asking her questions.

"So, Joe, I have some questions about this idea of bending time. Can I ask you now?"

"Sure, just speak up as Ken is doing all this pounding."

"I am not pounding too loud. This is how it sounds when banging on metal parts!"

"So here is my first question, Joe. How do you know where you will end up when you start this up, and say set it somehow to go to a certain date?"

"Mr. Brewster and I have set the program up so you can give it a geographical location, like a longitude and latitude, along with date and time. It wouldn't get you to an exact street corner, but it'd get you close."

"What if you're uncertain what was at the specific latitude and longitude in the time you wanted to go? Like what if you wanted that street corner, but the streets weren't there yet?"

"You would still end up there. It would just be fields or dirt road, or something else."

"So, does that mean you would need to know a lot about what the geography of a place was before you set this?"

"That would help a bit," Mr. Brewster injected.

"Ok, so try to explain to me how this, what did you call it, program works?"

"We set a series of mechanisms and levers and numbered sequences in place in the machine. That makes up the program. The program has some flexibility to set the date and time and the location. Then, when you start the machine up through a series of steps, the program runs. Simple enough for you?"

"Yes, that's simple enough, but how does that program translate into going to another time and place?"

"So, this is the big calculation we figured out and why it was set up in parts."

The pounding had stopped because Ken was now listening intently as he wondered about this as well.

"First you generate power, and run it quickly through a chamber and focus light to a point. Then, you create a strong magnetic field around the machine through friction of the air just around the machine and actual magnets. Inside the machine, the light explodes in the chamber, and the program interacts with this energy in the machine and generates enough power to move the machine faster than the speed of light. Then the air shifts outside the machine just inside the magnetic field, and it moves you backward or forward in time based on your settings and slows you down just to that date and time and location. It will be like a piece of paper that is folded up and when the two edges touch, you move to that other time."

"What if one of those mechanical things fails?"

"You might end up a long way from where you planned."

"Or you might end up at the wrong time or location," added Mr. Brewster.

"But the machine would be with you there, so you might have a chance to fix things and get home, right?"

"Yes."

"Ok, so let's say you go back in time and you do something, and you don't realize you have done something. Maybe you met someone that was about to meet the person they were supposed to marry and because they met you, they end up searching for you, and never meet the person they were supposed to. And what if that marriage that didn't take place was supposed to be your best friends' grandparents? When you get back, your friend won't be there and you wouldn't have known you set that in motion, right?"

"This is the very crux of the time travel mystery that no one has yet figured out. It leads to more and more questions about different dimensions, and all kinds of things. Yes, it is possible to change the course of history by doing this, but isn't that the point?"

"Yes, but Joe, we're going back to a time before we're born. What if what we do stops the accident from happening, but also stops our parents from deciding to have children or something?"

At this point, Kim, who had been reading in a big chair that Mr. Brewster had brought out for her to sit in while they were all here, looked up.

"I don't think Mom and Dad would have ever decided not to have kids. They always told me they wanted children, and they wanted four. That is why they had me. It just took a while cause they were so busy with you three. Mom told me this, like, a thousand times."

They all erupted into laughter, which eased the tension in Deb's questions.

"Ok, Joe, I think this is the last question for now. Let's say we go back and we do something to stop the accident from happening, and Mom and Dad are ok. And we get back into your really cool machine and we come back. We would come back here, right? If Mom and Dad weren't in the accident, we wouldn't be enrolled here. How does that work?"

"This is the one thing I'm not totally sure of, and any research I have done has not turned up anything except science fiction conjecture. We're changing time by doing this, not changing us, and this is the significant point. So, I think we'll have all of our memory of this place and what we did here, but no one else will, because we are altering the course of time. I think Mr. Brewster will know because he was here this whole time, but like Aunt Alicia will have no memory of having to go to our house and take control and bring us here. I think we would not be enrolled as students here, and we would have to make our way home from

Mr. Brewster's house when we got back here. That's my best scientific theory. But to be honest, it's more like a guess."

"When we step out of this machine after we do this, we won't know if what we did worked right away, will we?"

"I don't think so, but I don't know. I mean the events that happened between the date we change and today would happen, but I'm not sure when we would know if what we did worked or what the impact was."

Kim looked up again, and added, "Just walk through campus when you get back. If no one recognizes you and no one talks to you, and you can't get into the dorm building without the door monitor yelling at you, you'll know you changed things."

Ken thought this was a good idea and said as much. Mr. Brewster, however, suggested that might be a risky plan, as strangers on campus would likely be questioned, and then they would have some explaining to do, and how could they explain what had happened?

"Have you even powered this thing up, and not given it coordinates to move you and just seen what goes on inside it yet?"

"No, Mr. Brewster and I were trying to do that yesterday when we encountered some issues starting the magnetic field and had to stop. That is what we're trying to correct. By the way, Ken, why have you stopped pounding?"

"I wanted to hear this."

They laughed again and got back to work. Soon they had it ready to go and were deciding who should be inside. Joe and Mr. Brewster decided it would be them, and Deb agreed. They knew the most about it, and had worked on it so hard, but Ken was not sure he liked it. He didn't want anything to happen to Joe. In the end he agreed he would monitor things from outside, and the machine had both a communication mechanism so those inside could speak to people outside, and a recording device inside that would show them everything the machine was doing and monitor both Joe and Mr. Brewster.

Joe and Mr. Brewster went inside. They started up the machine and continued to talk to Ken for a few minutes. Then it got quiet, well, from the talking perspective. The machine was making a lot of noise, and stuff was swirling around in the barn like it was the center of a tornado in there. Deb was about to get worried when the machine slowed down, and all the noise came to a stop. The talking started again then. Actually, the whooping and hollering started then, as Joe was screaming and Mr. Brewster was laughing, and they came tumbling out of the machine like that.

"It works, it works!"

"I can't believe you did it, Joe," laughed Mr. Brewster.

Ken, the voice of reason, "Ok, let's make sure you both are ok. Can you get some readings on your monitoring, Joe?"

"Ok, yeah, let's check all the readings." He went back into the machine, and you could hear some paper printing out like a typewriter. He came out with a long stream of paper and put it on the big table. Kim came over to see what was on the paper and was unimpressed with the fact that it was just lines of sentences and numbers. She went back to her book.

The readings showed that both Joe and Mr. Brewster had registered elevated heart rates during the magnetic field generation, but beyond that, everything was relatively unchanged. The machine showed readings indicated it had sufficient power and a strong enough magnetic field to perform as they expected. They were all pleased.

It was getting late in the day, so the four of them went to head back to campus and agreed that they would move to the next level of testing as soon as they figured out who was going and where. They agreed to go back to the barn the next day to discuss this after church service.

That night, Ken drove Mary and Joe, and Christy into town for dinner and bowling. Deb stayed back with Kim and they did some drawing, which was the second favorite thing for Kim to do after ceramics. They talked about Ryan, missing mom and dad, Ken and Mary and Joe and Christy, classes and friends. Kim admitted that she sometimes went whole days without thinking about their parents now. Deb assured her this was ok, and how it was supposed to be.

At the bowling alley, Mary was again a little frustrated over not being able to spend time alone with Ken. Joe and Christy were right with them all the time. When she asked Ken if they could go get something to drink, Joe immediately said he would go with Ken to get drinks. When they got back to campus, Joe walked with Christy up the steps to the girls' dorm, but Mary stood by the car. Ken turned to her, "What's up?"

"Can we talk for a minute?"

Ken walked back to the car and came around to the side Mary was standing by. He looked down at her and waited.

"Ken, why don't you want to spend time with me anymore?"

"What are you talking about?"

"Well, last week we took the young girls to the movie and tonight we had to have Christy and Joe with us. Why don't you want to be alone with me anymore?"

"Mary, it's not that I don't want to be alone with you, but I have two sisters and a brother here. I have to watch over them."

"They all seem to be adjusting to being here fine, I don't see why you have to be with them all the time."

"You don't have to be jealous of my brother and sisters, Mary. I care about you in a way I won't ever care about them, but you have to understand that I feel responsible for them, and I have to watch out for them. It's not that I don't want to be with you. I do."

"Well, ok. I'm not jealous you know."

"It sure seems like you are," he said, but he was smiling as he said it, realizing for the first time that he might like her being jealous of what takes him away from her. He said as much and she stomped her feet and insisted she wasn't jealous. He reached for her and pulled her close, holding her for a minute. He said he was sorry if she thought he was making fun of her. She looked up and said, "maybe this was all I needed."

The next day, they all went back to the barn directly after church services. They sat at the table and discussed how they would proceed. Joe and Ken agreed that the next test should be to put someone in the machine and send them somewhere and bring them back. The time and place had to be such that the test subject would not meet themselves, and wouldn't interact with anything so as not to disrupt history too much. They also decided that they would go back in time instead of forward. When it came time to decide who, that is when it got more heated. Ken and Joe and Deb argued for several minutes over who should go, each of them concerned about the other having some sort of accident in the process or being hurt. Ken was pacing around the barn, and both he and Joe were yelling quite a bit.

Finally, Mr. Brewster ended the discussion by saying, "I will go. I'm older, and if something happens, it won't impact anyone else. Except you four for knowing. As this is a test, it is the best way to proceed. We don't know if everything will go correctly, so I am not risking any of you on this next step."

Ken agreed, so long as Mr. Brewster was willing. Now they just needed to determine the date, time, and location to set the test up. He said he would think about it a bit, and let them know. The four of them returned to campus and separated to finish homework. Ryan returned on the bus with the other hockey players and met up with Deb for dinner and to get caught up on homework. She told him what happened with the machine on Saturday and he told her about the game on Saturday and how they won again.

Ken came running into the main hall where Ryan and Deb had been working together on homework, and Joe and Christy were sitting playing a video game on the television. He said that he had just gotten off the phone with Mr. Reynolds, who was sending Michael to come and pick them all up on Friday and take them to the Hampton house for the week off for Easter. He had said he needed to be in Europe for the week and apparently Aunt Alicia was joining him, so they would be at the house with the house staff. Deb was disappointed that she wouldn't see Ryan for a week, but his parents were coming up, and were following the team around as they had games scheduled for Tuesday and Thursday and if they won then, there would be a championship game next

Saturday. Mr. Reynolds said they could call their respective girlfriends and boyfriend whenever they wanted, and Ken gave out the number to the Hampton house so they could be called there as well. They set their break plans. Hopefully, they could get the next test in before they left campus on Friday.

The next day, Mr. Brewster was working on landscaping near the building where Deb had class, and motioned to her as she left the building for lunch. Mr. Brewster told Deb he had figured out where he wanted to go and when, and gave her a piece of paper with some information on it. He asked her to research it a bit if she could, since she was the history buff, and make sure his details were correct. She said she would, and promised to get word to him as soon as possible, and to tell Ken and Joe at dinner that night. It turned out that Mr. Brewster wanted to go to a feed and hardware store in Iowa on December 12, 1941. It was the last day his father was working at this, his father's store, before he was set to leave for training and deployment in the army in the Second World War. That night, Mr. Brewster's father married his mother, and she became pregnant that night with their only son. Mr. Brewster's father never came home from the war, and he never got to know him. He decided he would like to go back there, go into that store, and talk to his father, giving nothing away who he was, and see what kind of man he was.

Deb thought it was a sweet idea, and she managed to check some records and found that Mr. Brewster's father served in the war and died during the invasion of Normandy. She found an old picture of him in a book in the library of all places, of people identified after the invasion and buried near Normandy. Mr. Brewster and his father had some resemblances, but Deb doubted it would do anything but make the older Mr. Brewster think they might be related. Ryan helped her locate an old survey map of Iowa in the agriculture center, and they found a small farm nearby with a creek that had a lot of tree coverage. They located the longitude and latitude for the general area of this farm and creek, and Deb got all this information to Joe the next day.

They all agreed that the test would be on Thursday afternoon. Ken and Joe had classes that were not even meeting that day because so many students were leaving campus early, and Deb and Ryan agreed they would get to the barn as soon as they could. Ken and Joe would go over and set things up with Mr. Brewster and be ready when they arrived. Deb reminded Joe to tell Mr. Brewster to make sure he located some older overalls, a long sleeve shirt and some work boots so he fit in, and gave Joe a picture she found in a book of a farmer from Iowa from the time period just before the date they had selected.

When Ryan and Deb arrived the next day, the machine was programmed, and they were ready to go. Mr. Brewster seemed excited, but nervous. Deb was really nervous, and she said as much as she and Ryan made their way to the barn. Mr. Brewster had been so nice to them all, especially Joe, and she wanted nothing to happen to him.

"Joe, how long will Mr. Brewster be there, and while he is away, how will time pass here?" Ken asked.

Joe looked at Mr. Brewster before he answered. "We expect that time will pass more quickly for Mr. Brewster than it does for us here. It won't seem that way for him, but that is what we are expecting the time lapse difference to be. We expect he will come back here in what seems like minutes when, in fact, it will be hours there."

"Remember, Mr. Brewster, you can't interrupt your father's plan for that night," Deb said gently.

"I know. All I want is to just go into the shop and seem like I'm a customer, and ask him some questions, find out what kind of man he is. I doubt I will stay over fifteen or twenty minutes."

With that, Mr. Brewster stepped into the machine, and Joe talked to him for as long as he could. Joe was surprised at the noise the machine made and the wind it created. It blew a lot of papers around in the barn. Then they sat and waited. They waited for what seemed like a long time, and then first the wind started, and then the noise started, and suddenly the machine was back, right where it had been, when Mr. Brewster stepped into it. Thankfully, at that moment, he stepped out of it, all in one piece.

Mr. Brewster was grinning when he announced, "That was amazing, Joe! I was tingling the whole time, over my whole body, and it seemed like my heart would beat out of my chest, but meeting my father, that was amazing. You have made me a very happy man, young man, very happy."

Joe ran into the machine to start the printout of the readings, and Mr. Brewster sat down. Deb asked him how it was. Did he meet his father and such? Mr. Brewster told them he exited the machine in Iowa just next to that creek and walked down the road to the store. He met his father and talked with him for about thirty minutes. Ken asked if his father asked who he was, and Mr. Brewster said he had, and that he had explained that his pa was buying a plot in the next county and he had taken a walk when the negotiations were going on, and ended up in the store.

"My father then offered me a bottle of coke, and we sat and talked. We talked about farming and seed, and he told me about his plans that night to marry his girl before he left for the war. It was wonderful. Then, he offered to drive me back, but I told him I couldn't keep him from his big date at the church, and I would just walk back. He tried to stop me, but a customer came in and I ducked out."

"Wow," that seemed to be all Ken could say.

"Clearly I'm still here, so I didn't stop him from getting to the church on time."

They laughed at that. Joe brought the readings out then, and they went over the data. It seemed it was a success, so they decided the next step would be to research when the next trip would be. Deb said she was formulating a plan and would have details for them when they got back from break. She said she would go over it with Joe and Ken, and they would review the plan with Mr. Brewster and Ryan, as he pointed out, when they got back to campus.

As the four of them walked back toward the dorms to get ready for dinner, Ryan asked, "Are you guys ever going to tell Mary and Christy what you're really building there?"

Ken answered first. "Not until we're sure of our plans. I'm still trying to figure out how to explain this to Mary. I don't want to lose her, and I think it's going to be hard to convince her my intentions were honorable when this started, but it seemed to get harder to reveal it as time went on. So please don't say anything around them, Ryan."

"No problem. I'm just glad I know. Deb told me about the questions she asked you Joe, and I would hate for your plan to work and you change something and then I don't know any of you. I think Mary and Christy might feel the same way. If you tell them, at least they will always have the memory of you both, instead of just you know, going to the dining hall that night and not know who Ken or Joe Fitzgerald is, or even knowing they should miss them."

"I didn't think about it that way. Ryan, what will you do if we come back and aren't students here anymore because we changed things?" Ken asked.

"I would find a way to find Deb and you all, and make sure you were ok, and continue with Deb for the next year until we graduate."

"The thing is, if we tell them, they'll want to be there too, and the more people that know about this, the better chance we have for the secret to get out. If people know, who knows what will happen, right?" Joe pondered.

They all kept it secret for now, but Ken was thinking he might tell Mary before they left on break. They all went to dinner and ended the night without another word about the machine. The next day, everyone else was leaving campus. Deb was able to see Ryan off and meet his parents. Then she and Kim and her brothers loaded up their things in the limousine that Michael had driven, and headed off for the drive and ferry to the Hamptons.

9

Michael pulled into the drive of the Hampton house rather late that night. Deb had to wake Kim to get out of the limousine and go inside. Michael carried their luggage in, with the help of Ken and Joe, and took it into some of the same rooms they had been in when there were here for Thanksgiving. Mr. Reynolds had set up a room for each of them now, and had someone come and redecorate these rooms to be more suited for teens, Michael told them. On Saturday, the cook had arranged for them to decorate Easter eggs. Kim was very excited because she still wanted to do this, but the others thought they were too old for this now, but eventually they too joined and ended up having a wonderful time.

Ken asked Michael to drive him into town that afternoon, and wouldn't tell the others what he was going for. Deb thought she might have an idea, but said nothing in front of Kim. It was a really wonderful warm day, so Deb suggested that Joe and Kim go with her down to the beach. Kim thought that was a great idea, and they spent the afternoon there making sand castles and hunting for shells. Ken returned and joined them, and it was a really wonderful afternoon, the four of them enjoying the break and the day together.

The next day, Kim woke Deb rather early, which she was not pleased about, but when they arrived downstairs, it was to find Easter baskets for Deb, Joe, and Kim. Deb thought that this was what Ken was doing yesterday, so she ran upstairs and got the things she had bought a few of weeks ago when she went into town with Kim to buy books. She wanted Ken to have an Easter too, but she forgot to buy a basket. She asked the cook, who quickly ran to retrieve one from the holiday storage cabinets.

Deb set the basket up and sent Kim up to wake her brothers, and placed the new basket by the others.

By the time that Joe and Ken got downstairs, Michael had appeared and was helping the cook set up a breakfast in case they wanted it between the baskets and the egg hunt. Kim asked where the other basket came from and Michael informed her, he found it in the other room. The Easter bunny apparently had misplaced Ken's basket. Ken was surprised as well. He questioned Michael, but Michael assured him he hadn't done this. They all received a small gift and candy. Kim received a sketch book and charcoals to do some artwork. Joe received a subscription to a mathematical journal and an original smaller version of a Turin machine. Deb received a journal to write her thoughts in and a ring that had her birthstone in it. Ken received a drafting set. After they went through the baskets, they had some breakfast and then went outside to find all the eggs. Later, they had a splendid meal and asked Michael and the cook to join them. During the afternoon, Deb spoke to Ryan, and he said that he had practice on Saturday. He wanted to see her, but they had a game on Tuesday. He promised to call her on Tuesday evening.

On Monday, Ken took them all into the city so that Deb and Joe could go to the library for Deb to do research on the history and spot that they wanted to go to, and Joe to do some research on any existing studies and experiments on time travel. Ken took Kim to FAO Schwarz to browse toys and bought her something. They all met for lunch and then Kim went back to the library with Deb and Joe so that Ken could meet with the lawyer again and get his bank account set up. Deb sat up that night for a long time, looking through the material she had from the library and Mr. Davis. She decided that writing out a plan would help them all, so she started on that.

The next couple of days Deb finished up her write up, and they went into town on the Hamptons, and to the beach. The four of them had a really great time together playing on the beach and Kim mentioned that this place was feeling like home. Ryan called Tuesday night and told Deb that they won the game and were headed to the next location for the Thursday game. If they won that game, they would be in the championship game on Saturday. He was not happy about that, and was very conflicted about winning Thursday because that Saturday was Deb's birthday. Ryan also called Ken, unknown to Deb, to plan something for her birthday. Ken talked to both Michael and the cook to plan for Saturday as well.

On Saturday, Deb was stirred by Kim, who had brought her breakfast in bed. This was an old family tradition for them, as their mother had done this for all of them for their birthday. Deb really appreciated it. Kim also gave her the first of her gifts, and as she indicated, was her new tradition of making gifts. Kim had made Deb a ceramic tray for her dresser to keep all the jewelry she had received from Ryan and Mr. Reynolds. Deb hugged Kim and told her it was a beautiful tray, and she would keep it always for her treasures on her dresser. They went downstairs and found both Ken and Joe sitting at the table. They all went down to the beach for some fun in the surf because it was very warm that day.

They had dinner, and then Deb opened her other gifts. She was so happy, and they enjoyed the cake that the cook made. From Ken, Deb received a set of archeology digging tools, from Joe she received a book on early American history and Kim gave her the book 'Gone with the Wind', saying it was about history, sort of. They all laughed, and it was a great night. Later the next morning, after breakfast, Michael took them all back to campus.

After they all unpacked, they met in the main hall. Deb had brought her plan document and wanted to go over it with Ken and Joe. Kim came with them and sat on the couch near the table they all sat at and was drawing in her new sketch book. Deb started by briefly reviewing everything she found out in the correspondence with Mr. Davis, and the research she and Ryan had finished on the Fitzgerald and Davis Holding Co. Because some of their original business plan was innovation in construction for housing for low-income and underprivileged people, Deb had decided if they could somehow impact the original meeting, they might change the business activities of their father and Mr. Davis, which might alter the movement to the other holdings they got involved in, and have them meeting with the set of clients they met with that fateful day of the accident. Deb reasoned that this would have the least impact on the overall timeline of the business, their parents, and the four of them.

"Ok, this sounds like a good idea and sound logic, Deb, but how are we going to impact that first meeting enough to change the business plan?"

"Ken, we have to find a way to stop President Kennedy from being assassinated that day. I figure that both Dad and Mr. Davis will end up in that bar even if they see the President and there is no assassination, but if they have only good things to talk about that day, they might not decide their first business venture is construction of affordable modular housing."

"And you think this is enough to change the timeline, and later keep them from this particular client meeting in Colorado?" Joe asked.

"I do Joe."

"But what about the idea that we do as little as possible so we don't impact so many other people's lives? This is a significant historical change, Deb," Ken asked.

"I think it might be for the better, though. If President Kennedy isn't killed that day, or he lives through that day, he enacts civil rights so much earlier, he had several initiatives for the economy that were never enacted, and he probably would keep us out of the war in Viet Nam, since his public comments up to his assassination showed, he didn't want to get further involved there, and this is just what he spoke about, imagine what other good things he might have accomplished? How can this be bad? Why can't we change something else for the better while we try to stop our parents' accident?"

"Some of what you are saying, Deb, seems like a great idea, but should we really be messing with history that much? And how are you sure it will change the outcome for our father and Mr. Davis?" Ken continued on his questions.

"Ken, in my letters with Mr. Davis, he spoke about the meeting in the bar in Dallas after the assassination, and how they talked about keeping his dream alive by doing something for the economy and civil rights. I doubt I can change the desires of either our father or Mr. Davis, but if there is no assassination that day, they might still meet and might still be motivated by the speech, but they would either wait to start their business because they would want to see what the President started, or they would not feel the strong desire to head toward civil rights and initiatives in housing."

"Dad had an advanced degree in physics. Perhaps he would have ended up in the space program or something if the assassination didn't take place," Joe said, remembering conversations he had with his father.

"Joe, that's a good point, but will this change also stop our mother and father from meeting? Don't they meet that same year?"

"Kenny, they meet that same year. In fact, a week later at that play, Dad had to see for a class that Mom was working at. I don't think this will change that event."

"Ok, let's say we do this. What exactly are we going to do to stop an assassination? This country still can't decide if it was Oswald or there were other people involved. How do we go about stopping this?" Joe asked, ready to move forward with her plan.

"So, here's what I've come up with. We can't just march in there and say we're from the future and we know the President is going to be assassinated today. Cancel the motorcade, please. However, we can figure out a way to get credible enough information to the Secret Service leading up to the day, so they close down the book depository building. That would certainly stop Oswald, and if there was a conspiracy, that alone should give that group enough pause to reconsider. Also, that morning, they're in Fort Worth at the Texas Hotel, and the President goes and speaks in the parking lot, and to a breakfast and Mrs. Kennedy comes down later. If we get right up to the day, I figure we can get into the hotel and try to speak to Mrs. Kennedy, and convince her to either change the route or leave the bubble on the convertible or change the event enough to impact the outcome," Deb explained.

"We could call the Dallas police from a pay phone and phone in the threat," Joe offered.

"Joe, that would work, but we'll have to be very careful about the phone we select to use and not stay on the phone too long."

"Also, we might get close enough to one of the Secret Service guys to pass a note or something," Ken offered, now believing in this plan.

"Ken, how would you do that?" Joe asked.

"Well, Deb said they are staying in a hotel the night before. The Secret Service should be at that hotel a few days before. We can wander around and find one, and slip a note in his pocket or something."

"Perhaps we can have Kim walk right up to them and say some man gave her a note to pass along or something," Joe suggested.

"That might raise too much suspicion, and might start questions on why we don't have parents with us. I don't want to put Kim in a direct line with police or Secret Service if we don't have to," Ken said authoritatively.

"I bet she could get Mrs. Kennedy's attention, though. If we end up in that situation, we could have Kim bring her flowers or something and say something to her," Deb suggested, smiling.

"These are all good ideas for getting the word out, Joe and Ken. For the next part of the planning, we have to figure out how much time we might need to be there, and then we're going to have to get clothing and a place to stay and Ken, you might need some identification since you're over eighteen, just in case. Also, we're going to need to make sure we have some money in case we need it. I think we're going to need to set our date and time a couple of days before so we can try to impact the motorcade, and then try to get out from Fort Worth, and not go to Dallas. That way, we'll have no chance of running into our father. I doubt it would matter because this is all before any of us are born, but Kenny, you look just like our father in the senior picture we have from the files that night, so he might come up to you or follow you if he sees you," Deb further explained her planning.

"So, we should set the machine for November twentieth. Deb, is that enough time or do you think we need to be there one more day? I think it is best if we are there as short a time as possible." Joe wanted to steer them to actual planning steps.

"Joe, I agree. I was thinking the twentieth myself," Deb replied.

"Ryan and I found an old map of Fort Worth, and there's a lake just a little southwest of a town called Benbrook Lake. It's not very populated in nineteen sixty-three, so if we can try for a spot on the northwest end of the lake, we wouldn't be too far from Fort Worth proper. I have the latitude and longitude in these plan documents."

"I can get money, but how are we going to get clothing that's appropriate for early nineteen sixties?" Ken asked.

"I think we can put together some outfits for all of us from the theater department. I just need to figure out how to get us in there, and get the clothes out of there," Deb suggested.

"Mary's best friend is into theater. Maybe we can use her to help us there," Ken remembered being dragged to a theater production and Mary introducing her.

"But Kenny, that means you'll have to tell Mary what's going on. Are you ready to do that?"

"Yes, I think it's time to bring her in. I don't want to lose her, and I've decided that's the only way I can ensure that we remember one another if this time-hopping does more than just save our parents."

"Ok, so Joe, you take the plan document and go over the dates and longitude and latitude information; I'll put together what clothing I think we'll need and what other supplies we're either going to need to bring with us, or have to acquire as soon as we get there; and Ken, you need to talk to Mary and get ready to 'borrow' some clothing from the theater department. Does this sound like the plan?" Deb asked.

"Yes. Mr. Brewster and I can have the machine ready to go this week. Do you both think we can be ready that quickly?" Joe asked.

"I'm not sure we can have all the clothing and everything ready that quickly, Joe, but how about we have a check back either Wednesday or Thursday?"

"Not Wednesday. I have a big test in my English class on Thursday and I'm going to need to prepare, as it's an essay test. It'll have to be Thursday evening," Ken said, remembering this test he was dreading.

"Did you wait until the last minute again, Kenny?"

"It's Sunday evening, Deb. It won't be last minute unless I wait to do any preparing until Wednesday night."

Joe laughed, and they all got up as it was nearly eight o'clock and they needed to get to the dorms. They agreed to meet in the library study rooms on Thursday at four thirty and they left for their respective dorms.

The next day, Ken told Mary during their walk from the dining hall to the building where their classes were held that he wanted to talk to her that night. They agreed to go for a walk after dinner. During that same walk, behind Ken and Mary, Deb was walking with Kim to her building that was on the way to the building that Deb's morning classes were in.

"Kim, you didn't say anything at all last night while we were discussing the plan. Why not?"

"You guys seemed to have it all under control and didn't seem to need me, that's why."

"Kim, are you upset with me for not having something specific for you to do?"

"Not just you Deb, Ken said he didn't really want me helping. I know I'm only ten, but I can do things too, you know. And if we're going to land somewhere near a lake with no actual idea where we are, you might need my navigation skills that I learned in girl scouts this year."

"Ok, first, Ken didn't say he didn't want you to help, he said he didn't want you in harm's way. But you're right about needing navigation help. You will be helpful with that. Especially if we have to make a quick getaway. We're going to need someone that can navigate us through what appears to be woods on the map."

"I just want to be included. If we're going to save Mom and Dad, I want to be included. I'm not a baby, you know."

"Yes, I do know that, Kim. I'm sorry. How about after dinner you come to my room and I can lie out the map that Ryan and I printed and we can go over it? You can help check my coordinates and we can talk about supplies you think would be helpful for us to have. How about that?"

"That would be fun. It would be like planning a camping trip. We haven't been on one of those since the accident."

"You're right. If we think about it like a camping trip, we won't forget anything we need, will we?"

Kim smiled up at here as she approached the door to the classroom building.

"I'll see you later then, Kim."

"Yeah, and thanks Deb."

"Hey, good luck on your geography test today!"

"Thanks Deb."

When the afternoon classes ended, Ryan found Deb and asked if they could have a quiet moment so he could give her the birthday gift he had for her. She said yes, but that she needed to get his Easter gift from her room to give him. They met a few minutes later and went for a walk toward the park near town. When they got to the park, Ryan produced from a bag he was carrying, a blanket and some snacks. They sat down, and Ryan gave her his gift. He gave her an exquisite charm bracelet. It had a dress charm, a heart charm and a letter "R" charm. Deb thought it was amazing and hugged Ryan. They talked about the championship game and Deb gave Ryan the gift she had for him for Easter. It was in a small basket and had some candy. Ryan had spoken regularly that he really wanted a jersey of his hockey mentor, Bobby Hull. So, Deb got him a jersey with Hull on the back and his number. Ryan really loved it. Ryan then pulled out a basket from his bag and gave it to Deb. It was also an Easter gift and had some candy and a framed picture of them from the formal. Deb really loved the picture, and they had a glorious afternoon.

After classes that day, Joe took off to the barn to go over the plan with Mr. Brewster and to get the machine ready. He was ready to push Deb and Ken to set the plan in motion this Friday. More importantly, he was more than ready to have his parents back. Of course, again, he barely made it to the dining hall just before the Reverend started doing the evening prayer. He slid into the seat nearest Ken and hardly acknowledged either his sisters or Christy, who was motioning him to come over by her. She looked down when he didn't acknowledge her and then started talking with her friends instead. During dinner, Kim regaled Ryan with stories of the Girl Scout camping trips she had been on, which he politely tolerated while making eyes at Deb. Ken and Mary spent dinner time going over plans for the English test later that week.

After dinner, Ryan walked Deb and Kim back to the girls' dorm, and then took off to work on a class project with some other classmates for his theology class. Ken and Mary left on their walk, and Christy caught up with Joe and asked if she could talk with him. He reluctantly agreed, and they went into the parlor of the girls' dorm.

"Joe, would you tell me what's bothering you?"

"Nothing is bothering me, Christy."

"Well then, why didn't you even look at me at dinner, and why didn't you come and sit with me when I motioned for you to?"

"I have a lot on my mind this week, is all."

"It seems like you always have a lot on your mind and you're always busy. If you don't want to see me anymore, I wish you would just tell me."

"It's not that Christy, it's just that I'm focused on this math project and it takes up a lot of my time."

"This isn't a project for class, is it?"

"No, it's just something I'm working on."

"Why won't you explain it to me, then?"

"Listen, before, when I used to go with my mom to Harvard and worked on the big computer there, I started working on some ideas with my father. That's all I'm doing, and there isn't really much else to explain. I'm sorry I don't have more time, but this is important to me."

"I get that it's important, and I'm not trying to pry Joe. Why are you getting agitated?"

"Because I'm being interrogated, like I'm at the police station or something."

"I don't think I'm interrogating you. I'm sorry."

They sat silently for a few minutes and Christy began to cry.

"Maybe we should take a break then, Joe, so you can focus on this project that is obviously so important to you. You know it won't bring your parents back, right?"

Joe stood up and jammed his hands into the pockets of his school uniform blue pants.

"Christy, you don't understand. You have both of your parents. You don't know what this feels like. And you don't understand how important this project is to me."

"You're right Joe, I don't have any idea what it feels like to lose your parents. I can only guess what that might be like for you. We could talk about it, you know, and maybe I could help you."

"I don't want to talk about it, and I know that talking about it will not make this better."

Joe circled the room twice, thinking.

"I guess you're right. We should take a little break. How about if I come and see you in a week or so?"

Christy looked down at her hands, folded in her lap.

"If that's what you want, Joe."

She didn't look up as Joe stood there a few minutes more, looking at her. Then Joe left. He headed straight for Mr. Brewster's barn even though it was nearly seven o'clock and he only had an hour until curfew.

Meanwhile, upstairs in Deb's room, Deb and Kim were looking over the map that Deb and Ryan had located of historical Fort Worth, Texas.

After reviewing Deb's plan and looking at the area around the lake that Deb thought would be a good place to land, they reviewed what supplies they would need.

"Are we planning on camping out at this lake?"

"No Kim, it will be November, and I don't think it'll be safe for us to do that. Kenny has some money saved up, and we're going to get a hotel room in Fort Worth to stay in."

"Well then, if we're not camping, we'll just need some maps and probably a compass or something to find our way away from the lake and back to it."

"That's a good idea. I was also thinking we might try to find a bus schedule right away or something so we can get around when we get into Fort Worth."

"I don't know how you can get a schedule now for bus routes that were going on in nineteen sixty-three, though."

"I don't suspect we'll be able to get the bus schedule until we get there."

"What are we doing for clothes again?"

"We're going to have to bring some clothing with us. Ken was thinking we would try to borrow as much as we can from the theater department, which is what he's talking to Mary about tonight, I think."

"I want to bring my sketchbook, too. Can I do that?"

"Yes, but not your camera. Those weren't available in nineteen sixty-three, so we can't risk having anyone see you with it."

"Ok. I want to go see Rebecca now if that's ok?"

"Sure, if you're done checking over the map for me?"

"Yes, I think everything looks good. Just be sure to get a compass and I think we might need to bring this map, and if we can find a road map from that time, it would be helpful, too."

"I'll work on the road map this week. I'm not sure where to find a compass, though."

"I think one of the girls from my troop has one. How about I ask her if I can borrow it? I'll tell her we're thinking of going on a hike next weekend or something."

"What a great idea. Let me know if that doesn't work and I'll see if I can find a store in town that might carry them."

"Doesn't Joe want to start up the machine and do this by Friday? Will we have time to get to town by then?"

"I'm not sure Friday is reasonable, but we'll see how our plans progress over the next couple of days. If we have to delay it to locate a compass, we will."

"Ok, see you tomorrow."

With that, Kim left Deb's room and returned downstairs to find her friend, Rebecca. Deb got out her homework and started on it, but kept thinking about the conversation that Ken was having with Mary right now and was hoping it went well.

Ken and Mary had walked around the outside perimeter of campus. There were fewer people there milling about, and Ken wanted to make sure he could speak honestly about what was going on without having to constantly check for people around them. They got around to the north side of campus and sat down to talk. At that point, Ken had told Mary about the machine and what Joe and Mr. Brewster and he had created.

"Ken, you don't really think you can bend time, do you?"

"Mary, I don't think we can do it. We have done it. Right before the Easter break, we sent Mr. Brewster back to nineteen forty-one to meet his father. It was amazing. The program ran and created this circle around the machine that had a strong magnetic field, and just around that a huge strong wind blowing. Then the machine just disappeared into thin air. About thirty or forty minutes later, the wind started first, then a bright light, a pop noise, and the machine appeared out of thin air."

"I'm having a hard time believing this, Ken."

"Yeah, I did too at first. I told Joe it was all science fiction. Then he showed me. Joe wants this so badly. He really felt, even before my parents died, that he had nothing special about himself. He told me before Thanksgiving last fall that I had muscles and athletic prowess. Deb was this history genius and was probably going to write some hugely successful book, and Kim was going to do something great too, but he had nothing. I really had to convince him he had the brains in our family. And he's had a terrible time missing my parents. He doesn't want to talk to any of us, and I think doing this is his way of connecting with my parents."

"He's the one that is going to be famous once you go public with this."

"Well, we aren't ready to do that yet, exactly."

Mary looked at Ken at that moment and saw something that frightened her.

"Why do I feel like this story isn't finished, Ken?"

"Well, there is more. We've decided to go back in time to do something to prevent our parents from getting on that plane that day."

"What?"

"We're going to prevent our parent's death."

"Ken, I guess we never talked about this, so I don't know what you believe, but you know there is a plan, right? God has a plan for all of us. We have free will and all, but you can't change the plan all that much."

"I'm not sure if I believe that, Mary."

"Ok, so what role do you think the Lord plays in our lives then?"

"I think He is here to guide us, and to be a sounding board for our decisions, and to hear our troubles, but I don't think that each of us is born with a plan, with a path that is already set and can't be impacted much. Why keep trying to always be a better person if you know the plan is already set? Does this mean that some people are born bad and commit crimes and some become doctors?"

"Ken, you keep trying to be a better person because that is how you honor the blessings you have been given. Your brother, your two sisters, your athletic ability, your intelligence, your kindness and caring nature, those are your blessings. I think we're all born with a plan that has us all being good and successful. Some people end up bad and commit crimes because of the choices they make, the free will that takes them off their plan."

"Mary, you are the kind one sitting here."

"Don't be ridiculous, I've seen you with your sister Kim, and I've heard you speak of your drive to care for your brother and sisters."

"Maybe. I'm thankful for the good things in my life, you, for one. I just don't know if I buy into what you're saying."

"Well, that might be the problem, Ken. You don't buy into it; you have faith in it."

They sat quietly for a few minutes, holding hands. Each thinking about what the other had said. Then Mary said, "This is why you been spending so much time in discussions with Joe and Deb isn't it? You've been discussing this?"

"Yes."

"Sometimes I see Ryan with you though. Does he know?"

"He knows. Deb told him a while ago."

"Why did she tell him and you not tell me?"

"Here's the thing, Mary. We weren't sure what was going to happen at first and we didn't want to tell anyone, but then it started to get bigger and by that time, I knew I hadn't told you and worried you wouldn't understand."

"Well, I'm not sure I do understand. You keeping this from me, and plus, Deb telling Ryan. I mean, don't you trust me?"

"Mary, I do trust you. I wanted to tell you, I just suspected you would think we were all crazy or something. Please don't be mad at me."

They sat quietly for a few minutes and then Mary changed tactic. "I don't think this is a good idea, Ken. What if something happens to one of you while you're in another time where you don't belong?"

"So, you believe me now?"

"I will always believe you, Ken, and I will always believe in you. I just don't think this is a good idea."

"I need to do this, Mary. If for no other reason than to help Joe through his grief. And while I'm telling you all of this, I might as well tell you everything."

At that, Ken told Mary all about the letters from his parents, the trust and the business. He had not told her all these details from the meeting he had at the lawyer's office and thought it was time to come totally clean. When he had finished, Mary had a better understanding of why Ken felt he had to do this.

"So how can I help?" Mary said this with some resignation in her voice, as she was sure she couldn't talk Ken out of this.

"Mary, before we go any further, I have one more thing to tell you. I love you."

Mary smiled and hugged Ken. She whispered in his ear that she loved him, too.

"This is partly why I told you all this. If we succeed and keep our parents from this accident, it is possible that when we come back, we won't be students here. I don't want to lose you, and if you know all this now, I'm hoping you'll have memory of it if we change things, and we can find each other again. Listen, I'm sorry about keeping this from you. This isn't an excuse, but I hope you understand that in the beginning it was to ensure Joe had the time to complete his research, and then it just got harder. I never want to keep anything from you again. I hope you know that and can trust me. Also, we do kind of need some help. You see, we have to have time appropriate clothing and we need to figure out how to borrow some things from the theater department. Can you help?"

"I know why you kept this from me, Ken. You know, right, that you could tell me anything? I will always believe you. Have I not told you that? And, of course, I will help you. What kind of clothing do you need?"

"Well, I think I will need a couple of 1960s style suits, and also some dress slacks, shoes and maybe a blazer or something. Joe will need the same and Deb and Kim will need dresses. We're trying to be in the hotel where the President and First Lady are, so we have to look more conservative, I think."

"Ok, tomorrow I can go to the theater department and check out what they have, and I will let you know. But one last thing, Ken, before you do this, I think you should tell Joe and Kim about the will and what happened at the lawyers, and give them their letters from your parents. You owe it to them to share that before you all go through with this."

"I had been thinking about doing this. Just hearing you say it makes me sure I should. I'll ask Deb what she thinks first, and we'll figure out when to do that. Thanks for being so understanding, Mary."

They walked back to the dorms and Ken left Mary at the girls' dorm and went to his room. All three of the older children went to bed that night with their thoughts on the plan, their parents, and what had transpired that night.

The next day, the news about Joe and Christy was out by the time breakfast was over. Joe didn't appear at the dining hall, so Ken took off as soon as he ate something to check on Joe. He was not in his room either. Deb caught up with him at the end of morning classes as she was leaving the building. She saw Joe and ran after him. She caught him as he was headed toward the boys' dorm.

"Joe, wait up a minute!"

Joe turned and saw Deb and looked up to the sky for a minute, but waited for her to catch up to him on the sidewalk.

"I suppose you heard right. That's why you're after me?"

"I just want to make sure you're ok, Joe."

"I'm fine. I didn't want to tell Christy about what we're doing, and she was really bugging me about not talking to her. It was getting annoying. All she ever wanted to do was talk, talk, talk."

"Joe, I'm sorry you had to deal with that. I know you haven't been in a very talkative mood with anyone except Mr. Brewster since we got here."

"It's not that bad, Deb."

"Ok, maybe not, but you can't start avoiding the dining hall because of this."

"Tony, that kid from my floor, asked me in the hall this morning if it was true, if Christy and I broke up, and he asked if he could have a go at her. Is it wrong that I just didn't want to sit and watch that today at breakfast? I still like her. I just can't deal with it right now. So, I don't want to watch her go with another guy today, ok?"

"Seems perfectly logical to me. Come to lunch with me then."

Deb put her arm through Joe's and started steering him toward the dining hall. He laughed a little and went with her, saying he might as well as he was starving at this point. While they walked, Deb told Joe that she straightened everything out with Kim the night before, and about Kim's contribution for the need to locate a compass for the trip. Joe said he thought someone from his floor had one and he would ask, even though Deb had said Kim was checking with a girl from her troop. They had lunch off together, and she had him laughing and in better spirits by the time they left the dining hall.

While Deb was walking back to the dorms after the afternoon classes, Mary pulled her off the sidewalk to the dorms onto the sidewalk leading to the perimeter of campus. They walked a few paces away from all the other students, making their way back to the dorms before Mary started speaking.

"So, Ken and I had a long talk last night."

"I know. He told me he was going to talk with you."

"He told me everything."

"I figured."

"You don't want to give away anything, do you, Deb?"

"What are you saying, Mary?"

"I don't understand all the secrets you keep, that's all."

"Well, Mary, why don't you tell me what you think first?"

"Are you mad he told me?"

Deb stopped walking and faced Mary.

"No, I'm not mad. I just feel you aren't happy about what you heard, and I thought I would see what you were thinking before I said anything. Why would I be mad that Ken told you?"

"I don't know, maybe because you're used to him always being close with you."

"Mary, you're becoming a very good friend of mine, and I'm really happy that you and Ken are together. I'm not worried about him being with you or telling you anything."

"Ok. You're right. I have some feelings about what I was told. Here it is. I think none of you should do this. I think it's really cool that Joe figured this out and that you have this cool machine, and Mr. Brewster got to meet his father and everything, but I don't think four kids from Cambridge should go jumping through time to see if they can keep their parents alive. That's what I think."

"I'm not sure we should either, Mary, but we all miss our parents so much, and the letters they wrote to me really made up my mind to do this. I don't want to miss them my entire life. And Joe seems to have attached this machine and trying to save our parents to his grief and I know he would go without us, so we have to go with him."

"Have you thought about the implications of this? What if you save them from this one incident, but since it seems to be God's plan to have your parents not with you, what if it happens two weeks later than it did, or a year or even ten years? Are you going to be jumping through time each time that happens just to protect Joe's feelings or to keep changing God's plan?"

"Well, to start with, we aren't jumping through time, we're bending it. Joe explains it like a piece of paper that we sort of roll up and then when the page touches itself, we can slide onto that other part of the page. So, time is like the page. See?"

"OK, but that wasn't really the point."

Deb sighed heavily, and then turned and sat down on a bench that was near the sidewalk, motioning for Mary to join her.

"I've thought a lot about this. I have many doubts about doing this. Where Joe is concerned, if we do this and we don't succeed, what will that mean for Joe? Will he feel like he failed, like he lost our parents all over again? I don't know. And for me, the even bigger issue is that if we succeed, we won't be students here, probably. I won't know you. I wouldn't have met Ryan, and that doesn't feel right any more than not seeing my parents every day. And yes, I do feel like we might mess with God's plan a little too much here. "

"Perhaps you and Ken should go talk to the Reverend before you go any further. Wouldn't it be a good idea to discuss the implications of altering the path God set for you and your family?"

"I wouldn't mind that, but Mary, Ken has genuine doubts about his spirituality and is really questioning the lessons of Sunday school and our grandfather. You know he was a minister, right?"

"Yes, Ken told me that some time ago. Why do you think he is questioning it so much?"

"I don't know. Maybe because of our parents' deaths. I know I've struggled with the idea that God watches over us and wants us to be good people and blesses us with life, but then why would my parents die suddenly? How can I look at that as anything but punishment? How can it be God's plan for my parents to die suddenly and leave us like this?"

"I don't have the answers to that. But, if you were supposed to meet Ryan, and I was supposed to meet Ken, and Joe was supposed to make this monumental discovery, how could that have happened if your parents were alive? Maybe that's the reason they're gone, so you four can go on as you're supposed to."

"By that logic, isn't it God's plan that we do this time travel?"

"I don't know. This is all so confusing and feels wrong for some reason that I cannot explain."

"I have that little voice in my head, too. I just can't abandon my brother."

They sat there in silence for a long time, each with their own thoughts, trying to sort out what they were dealing with.

"You said that you decided this was the thing to do when you read your letters from your parents. Do you know Ken hasn't given the letters to Joe or Kim yet?"

"Yes, I know, and I was going to encourage Ken to do that this week."

"Good, because I told him to do that, too."

"I'm worried about them getting these letters, though. Given what was in my letter, I don't think it will make Joe not want to do this. I think it will make him convinced this is what he must do."

"I'm worried about that too now. I told Ken last night that, although I think you shouldn't do this, I'm ready to help."

"Thanks for understanding, Mary. I know you mean a lot to Ken, and I wouldn't want this to come between you two."

"Not like with Joe, huh? I saw you with Joe at lunch. I stayed away so you could have some time. Is his heart broken?"

"I know he still really likes Christy, but she was bugging him to talk all the time and was angry with him for not talking and spending so much time away from her, so who knows? Maybe they will work it all out later this week?"

"Probably not. I remember liking boys when I was fourteen, and you were dating for about a week and then never spoke again."

"Yeah, but the good news is there will be another girl for Joe."

"Yeah, in another week or so."

They laughed and got up and started walking back toward the dorms.

"By the way, I have some clothes stashed in my room for you to look at and see if they'll work. I took them from the theater department earlier today."

"Great, can we go to your room right now?"

"Sure."

The girls headed back to Mary's room and looked over the clothing. Deb thought they would work and showed Mary the pictures she had found in the library. Mary agreed they would work and agreed to keep them in her room until they needed them.

Ken found Joe at the pool tables in the main hall just after classes let out. He and Ryan walked up to the table where Joe was playing, and Ken pulled Joe away. Ryan stayed and played for Joe.

"I heard about you and Christy."

"Ken, don't bug me about this. It wasn't working out, all she wanted to do was talk and was mad at me for not spending more time with her, and all she could talk about is about how you spent time with Mary and Deb spent time with Ryan even though you both seemed to work on the something with me. I just didn't want to deal with it anymore, ok? I want to focus on this machine and this trip we are planning."

"That's pretty funny considering I heard the same argument from Mary the other day."

"What do you mean?" Joe asked.

"She said she thought I was avoiding spending time alone with her while I was doing things with all of you. I told her she might be jealous but she had no reason to be."

"I bet that went over good," Joe said laughing.

"Thanks a lot. I come to check on my brother and this is the thanks I get."

Hey, I guess all chicks are crazy about that time together issue. But you shouldn't mess with Mary, ok?"

"Yeah, that's ok, I just want to make sure you are ok, ok? This is what big brothers are supposed to do. Check on little brothers after their first breakup, ok?"

Ken exaggerated the last couple of ok's for effect and then wrapped his arm around Joe's neck and put him in a headlock for more effect. Joe pulled out of it and said they needed to get back to the game since Ryan could play hockey, but not pool, and Joe had a pool reputation to uphold. Deb found them at the pool table after she left Mary's room and, after greeting Ryan, asked to talk to Ken.

They walked away from the pool table and sat down at a small table.

"I think we need to have a long talk with Joe and Kim, and you need to give them their letters this week before we do anything else with the machine, Ken."

"I've been thinking about that, too. And Mary thinks I should too."

"I know. She told me today. I'm also not sure we should mess with history like this, and although I hated the idea of coming here last fall, I really don't want to leave here, but at the very least, Joe and Kim deserve their letters, and we need to talk about this one more time before we go through with this trip through time."

"I agree. Wednesday night when we get together in the library, I'm starting with the explanation of the lawyer's visit and the letters."

Deb and Ken went back to the pool table, and they all played until it was time to go into the dining hall. They all walked over together and had dinner and then separated to finish homework in their separate dorm rooms.

When the four of them met in the library on Wednesday evening, Ken went through his meeting with the lawyer and what he learned about the wills. He explained the trust to Joe and Kim and then told them about the letters from their parents. Joe at first had a shocked look on his face, and Deb was not sure he would even want the letters, but he asked to have his. Kim, of course, wanted hers, as she was likely thinking this was one more moment with her parents. Kim read hers rather quickly and started crying as soon as she had finished the opening sentence of her father's letter. After she was finished, she climbed into Ken's lap and hugged him, and asked what had been in Ken's letter. Ken said he would wait until Joe was finished and go over that.

Joe took much longer to read the letters he had received. He turned away from the others to read his because he didn't want them to see him cry, and he wasn't sure he could hold it in through both letters. His mother's letter spoke of how proud she was of his skills in math and science and how much she enjoyed their weekends at the lab and just working together in her office at Harvard. She said she knew he would accomplish great things in his life and she was sorry she would not be there to stand in the crowd and cheer for him. She told him not to fret too much over his size or his lack of interest in sports, as everyone had to find their own way, and he would grow into his adult body over time. His father's letter was something else entirely. His father spoke of the computer plans, and that he had set aside money in his will just for Joe to use as his seed money for his business plan and inventions. He said he knew Joe would change the world with his plans for computer usage, and he had hoped to be a part of that with him.

Joe shed a few tears, but it wasn't as bad as he had thought it would be. He turned back to his brother and two sisters after wiping away the signs of his tears.

"So, what was in your letter, Ken?"

"Well, both Mom and Dad told me to look after you all. They told me to wait to do anything about custody of you until after I had finished college. As you know, right now, Aunt Alicia has custody of the three of you."

Kim looked up at Ken then. "Are you going to be in charge of us now?"

"No Kim, I'm going to leave things the way they are with Aunt Alicia in charge of you and Deb and Joe until I am out of college."

"By then, Deb and Joe will be eighteen years old, won't they?"

"Yes, they will, but you'll be fifteen years old. So, in those last three years, I might have custody. We'll wait and see how you feel when we get to that point, ok?"

Kim nodded in agreement and nuzzled back into Ken's arms.

"Did you get letters too, Deb?"

"Yes, I did. Mine spoke of helping Kim find her way as she grew up, and helping Ken deal with the fact that he would feel totally responsible for us all."

"In mine, Mom and Dad both said they were so very sorry they would not be here to see so many of my first events in my life, and that they were sorry they couldn't see me out of childhood, but they knew I would grow up to be a beautiful and smart young lady with the help of the three of you. What did your letters say, Joe?"

"My letters were about making my inventions and ideas a success. Dad said that he set aside money for me to use for the ideas later. Mom said she was glad we got to spend weekends at the lab and stuff."

"Yes, Joe, the will has a term and special offset of the trust of money to be given to you when you present a business plan or when you turn twenty-one years old, whichever comes first."

"How much money?" Kim asked.

"Well, Kim, the principal amount is one million dollars, but since it is sitting in a trust, it's earning interest, so if Joe waits until after college to start this business, it will be a lot more money than that. If he starts it based on when the market is ready and he is ready, it might be just the million."

"Wow Joe, you're set to launch right now if you want to."

"It'll probably be two years before it is really ready, but like Ken said, if the market is ready, I wouldn't want to wait until I was twenty-one."

They all sat for a minute in silence, then Deb looked at Ken and nodded.

"Ok, I think we need to talk about some things here. First, I know we're all feeling the weight of missing our parents right now. But I think we need to really talk about what that means for each of us, and be really open and honest with each other. The theme of all the letters seems to be helping each other reach our goals even if Mom and Dad aren't with us, and stay a family," Deb said to steer them in the direction that she thought would help.

"I'll start," Ken said resignedly.

"When we first got here, I thought about Mom and Dad every day. I was angry because of the accident, because Aunt Alicia dumped us here and how that went down, and I was sure I could never take care of you all. Each day, I was worried about going to college and leaving you three here, and it bothered me every day, almost all day. I was sure I was going to go get custody as soon as I graduated high school here, and get a job and support us all so you three could go to college. Now, it's different. Since I saw the lawyer and got set up to deal with the trust, and since we've all found friends here and adjusted to the classes and living here, I feel more in control. I feel like we're closer than we would have been if Mom and Dad were still here. I would never have spent weekends helping Kim with homework or taking her to the movies, and Joe, I would have been too busy with my friends to bother with whatever machine or math problem you were working on, and would never have learned how smart and dedicated you are. And Deb, I would never have known what a caring and smart person you've become, and never would have spent time with you or gone skating on my birthday because of you. So, in some ways, I think my life has gotten better. I know I shouldn't feel this way, but I do. I still miss Mom and Dad, but I wonder if maybe we're moving forward and it's getting better now, and we shouldn't do anything to mess that up."

The other three looked at each other, and Kim held up her hand.

"I felt like I would never find another friend as long as I lived when we first got here. Everything reminded me of Mom and Dad, and I was sad all the time. The books people read out loud on my floor, the smell in the dining hall, the desks in the classroom all reminded me of Mom. My geography teacher totally reminds me of Dad, so every day I walked into that classroom and wanted to cry. But now, I go whole days without thinking about them. Now, I have lots of friends, Girl Scouts, and all the activities we get to do here. Each day, I get to spend time with all of you, and that's been the best part. I hope you aren't mad at me for not thinking of them every day, and I don't think I want to go back to our old house or my old friends or old school now. I really like it here."

Ken hugged Kim a little tighter. "No one is going to be mad at you for trying to find some peace here and making new friends, Kim."

"What if you could have Mom and Dad back and still be here, though, Kim?" Joe asked.

"Joe, you know that Mom and Dad would never have sent me here before high school, even if they were thinking of it for you. And why would they take Ken out of his senior year of high school and the football team, and Deb was already in high school? I doubt they were thinking of sending her? I doubt any of us would have ended up here if the accident hadn't happened. Besides, then Ken wouldn't have met Mary and Deb wouldn't have met Ryan. That makes me almost as sad as missing Mom and Dad."

"That would make me sad too, Kim. Meeting Ryan has been really important to me. I too missed Mom and Dad terribly when we first got here, and was lost after being sent here. Do any of you know I wasn't even able to talk to Denise before we left? We found out we were leaving just after the funeral, and she was busy with her family, and then we just left that Sunday morning. Now, I can't imagine my life without this place. Kim, before we got here, I was more annoyed than anything about having you try to tag along and do things with me. Now, we spend time together and I've found out that you are insightful and fun to be with. Would we ever be this close if we hadn't come here? I don't want to lose this. I'm really worried that we might succeed in stopping the accident, which on the one hand would be great because we wouldn't lose Mom and Dad, but on the other hand, that would mean we wouldn't have this place and we wouldn't have these friends or be this close."

"I agree with you all that coming here has not turned out as bad as I thought it would when we first arrived. Everything felt wrong when we got here," Joe started by acknowledging what they all thought.

"You would never have met Mr. Brewster and learned so much about the nuclear program if we had not been here, Joe," Deb said.

"Yeah, and I would never have discovered the formula or the machine if we hadn't come here. It's been fun spending time with you all, and I have finally gotten to know my brother and sisters. I know that wouldn't have happened if we had not shared this terrible event."

Again, they all sat for a few minutes contemplating what they said. Deb looked at each of them and decided now was the time to bring this up.

"With everything we've all said, I have to ask, do we still want to go through with getting into the machine and going back in time to try to stop what happened to Mom and Dad?"

"I do. Even with all that has been good about being here, I would rather find out the good times we could have with Mom and Dad than not try at all."

"Joe, are you sure?"

"Yes Deb, I am very sure."

Kim climbed off of Ken's lap and went to stand next to Joe. "Joe, I want to have more fun times with Mom and Dad too."

"I know we all want the opportunity to have our parents back, but Joe and Kim, we have to be prepared for the fact that if we do this, our lives here are gone. Are you ready for that? And furthermore, what about everything that we learned in church and everything Grandpa Joe taught us? We're supposed to accept God's plan. We know from Sunday school that sometimes there is pain, and it's through that pain we get closer to God."

"Deb, I am prepared to give this all up. I think with what I have learned from this machine and what I have learned from Mr. Brewster, I can move forward on the computer business and make it successful. That is what Dad wanted me to do."

Kim put her hand on Joe's shoulder, and tears formed in her eye as she said, "Joe, do you hear yourself? I want you to be famous and successful, but what about the rest of us? Do you even care that Ken will probably lose Mary and Deb will probably lose Ryan if we do this?"

"Are we really comparing this girl and this guy that have been in their lives for a mere few months with having our parents back?"

"It's not just that Joe, what about all the Sundays we sat in church and heard about how we don't know what God has planned but we have to accept some things even if we don't like them, or don't agree with them, and especially when we don't understand them," Deb said, trying to ensure they thought about these implications.

"Do you really still believe that, Deb? Do you Ken? We LOST our parents. How can that be something God thought was a good idea? I do not, and cannot, and will never, accept that there was a point to this."

"Joe, calm down. I don't know if I still believe it, but I have to say after talking to Deb and talking to Mary, I'm thinking that I have let my anger and grief impede what I believed for my whole life."

"Geez, Ken, I thought you were smarter than this. Science disproves God at every turn. All the so-called facts that people believed throughout history have been explained by science."

Ken turned to face Joe fully and looked him directly in the eyes when he said, "Science doesn't explain everything, Joe. You know this, deep down, you know this."

Joe looked down at that. He could barely keep from crying. He wondered how his sister and brother could not want this as badly as he did. It couldn't just be the girlfriend and boyfriend, and he finally said as much.

Deb was first to respond, "Joe, you're right, this isn't really about Ryan or Mary. It's about the fact that Ken and I are moving forward and letting the grief go. We can see this from a perspective you can't because you can't let go of your grief."

"She's right Joe, we're just able to look at it without the pain that is giving you tunnel vision," Kim added.

"Joe, I'll tell you what. I will not abandon you just because I might disagree with you. You're my brother, and if there is one thing I've learned since we got put here, we're nothing without each other," Deb said.

"Me either bro, I have your back, even if I think it means we're going through fire," Ken said, smiling at Joe.

Ken pulled his chair more directly up to the table at this point, all business-like, and switched the subject.

"So, I know I can find Mary again if we change things, and Deb, I know we can find Ryan again. We know exactly where they'll be if we come forward and things have dramatically changed and we're not students here, because they will be here. I doubt anything we do in nineteen sixty-three is going to change what Mary's and Ryan's parent do in their lives. We think they will retain memory of us, and we'll retain memory of them because we've included them in the planning and told them everything. And, I don't think we'll lose the memory of what we have shared these past few months together, so I'm not worried about losing that either. I know at this moment I will always want you three in my life, and want to support you all in everything you want to do, and I don't expect that to change ever. But here's my question: what if this is God's plan, and no matter what we do, we can't change that? At what point do we say enough and go about the business of living our lives without them?"

"Ken, why don't you believe God has a plan for each of us?"

"Kimmy, I'm not saying I totally don't believe. I'm just saying that I find it hard to have free will and a plan already in place at that same time."

"I have another point. If we don't succeed with this trip, will there be other trips and other plans? When does it end, Joe? It feels like doing this, trying to stop the accident, is keeping us all locked in the grief and not able to move on."

Deb then looked at Ken, "Ken, what if we change something back there and it changes our father enough to change everything about how his business progresses and it changes our lives? What I don't understand is if we go back in time, impact our father, and it changes his life enough, it will change our upbringing, and then how do we know we remember this place at all? I think we should all take some time to write out, kind of letter to ourselves and maybe I'm going to write a letter to Ryan and you should write one to Mary, Ken."

Joe held up his finger at this point. They all looked at him as they were hoping he would have a scientific answer for Deb's question.

"All the theory says that time travel works like this. We go back, change one thing, and everything from that one change forward changes. So, let's say that Dad and Mr. Davis meet, but they don't start this bond that leads to their business. Maybe Dad goes back to school and meets someone else whom he forms a business with. But everything else about his business is the same. He meets and marries Mom and we're all born. That would mean no accident, because of no business trip to Colorado on Mr. Davis's plane. But all the theory also states that if we go back, make this change and then come back, we have to have memory of doing this. Even if we change our history by changing Dad's history, we'll still have memory of the other events and going back and changing things."

Joe paused, and because no one asked another question, he continued.

"Second, I think there is a plan for each of us, and let's face it, we all have to die sometime, right? But the free will thing makes each of our plans flexible, doesn't it? Can't the choices we make change the course of our plan? Doesn't God account for this somehow? I think there is a kind of road map, with some forks in the road and the free will allows us to shift off onto those forks in the road and end up a bit off the main road."

Ken was first to respond, "So I'm clear on the theory Joe, but since no one else to my knowledge has time travelled except Mr. Brewster, we don't know for sure, and I appreciate the fact that Deb is a little worried. And as far as your theories about God's plan, all I can say is that my questions are kind of my own, and maybe I think that the free will allows us to make drastic changes from whatever God intended for us, and that has to mean there is no real definitive plan for any of us. I think God wants us to choose the good or right or Christian way with each decision we make, but we always have a choice to turn the opposite way. That has to mean there is no real roadmap or plan," Joe said.

"So, I see both your points, Ken and Joe, but at the end of the day, only our testing the machine will provide some elements of proof, right? If we go back and stop the assassination of President Kennedy and come back here and find out he died anyway but at a later date or something, or if we change the way Dad and Mr. Davis started out, but they still end up in business together and the accident still happens, doesn't that prove my point?" Deb said.

"And mine," Kim added triumphantly, as she wholeheartedly believed that God had a plan for each of them.

"I guess we shall see then, won't we?"

Joe thought it best to move on to the other point made, "I don't think we can keep going back to the same event and try to change it repeatedly hoping for a different result, so I don't think we will be stuck in this state forever."

"Joe, I don't think we would go back to the same event, but what if we kept trying to find other events to impact to change the outcome? Remember, we're starting with the event where Mr. Davis met our dad. There are a million events after that first meeting, we could impact. Are we going to keep trying until we get your desired outcome?"

Deb continued before anyone could start talking, "I, for one, think it's ok to talk about trying once, but not over and over again. We run the risk each time we go back to impact other people's lives, and messing something else up in our lives, so I don't think we should ever think of trying over three or four times. What if we do something we're not aware of then we come back here and someone isn't here that we expected to be here, or the world has changed so much because of something we did, that nothing is the same for us or anyone else?"

"I think we might want to be thinking about how and when to introduce your formula and machine to the outside world and get you the recognition you deserve for it. Maybe this is your path to the computer business you want to accomplish later," Ken suggested.

"Ken, do you just want me to write this all up and work with Mr. Brewster to announce it to the world and not try to save our parents?"

"At some point, we have to prepare for that."

"Ok, let's lay out the points for and against this on a piece of paper," Deb suggested, to organize their thoughts.

"Let's start with the positives," Joe said, hoping for the best.

"We get to have our parents back."

"Yes, Kim, that's the big one."

"We get to see if Joe's machine really works and test out other theories, like the changing history theory," Deb offered.

"We know the machine works. Mr. Brewster met his father," Joe said, smirking at Deb.

"So only one point for that, Deb," Ken added, also smiling at Deb.

"There are other theories we will be testing. Like who will have memory of us, and will we have memory of the time we spent here," Joe added.

"These theory points will go toward a positive impact on Joe's scientific journal report and career," Ken said, brushing his hand across the table to show them gathered up.

"We will get to meet some important figures in history first hand."

"Only you would come up with a history positive point, Deb."

"Joe, you get the accolades for the math. Don't I deserve some for the history?"

They all laughed.

"Ok, now the negatives."

"We might not impact history enough to stop the accident," Joe started.

"We might mess up something bigger than just the accident," Deb stated.

"We might come back here and no one would remember us," Ken said, as this was his worry now.

"Kimmy, we have all added a negative. Do you have any?"

"Yes, we might find we don't like each other again."

Ken sighed. "Well, any other additions to the list? If not, can we decide tonight, or do each of you want some time to think about this before we call a vote?"

Joe responded first, "I want to decide tonight and then not change our minds again or question what we're doing. Let's put it to a vote and get it over with."

They each thought for a minute and looked at each other. Kim spoke first.

"I think we have to try. We have to go, and we have to right now set a limit on how many times we'll try."

"Your vote Deb?"

"Joe, I think we need to try, too."

"I do too. So, we're agreed. We are going."

"Ok, then what is the number of times we'll try to change history to bring our parents back?" Deb asked.

"But first, we need to agree that when and what we try to change will be up to Deb to sort out, so we are not going back to the same event over and over again," Ken added.

Kim held up four fingers. "Four times. No matter what has happened, if we don't succeed at four times, we stop."

Deb nodded her agreement. Joe added, "Four times is good with me."

Ken looked around the table. "Ok, we're going, and we will only go four times. We are agreed. No questioning, no doubts."

Everyone nodded.

"If that's the vote, then I can tell you Mary got us some costumes, and she has them in her room. I have confirmed with Kim the coordinates on the map and given those to Joe. Did either of you get a compass?"

"I got one from my friend in Girl Scouts."

"I got one from Mr. Brewster as well."

"All we have to decide then is when we're going."

"Friday night."

"Joe, I would rather wait until Saturday morning. We can get the costumes and supplies to the barn on Friday and then go first thing Saturday. I think that would be less suspicious, and I'd like to have one last evening with Ryan in case our theories are all wrong."

"I think that's a good plan. We go on Saturday morning. Friday after classes, each of us should gather up supplies we think we need. Deb, I'll help you get the costumes from Mary, and we'll get that all to the barn before dinner. Then we will get up Saturday and make like we are going somewhere and head to the barn instead," Ken summarized.

"Just in time, too, as it is seven forty-five, and we have to get back to the dorms."

They left the library, each carrying their letters and Ken carrying the envelope with the will and trust papers. The girls headed in one direction, the boys in the other. As they left one another, Deb reminded them all, "Don't forget you have to write a letter to yourself with all the information and memories and things you want to be sure you remember. Ken, write one to give to Mary."

They all indicated they would work on them the next day.

Ryan found Deb on the way to the dining hall for breakfast and took her hand and then whispered to her, "So, how did it go last night?"

"A little difficult at first."

"I suspected it would be difficult."

They walked into the dining hall and sat down near Kim. Joe and Ken were not in the dining hall. After the Reverend gave the prayer, they all started eating.

"How did Joe and Kim handle the letters from your parents?"

"They both were upset, but not as much as I expected. Kim climbed into Ken's lap after she read hers. That was unusual, and not something she's done for a long time. And then we all shared how we felt when we came here, and how each of us felt now about losing our parents and being here at Choate."

"Wow, what prompted that?"

"I thought it would be a good way to open up about why we're thinking of going back and trying to stop the accident, and to help us talk about whether this was really something we wanted to or should be doing."

"And?"

"We all were in about the same place when we got here. Angry at how it happened, really missing our parents and being here making that harder. But we all acknowledged that it had changed, and we liked it more here. Joe was not as enthusiastic as Ken, Kim and I about that part, but he said it was better now. Then we talked about some of the other big questions."

"Like, whether you should mess with history and your lives like this?"

"Yes, that was one issue. Also, about the risk of messing up something bigger than we planned, or changing history in some big way. If we would remember being here, if we thought you and Mary would remember us, and then finally how many times we might want to try this if it is unsuccessful the first time in stopping the accident?"

"And how many times are you going to do this?"

"We agreed on four times."

"Deb, I'd like to discuss this some more if that's ok? I'm worried about you doing this. I don't want anything to happen to you, and I really don't want to lose you."

"Ryan, I don't want to lose you either, but I have to support my brothers and sister in this. Please understand."

"Can we talk more later?"

"Sure."

They went to class, met later at lunch, and saw both Joe and Ken at lunch. Ken sat with Mary, whispering back and forth the whole time. Whenever Deb looked over at them, she thought she sensed Ken trying to calm Mary down and Mary kind of berating him. Joe sat with some guys from his floor and Kim was with her friends, so Deb and Ryan got to sit and talk more.

"Deb, I'm trying to understand what you all must be feeling. It's hard for me to imagine not having my parents around. When I try to think how that might be, it makes me feel sick to my stomach, so I know it must be really hard for all of you. All morning I've been thinking if I was in your shoes, and I found some way to go back and stop the event from happening that made me lose my parents, I would want to take the chance and try to fix it. I get all that. Here's the issue for me though, Deb, I think I love you, and it feels like this might mean we can't be together if you do this."

"I don't know what to say, Ryan. We're sitting in the dining hall, remember?"

"Yes, I realize this isn't the most romantic place to tell you I love you, but I was sitting in history class when it hit me that this was why this plan of yours seems wrong to me."

"Ryan, I don't want to lose you either. We all talked about this yesterday, how we were really upset when we first got here, how things have changed, how we met people and how important those people have become to us. Even Kim said she was sad, thinking that Ken wouldn't have Mary and I wouldn't have you if something happened."

"I knew she would be on my side!"

They both laughed, but got up as it was time to go to afternoon classes.

"Let's meet right after class, ok and finish this discussion?"

"Yes, I want to do that, Deb. Can we walk into town and get some ice cream or something?"

"That sounds good. Can you meet me at the girls' dorm so I can drop off my books?"

"Meet you there."

The afternoon dragged on for Deb as she anticipated finishing her talk with Ryan and thinking about what he said to her. She wondered why she hadn't told him she loved him back, and was thinking about this when she was called on in literature class. She fumbled to get the answer, and some of the other kids in the class snickered at her. Ryan was sitting a few seats back and a row over from her and he whispered loudly for them to cut it out. He sensed that their conversation distracted her and was trying to help. The last class of the afternoon was history, and Deb enjoyed this, so she could concentrate a little better. She was relieved, though, when class was over, and she headed back to the dorm to drop off her things. Ryan was waiting in the dorm's lobby when she got back downstairs and they headed out the door silently together.

After getting down the drive and to the entrance of campus, Ryan started the conversation up again. "What happened in Literature? You're usually so on top of class discussions."

"I was thinking about what we talked about at lunch and was distracted."

"I figured as much. Sorry for distracting you."

Deb stopped walking, and Ryan stopped and turned toward her.

"First Ryan, I want to apologize for not reacting better to what you said."

"Deb, you don't have to apologize. I know this is all very important to you, Ken, Joe, and Kim."

"Not that, about you telling me you loved me."

"Oh."

Deb stepped closer to Ryan and reached for his hands. "Ryan, I think I love you, too. And I know that you're very important to me, and I don't want to lose what we have."

Ryan smiled and put his arms around Deb. "I have to say, now, that I was a little worried all afternoon that maybe you didn't feel the same way about me I felt about you."

"No, just slow to react, I guess."

They started walking again and discussed the objections that Deb and the others had brought up yesterday. Then Deb explained what Mr. Brewster and Joe thought about others knowing about them if they changed history and were no longer students here at Choate. Ryan listened to everything Deb told him, made some points about agreeing with the idea that everyone has a plan and free will can only adjust that plan and maybe they won't impact anything if they go back in time.

While they ate their ice cream, they talked about when and how the plan was going to work. Ryan asked if he could be there when they left, and Deb told him that Mr. Brewster had suggested that both Ryan and Mary come over the barn after the kids had left, and wait for them to return so they didn't raise any suspicion with so many of them heading over to Mr. Brewster's place on Saturday morning. As they walked back to campus, Ryan told Deb that he wanted to have one last night with her on Friday, so would she please try to meet him? She agreed and said she would talk to Ken about Friday's activities.

Later that evening, Deb found Ken in the lounge of the girls' dorm with Mary and told him about her wanting to go out with Ryan on Friday night. Ken agreed, and said he too wanted to have a last night with Mary, so he was going to arrange for Joe to take Kim to the movie night at the main hall. Two days later, on Friday, they all gathered their supplies, with Ken and Mary and Deb taking the clothing, and Ryan carrying some of the other items Deb had acquired and Kim bringing her girl scout supplies to the barn. They packed them all into several compartments built into the interior of the machine, and then they all headed back to campus. Ken and Deb gave all the letters they had written to Mr. Brewster to deliver to Mary and Ryan after they left, and to hold the others until they returned. Joe had written one to Mr. Brewster as well, but he promised to not open it until after they left.

Ken and Mary went into town and had dinner and then went to a movie playing at the theater in town. Ryan gathered up food, a blanket, and a radio, and took Deb out to park on the outskirts of town and had an evening picnic. They laid on the blanket and looked up at the stars, listened to music on the radio, talked about what they wanted to do after high school, where they wanted to go to college and what they wanted to do in life. They got up and danced to several slow songs, but then laid back down and watched the stars again. Ryan walked Deb back to the girls' dorm around ten and stood on the steps, holding her for a long time. When they parted, he said, "You be careful tomorrow and watch out for your sister and brothers. I will think of you tomorrow, and then I expect to see you soon, Deb."

"I will. I can't wait to see you again, Ryan."

11

S aturday morning Deb and Kim got up and met Joe and Ken in the dining hall for the earliest breakfast time. They ate silently, each thinking about what they were about to do. Ken drove the car over to Mr. Brewster's after breakfast and put the car into one of the Morton buildings on Mr. Brewster's property. They all changed into the clothing that was appropriate for nineteen sixty-three and got ready to go. Mary and Ryan walked over after they finished breakfast and see Ken and Deb off, even though they had promised to wait to go to the barn. When they got to the barn, they were amazed by the machine and were intimidated by the whole thing. Mary hugged Ken and Ryan hugged Deb as Joe and Mr. Brewster confirmed the setup of the machine program they did last night, and the four of them climbed into the machine.

"It seems awfully small in here, Joe."

"Kim, it isn't meant to be a first-class plane ride. Please sit down in one of the two back seats here and let's get you harnessed in."

Ken and Deb got into the machine and got harnessed into their seats. Joe turned the machine on and turned the communication system on so they could talk to Mr. Brewster while they started the machine up.

"Joe, you all buckled in there?"

"Yes, Mr. Brewster, we're all in our seats. I set the program. We have powered up the machine. I'm ready to start the system now."

"Ok, good luck, and I will see you all soon. You all take care of each other and watch out. Don't do too much, ok?"

They all answered back that they would see him soon and thanked him for everything. The machine's systems started up, and it got very noisy both inside and outside the machine. The wind picked up outside as the magnetic field formed and the lights focused. Inside, Ken and Joe were monitoring the systems on the small screens, and then the light became too bright for any of them to keep their eyes open. The noise went away, but the light was very intense, and Deb felt like her heart was beating right out of her chest. This lasted for what seemed like a long time, but probably was only a few moments, and then it got dark and quiet inside the machine. The system screen indicated they were outside of Fort Worth, Texas, at 10:15am on November 20, 1963. Joe powered down the systems after running the printout of the system activities. He turned on the internal lights and he and Ken looked over the prints.

"Wow, that was so bright!"

"Yes, Kim it was, and I felt funny, like my heart was beating fast."

"That's what Mr. Brewster, and I felt when we first tested the machine. The fast heartbeat, and it felt like we were moving up on a roller coaster or something."

"Yeah, and never reaching the top to go down."

Joe indicated that the printout looked normal and the system check showed the machine was in good shape. Ken unharnessed himself, then Deb and Kim, and then he peered out the small portal window in the door. He said he didn't see anyone or anything and he opened the door. The four of them climbed out of the machine and looked around.

"We should put some brush and tree limbs and stuff around the machine if we can, to make sure no one sees anything if they come by here."

"Is that the girl scout way, Kim?"

"Joe, I'm just saying you don't want someone climbing in here and taking off with your machine, do you?"

"Luckily, your coordinates put us into some tall brush to begin with, so we can just put some of this around the machine. Kim, it's a good idea."

Ken and Joe collected some more branches while Deb and Kim took their bags and supplies out of the machine and stood the brush up against the machine. After they were done, Kim pulled out her compass and gave them the direction they needed to go to get to the road. They walked for about a quarter of a mile and found it. Then they walked along the road until they got into town. They found a bus stop and rode the rest of the way into downtown, and got off the bus about a block away from the Texas Hotel. They entered the hotel, and Ken went to the desk and requested two adjoining rooms and paid cash for the three days they would be in town. Up in the room, Kim was having great fun going from one room to the other and looking out the windows on the downtown of Fort Worth while Deb sat down at the desk and pulled out her documents with the ideas they had to stop the assassination.

"The Secret Service should be here at this hotel already. We have two choices to start this process. We can either get some information to the Secret Service that there is a threat at the book depository building, or we can notify the Dallas police department."

"How would we notify the Secret Service?" Joe asked.

"Well, we could slip a note to one of them. We could leave a message for them at the front desk, or we could hope that calling into the police department might connect us to the Secret Service."

Ken, the ever reasonable one, said, "Let's try leaving a note at the front desk. Deb, you can write it out and then put it in an envelope and take it to the front desk and say you found it on some papers in the lobby. I think you would look the most unsuspicious."

"How can I look unsuspicious?" Deb asked, laughing a bit.

"You put on a sweet smile and say please and thank you a lot," Kim suggested on one of her laps around the two rooms.

"Ok, but I think we should also call in a tip to the Dallas police from a pay phone somewhere," Joe added.

"I agree Joe, but it needs to be a phone not near this hotel, and not in Dallas and not near anywhere where there might be too little activity, so we will be noticed or something."

"So, we'll go out and find a place to have some lunch, and then walk around a bit and find a busy place with a pay phone. We'll call into the

Dallas police tomorrow morning and leave the note tomorrow as well," Kim stood up to say.

"I'm wondering if we should also get some information to the newspaper. I wonder if they would print something if they got an anonymous tip," Deb wondered out loud.

"It's worth a try, isn't it?" Joe asked.

"Ok, Deb, start writing. Let's go over your notes before we head out for lunch. We can find the paper's office today as well and drop it off at their office. This way, if they decide to print something, it'll get into the papers tomorrow."

"I'm going to unpack my clothes."

"Good idea Kim, and while you're doing that, Joe and I will walk around the hotel. Remember, we're in nineteen sixty-three, so Deb and Kim, you shouldn't go anywhere alone. It wouldn't be likely that a girl or young woman would be unaccompanied in this time. Remember that."

"It's not colonial America, Ken. Women were doing more in the sixties!" Deb said, looking up and rolling her eyes, "I think we'd be ok inside the hotel. Kim, we probably need to change the style of your hair before we go out again and I should, too."

"We'll be back," Ken said as he and Joe left the room.

Deb sat down to write out the note to the Secret Service, and to write something to the newspaper using the research notes she had brought with her hoping her understanding of the history of what happened here would make a convincing enough argument to cause the Secret Service and police to act, and the newspaper to print something. She was done with the Secret Service note when the boys returned. She let them read it over while she worked on the newspaper letter.

Ken read over the Secret Service note and sat for a few minutes while Deb finished the newspaper letter.

"Deb, this is great. It looks just plausible enough for them to act on, but not too telling to indicate who wrote this note. Your handwriting is clean and besides, you aren't born yet, so they will not be able to match it to anyone."

"Thanks, Ken."

"Maybe we should indicate that the person in question is an employee of the book depository?" Ken asked.

"I thought of that, but since I don't name anyone, can I say that?" Deb questioned.

"I think you can. Just add it here."

Ken indicated by handing her page two of the letter for the Secret Service.

"I can add that at the end here, and just have a new page three."

"Good. Are you going to provide the same information to the paper?"

"I think we should leave out the book depository part, don't you?"

"I think so. You don't want to create too much panic, right?"

Deb corrected the Secret Service letter and finished the newspaper letter. Ken then suggested they write out the Secret Service letter again to use as a script for the call to the Dallas police. When they had all the notes ready, Deb put them all in her purse. Ken then mentioned that he had bought a Dallas newspaper and that Deb might look through it to see if there was some specific reporter they should direct the letter to. She thought that was a great idea, and they all started looking through the paper.

"Hey, this guy wrote an article about the corruption of the garbage company here. Maybe he would be a good one to get our letter. It says Daniel Cryer."

Deb looked over Kim's shoulder and read over the beginning of the article she was reading.

"Kim, that's a great idea. He's going to get our letter."

Deb took out the newspaper letter and wrote the man's name on the front of the envelope. They then left their room and headed down to the street. Down the block, they got onto a bus that went into Dallas. It took them close to an hour on the bus. When they arrived in downtown Dallas, they first found a place to have some lunch. Joe commented on the decoration of the hamburger joint. They found it seemed like it was more out of the nineteen fifties than the nineteen sixties, but the food was good. They then walked a few blocks and found the newspaper offices.

Ken suggested that Deb go in alone and he, Joe and Kim waited across the street. Deb walked into the lobby of the newspaper offices and approached the receptionist's desk. She pulled out the letter from her purse as she walked up to the desk. The receptionist asked Deb what she could do for her. Deb put the letter on the counter and indicated that she just needed to leave the letter for Mr. Daniel Cryer. The receptionist asked if Deb would like to speak to Mr. Cryer and Deb said that would not be necessary. The receptionist smiled at Deb and said she would make sure Mr. Cryer received the letter that afternoon. Deb thanked her and turned and left the offices.

When Deb got outside to where Ken, Joe, and Kim were waiting, she took a very deep breath. Joe looked at her expectantly, and Deb said she had no trouble. They just needed to wait and see if Mr. Cryer wrote anything in the paper. They decided to walk around Dealey Plaza, so they walked the five or six blocks down Main Street and sat in the park across from the book depository. There were people walking up and down the sidewalk and people going into and out of the book depository.

"It's so strange that in a few short days, this is the scene of where President Kennedy is shot. It looks so normal."

"But Deb, if we succeed, it won't be the scene at all."

"You're right Joe, if we succeed it will just be another location in Dallas and that building will probably become something else instead of a memorial museum."

"I wonder if Dad is here in town yet."

"Kim, we can't think about that or try to look for him. If we do, and we find him, we might mess the whole thing up."

"Couldn't we just find him and watch him a little? I want to see what he was like when he was younger."

"No, we can't do that. Like Deb said, we want to only change the one thing we came here to change. If we see Dad, we might do or say something that causes him to change his whole course, and since we have no idea how little of a thing, we would need to do to effect change, we're going to avoid him, not go look for him. Which means, since he is headed for Dallas today, we need to get back to Fort Worth and stay out of trouble," Ken said.

"Right Ken, and we need to figure out how we're going to unsuspiciously deliver a letter to the Secret Service," Deb added.

"Then let's go."

"First, let's go to the book depository, Ken, and see if we can get inside and walk around."

"Joe, why do you want to do that?"

"Well, if I was planning to assassinate someone from this building in two days, I would probably have already set up the boxes and hidden the gun, or at least some things I needed, so it wasn't so obvious."

"Yeah, Joe, that's a good idea. Deb and Kim, you stay here and we'll be right back."

"Be sure to not talk to too many people and do nothing suspicious. Remember, we're trying to not change anything but what we came here to change, and we have no idea who works there, and what else it might impact if you say the wrong thing. And, you might not even think what you are saying is the wrong thing, but it becomes the wrong thing later. Ok?"

"We'll be careful."

Ken and Joe went across the street and entered the book depository from a side entrance. They walked around the first floor and didn't see anyone but several women working in a big room with a bunch of typewriters. They went up the first flight of stairs and the second floor had offices and the break room. There were several people in the break room, but no one noticed or said anything to Ken or Joe. They were dressed in suits, so they might have been mistaken for business visitors. They continued up to the third floor and found men working on moving boxes and packing up books into boxes. The room looked like a maze of boxes stacked as tall as Ken. They went up another floor and the same thing was going on there. On the fifth floor, there were not all the workers, but boxes and boxes stacked in sections around all the walls. They cautiously went up to the sixth floor and again, boxes stacked in sections, but this time on pallets so they were not stacked just against the walls. Ken knew that this was where Lee Harvey Oswald was supposed to be firing from, so they looked around. As they got close to where the windows were looking out over the plaza, several people came up the other stairwell and entered the floor.

"Can we help you?" asked one man that looked not much older than Ken.

"We are so sorry. We are visiting from up East and were hoping to locate a young man that works here. Lee Oswald?"

"Yes, he works here, but he works on the fourth floor."

"My apologies again. We are just fascinated by all the books you store here, and how so many books can be organized for shipments all over the country. We certainly meant nothing by looking around."

"We are always ready to welcome visitors to our facility. Who are you with, may I ask?" said one of the other gentlemen that had come onto the floor.

"I am with Davis and Fitzgerald out of Boston. We design and manufacture machine parts for companies like GE and Bell Telephone. And this is my younger brother. He is a student at Harvard."

"We don't have many machining books. We generally focus on textbooks for high school and college academic programs. What are you studying, young man?"

"I believe I will go into the law program at Harvard, Sir."

"Well, very good. Would you like one of us to take you down to find Mr. Oswald?"

"No, we can find our way. We don't want to interrupt your work here."

Ken and Joe made their way toward the stairwell. Ken then had a brilliant idea. He stopped, and looked back toward the men.

"I noticed you have a bird's eye view of the plaza. Are you offering to allow people to come and watch the President later this week from your building?"

"Why, we had not thought of that. We might consider it now that you mention it. Thank you."

"Certainly. I presumed you might be doing that given that the book boxes near the windows appear to have been moved around."

"That shouldn't be like that. We will have to send someone up here now to inventory and re-stack up here. Thank you so much for bringing that to our attention.'

"Certainly. Have a good day, gentlemen."

Joe patted Ken on the back as they entered the stairwell. He whispered that Ken was a genius. They made their way down to the fourth floor. Entering the only room on the floor, they asked someone where Lee Oswald was. The man they asked pointed to a man across the room, and Joe and Ken made their way over to him.

When they got to Mr. Oswald, Ken held out his hand as he said, "Mr. Oswald, my name is Aaron Banks. I work for Crescent Firearms, the company you recently ordered a rifle from, and should have received."

Mr. Oswald appeared to look a bit nervous and looked around at the other workers nearby to see if anyone heard what was being said.

"I don't believe I'm the one you are looking for."

"I am terribly sorry. My office indicated that they tracked you down via a post office box you had back in March when the Carcano Italian Carbine rifle was ordered. If we have made a mistake, I apologize."

Mr. Oswald continued to look very nervous and seemed more concerned about getting linked to the gun rather than owning it. Ken wondered if he had made a terrible mistake. But then, Mr. Oswald nodded yes to the question Ken had asked him, and shook his hand.

Ken continued, "Well, we are in town to meet with several suppliers and to address a recent issue that several other customers have brought to our attention regarding recent shipments. Several customers in the Dallas/Fort Worth area have received rifles with a faulty firing pin that does not fire correctly. Have you tested your rifle and found any issues?"

"I have not tested it yet. I was planning to go to the firing range later this week."

"Well, Mr. Oswald, if you would like, we could meet you here tomorrow morning and look at the firing pin, and if it has the same fault in the metal, we can take the firing pin from you, and then ship you a replacement. Is that something you would like us to do for you?"

"Well, you probably are not aware I'm ex-military. What exactly is wrong with the firing pin?"

"Mr. Oswald, I am not from the design team, so it might not be as detailed an explanation as you might be used to, but apparently the metal does not have the tensile strength and as such, sticks even when it has fired fine for several shots. The design team has gone over the requirements and we have changed suppliers, so the new firing pins we are shipping out do not have the same issue."

"Is there no way to identify it, then?"

"Mr. Oswald, the only way is by the serial number on the firing pin, so it must be removed and checked against a list that I have."

"If I cannot bring it tomorrow morning, what then?"

"Well, we were hoping to resolve this issue for all the customers in this area while we are in town. Is there any way you could reconsider?"

"I would like to check the rifle out first. Can I contact the company if I have any issues and get it replaced later?"

"Certainly, but as I said, we are hoping to resolve this for you while I am in town. We hope to ensure you have a rifle that meets the standards we guaranteed, and to ensure safety for you."

"With my experience, Mr. Banks, I'm sure I will be fine. I will confirm the rifle later this week or this weekend and let the company know if there are any issues. Thank you for the personal attention."

"If you say so, Mr. Oswald. We thank you for the purchase of this rifle and welcome you back as a continued customer if you have other needs."

Ken held out his hand and Mr. Oswald shook it again, and then turned away from Ken and Joe. Ken and Joe went out the side entrance they had originally entered the building from and made their way back across the street to the plaza, where Deb and Kim were waiting.

"What happened? You were gone a long time," Kim asked.

Joe was smiling as they walked up. "You should have seen Ken; he was so cool as a cucumber. We were checking all the floors out, and we went all the way up to the sixth floor. We walked right up the window where the shots were supposed to be fired from. Then some men came up to that floor, and Ken, very cool like, said he worked for Davis and Fitzgerald, a manufacturing company in Boston and I was a student at Harvard. The men thought nothing of us wandering around their business. Then as we were leaving to go down and look for our friend, Mr. Lee Oswald, he mentioned the windows would be a great place to watch the President, and that the boxes appeared to have been moved for that purpose. One guy said that wasn't right, and they were going to send someone up to fix the boxes."

"You're kidding. You actually told them they organized the boxes up there and drew attention to it?"

"It gets better, Deb, then we went to the fourth floor and Ken talked to Mr. Oswald! He told him we were from the company that sold him the rifle! He told him we were talking to every customer in the area to replace the firing pin. It was genius. Pure genius! Ken wanted to meet Mr. Oswald tomorrow to check his firing pin and then take it from him and send a replacement. Can you believe the idea of that?"

"Did you get him to agree to that, Ken?"

"No Kim, I didn't."

"That's a shame."

"I think it made him nervous that we knew he had the rifle and something might be wrong with it. Also, he hasn't even fired it yet."

"Wow, you got a lot of information out of him, Ken. It's a shame you couldn't get him to meet you tomorrow. That would have ended this whole thing right there."

"That's what I was thinking, as I was making all that up."

"Did you give him your name, Ken?"

"No, I gave him a made-up name."

"What name did you give him?" Kim asked.

"Aaron Banks."

Joe started laughing. He doubled over with laughter, in fact. Ken rolled his eyes at Joe's antics.

"Why does that name sound so familiar?"

"Maybe because you know this name as Ernie Banks and Hank Aaron!" Joe said, still laughing.

"Ok, well, maybe we should head back to Fort Worth and the hotel now?"

"Good idea. Let's get back before we talk to anyone else, huh, Mr. Aaron Banks?"

They walked back down Main Street and to the bus stop that brought them over to Dallas this morning. By the time they got back to the hotel, it was nearly five in the evening. Ken decided that they should have dinner in the hotel restaurant and hang out in the lobby for a while to see if the secret service people were milling about at all. After dinner, they went to the lobby and sat down. Deb read the paper to check for any of Mr. Cryer's stories, Ken looked at a magazine that was sitting on the table, Kim read one of her books that she brought along, and Joe wandered around the first floor of the hotel. With nothing much to see on the first floor, he went up to the second floor, where all the conference rooms were located. The first few rooms were being set up for tomorrow, with chairs and tables. Toward the back of the hall, there was one room with the door only partially opened with people in it.

Joe made his way toward that room to take a look, and was surprised that the room had a few tables and about six men, all in black suits, going over maps and notes. Joe knew he had found the secret service. He watched for a minute and then made his way back to Ken and Deb and Kim.

"I know where the secret service guys are hiding out."

"Where Joe?"

"Up on the second floor. They're in a conference room going over maps and notes right now."

"Show me. Deb and Kim, you wait here."

Joe took Ken upstairs to the second floor and walked him toward the door of the conference room. They stood nearby for a few minutes and heard the men talking about the travel route and the itinerary for the days here in Fort Worth and Dallas. Then one man said that they were done for the day. It was time to get some dinner and pick it back up in the morning. Joe and Ken made their way quickly to the public bathrooms nearby and snuck inside. They heard the secret service men leave the room and then one of them called to another to make sure they locked the room.

After a few minutes, Joe and Ken left the bathroom and went downstairs.

"It was definitely the secret service. We heard them talking about the parade route, the flight from here to Dallas after a morning speech here at the hotel, and some breakfast or something. They have a room set up for themselves and have a lock on the door and they have the key. I'm sure the hotel let them set that room up for their preparation and use."

"So, do you think we can get the letter to them?" Kim asked.

"I was thinking we could go up there a little later and slide it under the door to that room. What do you think about that, Deb?"

"I think that's a great idea. No one will have to try to slip it to them, and we don't have to bring attention to ourselves at the front desk. Let's head up to the rooms and I can get the letter and we can go down there after about an hour or so."

"Wait a minute. They said they were going to get dinner. Maybe we should go right away and slide it under the door in case they come back after dinner."

"That's probably a better idea, Joe."

The four of them went to the elevators and went to their rooms. Kim sat down in front of the television and Ken and Deb left right away to take the letter to the secret service conference room. They crept down the hall, even though it all seemed quiet, and closed up for the night. They got to the room Joe had found, and Deb knelt down and slide the letter under the door. On the envelope they had written Alert to Secret Service.

As they made their way back to their hotel rooms, Deb asked, "Do you think they might identify us from this letter, Ken?"

"I don't think so. Walking around, I've checked the hotel and there are no cameras anywhere, and our fingerprints can 't identify us, since we haven't been born yet in this time. I think we're safe."

They went into the room and talked over what to do tomorrow if the secret service did nothing and the newspaper showed nothing, and then they all went to sleep.

The next day they all went downstairs and found a bunch of police in the lobby and most of the secret service people that had been in the room last night in the office next to the registration desk. Deb was excited because clearly, they had seen the letter, or at least that's what she thought had caused all of this action. Deb suggested they leave to get breakfast today so they don't get asked anything. They left and walked a block or two to a diner and had breakfast. While they were eating, they decided to go back to the hotel and check for a newspaper and then get back on the bus over to Dallas to sit in the plaza to see if anything was happening over there.

When they got back to the hotel, the police had left but the secret service people were still in the office talking to staff from the hotel. The lady that worked on the registration desk came over to the four kids as they were sitting in the lobby area and asked if they had seen anything suspicious last night as she had seen them in the lobby then as well. They said no, that they had seen nothing out of the ordinary. They asked what was going on, since they had seen the police when they came down today. She indicated they were just in preparation for the President and First Lady to arrive later that evening.

Deb found a newspaper and held it up. Ken had the rest of them get up at that point by motioning to Joe and Kim. He then said goodbye to the registration desk clerk, saying they had to go to a family appointment. They left the hotel and went down the street to catch the bus to Dallas. While they were riding on the bus, Deb scanned the paper for a story from Mr. Cryer. Sure enough, he had taken the bait and had written a piece about unconfirmed reports of a possible assassination plot against the President and First Lady. He put just enough details in the report regarding the probable location being in Dealey Plaza and that the assassin was rumored to have access to one building on the plaza. Deb read the report out loud to her siblings. They were thrilled.

When they arrived in Dallas, they walked down Main Street again to the plaza and found Dallas police all over the place. They were coming in and going out of buildings along the parade route as well. Since one side of the plaza held the county offices, jail, and other municipal buildings, there did not appear to be much activity there. All the police activity seemed to be centered on the book depository and several business buildings that were across Houston Street from the book depository and cornered on the plaza parade route. There were also police officers and some secret service men walking along the grassy knoll area of the plaza that was also directly on the parade route. Deb was pleased by what she saw.

They sat there for some time, and then suddenly a man walking across the street in front of the book depository with a police officer stopped and pointed straight at Ken. Wanting to run, they decided that would not be a good idea. They waited quietly for the officer to get over to where they were sitting on the plaza.

"Excuse me, my name is Officer Daniels. I am with the Dallas police department. I understand you were in the book depository yesterday. Can I ask what you were doing there?"

"Officer, my name is Kenneth Fitzgerald. I went to the book depository yesterday with my younger brother here because I work for a company in Boston that represents Crescent Firearms. The company has had several reports of issues with one rifle that Crescent wholesales to several stores, and one of them was purchased earlier this year by Mr. Lee Oswald. We tracked the purchase to a post office box that was owned by a person noted with the US postal service as A. Hidell. I am not at all certain why my company connected this postal box with this name to Mr. Oswald, as a matter of fact. In any cases, my company has asked me to contact owners of this rifle to inspect and replace the firing pin. As I was travelling to the Fort Worth/Dallas area with my brother and two of my cousins for a family matter, I was asked to contact Mr. Oswald to inquire if he had any issues with the rifle and to offer to inspect and replace the firing pin."

"Do you have identification with you, Mr. Fitzgerald?"

"Yes Sir, I do."

Ken took out his wallet from his inside suit jacket pocket and then pulled the Connecticut driver's license out he and Mary had made prior to this trip through time. He handed the id to the police officer and waited.

"I thought you said you were from Boston?"

"Yes, the company I work for has its main office in Boston, but I work from an affiliate location in Wallingford, Connecticut."

"And what exactly brings you to Dallas?"

"As I said, we have some family business to attend to. You see, Deborah and Kimberly, my two cousins sitting there, have recently lost their parents to an accident while they were overseas. I am here with my brother to attend to legal matters concerning their custody and such."

The officer looked over at Deb and Kim, sitting on a park bench, and touched his police hat. "I am very sorry for your loss, young ladies. Apparently, you have a very caring and responsible cousin in Mr. Fitzgerald here."

The officer paused and then said, "Did you notice anything unusual about the book depository when you were there yesterday?"

"Well, we met several gentlemen when we were wandering around the building trying to locate Mr. Oswald and commented that the book boxes seemed to be organized for viewing the Presidential parade, and we wondered if they were offering public viewing as I wanted to bring my brother and cousins to see the parade, but wanted to ensure the safety of my two young cousins. The gentleman that responded indicated that they had not set up the floor for viewing and it was unusual that the boxes would be out of order. He said he was going to send someone to look at that. Is that what you meant?"

"What floor did you encounter these gentlemen?"

"On the sixth floor, I believe."

"Did they announce themselves as being employed by the company?"

"Not exactly. We apologized for roaming around. I explained who I was, and that it impressed us with the volume of books the company appeared to manage. We identified who were looking for, and one of the other gentlemen said that Mr. Oswald worked on the fourth floor, so I simply presumed they were employees of the company. They did not provide me with their names."

"How did you find Mr. Oswald?"

"We found him on the fourth floor after asking for someone to point him out when we arrived on that floor."

"Excuse me, I meant did you see anything unusual when you spoke to Mr. Oswald?"

"Well, he seemed concerned that we had located him at all. I presume that was because of the post office box being noted with another name. And he seemed nervous speaking to us about a rifle while at work, which may be understandable depending on the environment at the company."

"How did you locate him at his place of work?"

"As I stated before, I am uncertain of that. The company provided me with the information through my supervisor at Davis and Fitzgerald and I simply followed up. They provided me his place of work and his home address."

"It's interesting that you work for a company with your last name in it."

"Is that a question, Sir?"

"It is now."

"My uncle, who recently passed away, and a business partner of his own the company, or did until this accident occurred. My uncle had moved to Texas several years ago, as he was retiring early. So, yes, I worked for my uncle's company."

"I see."

"What else do you know about Mr. Oswald?"

"He mentioned while we spoke yesterday that he had not yet fired the rifle and that he was ex-military. He said that would sufficiently make him knowledgeable about whether he had an issue with his firing pin so he refused my offer to meet him here this morning for me to inspect and take the faulty firing pin if necessary and order a new firing pin to be shipped to him."

"Did he say what branch of the military he had been in?"

"He did not."

"Did you get the impression he was a foreigner, Mr. Fitzgerald?"

"He had a slight accent to his speaking that did not seem like it was Texan, but then I am from the East Coast, so most people speak with an accent to me."

"We feel the same way about those of you from up North, Mr. Fitzgerald."

"I imagine it is all in what you are used to."

"Yes. Did Mr. Oswald indicate he might meet you today? Is that why you are back in the plaza today?"

"He actually said he would not meet us today. We are here simply to show my brother and cousins the plaza and where the President will be. We are leaving town later today."

"Very good. Thank you for the time, Mr. Fitzgerald."

"If I might ask, what is all the activity here in the plaza about today? Could it be related to the story we saw in the paper this morning about a possible assassination plot?"

"Well, most of this is precautionary. It is just what we do prior to a dignitary like the President visiting. However, we are looking at the buildings here on the plaza, and your visit yesterday seemed significant and was pointed out to me by a manager at the book depository who pointed you out across the street, and given that Mr. Oswald did not report for work today."

"I see. Well, unfortunately, my interaction with Mr. Oswald was brief."

"Yes, so it would seem. Have a good day, Mr. Fitzgerald, and safe travels to you and your family."

"Thank you, Officer Daniels. Good luck with the Presidential visit to your city."

The officer walked off. Deb held her breath until he got back across the street.

"Whew, that was a close one."

"Yeah, it sure was. I thought they were going to drag you in Ken."

"Joe, Deb, and Kim, you too, there's no need to worry. Dad told me a long time ago that people will believe you and will always respond favorably if you speak with authority. That's all I did."

"Well, it seems to me like it might be a good idea for us to make a quick getaway today and get back to the machine. We don't want to press our luck anymore."

"Deb, we need to see this through. I think we lie low for the rest of the day today at the hotel and see what we can find out there and leave tomorrow as planned. We're just leaving Dallas and not coming back here."

With that, they all got up and walked to the bus stop and went back to Fort Worth and the hotel. When they arrived at the hotel, there were even more secret service men in the lobby and several Dallas police officers and several generals from the Army. They went to get lunch and then came back to hang out in the hotel rooms for the remainder of the day and venture out to see what they could learn after all the activity settled down. After lunch, they sat for a few minutes in the lobby and the desk clerk approached them again.

"I know you were all asking about the President and First Lady visit. It appears it is still on, but they are ramping up some security. They will clear the lobby at five o'clock today and you cannot sit in the lobby until after the President gives his speech and they head to Dallas tomorrow. "

"Thank you for telling us."

"Certainly. Also, I heard they were closing several businesses on the parade route tomorrow because of that supposed assassination plot that was in the paper today. I think the secret service found out about it, too, last night or early this morning. It must be a genuine threat if they are doing all of this, don't you think?"

Ken answered her, "I would think so. It's amazing that they discovered this plot. The paper didn't have many details."

"Well, apparently someone slipped a note to the secret service last night."

"How does anyone know where they are located? They seem to appear and disappear like magic."

"They have a base of operations here in the hotel."

"Oh, well, maybe someone involved with the plot got cold feet and left the note?"

"Do you think? That means they were in the hotel last night. How frightening."

"That might explain why there are so many police here today."

"Yes, and they are not telling the staff anything."

"I think I will take my sisters upstairs to keep us all out of the way, if you don't mind."

"You are so protective of your sisters. That is lovely to see. Goodbye Mr. Fitzgerald."

"Goodbye."

They left the lobby and went up to their rooms. As they entered the room, Kim looked up at Ken and said, "That young lady likes you, Ken."

"No, she doesn't, Kim. She was just being nice."

"I think Kim's right, Ken. She was smiling at you whenever we've been down there. And, I might add, she didn't give that special attention and information to anyone else sitting in the lobby," Joe said, laughing a bit.

"Don't be ridiculous. That wasn't what was going on."

"Ken, they're right. She liked you. I know you don't notice it, but I've been asked by other girls since I got to high school with you. They come up and ask me things about you and want me to help them get close to you. I see the way they look at you too." Deb revealed something that had been going on for years, apparently.

Ken sat down in a chair hard and looked up at Deb as he said, "Geez, I had no idea that had been going on. Does it mean I'm really dumb that I don't see that? And by the way, I'm with Mary."

"You're not dumb, big brother, you just don't seem to realize how the girls fawn over you," Joe said, laying down on the bed and laughing.

"You probably should stay away from her now, Ken. You don't want to make her look for you and stuff like Deb said could mess her life up," Kim added, patting Ken on this arm.

They settled down and tried not to think about what was going on outside their room. It was only three in the afternoon, but it seemed everything was going exactly as they hoped. Mr. Oswald was not coming to work. They would lock the buildings down, and the President was probably safe. They played cards and watched some television until six and then went down to the hotel restaurant for dinner. The lobby was deserted except for the secret service guarding doors and access points, like the elevator hallway. After dinner, Deb wanted to walk around the lobby but the secret service said they could not stay, so Deb took Kim to the lobby shop and they looked for some magazines and snacks to take to their room.

The next morning, they went out to the parking lot to see the President give his speech. It was raining, but they stood under umbrellas and listened to him. After the speech, they went back into the hotel and Kim asked if she could go to the lobby shop as they were selling commemorative items of the President and First Lady. The boys went up to the room to finish packing up. When the girls got into the elevator to go up and get the boys to leave, the doors opened suddenly on the second floor and Mrs. Kennedy and two secret service men entered the elevator. She smiled at Deb and Kim and looked at what Kim had purchased.

Mrs. Kennedy then asked, "Did you see the President downstairs?"

Kim answered because Deb was a little dumbfounded, "Yes, Ma'am we saw him."

Deb then found her voice. "We were so glad we got to see him in person, well, on the stage anyway. He is such a great man, Ma'am, and we're lucky to have him as our President."

"Well, thank you. What is your name, dear?"

"My name is Deborah, and this is my sister Kimberly. It is a real honor to meet you, Ma'am."

"The honor is all mine. My favorite part of being First Lady is getting to meet all the young people touched by my husband and inspired to go out and change the world. You will do that, won't you?"

"Yes Ma'am. We are planning every day how we can contribute and help change the world."

With that, the elevator door opened and Deb and Kim got off. Deb turned as the secret service gentleman that got off the elevator when it arrived at Deb and Kim's floor, got back onto the elevator and said, "It was a real honor to meet you Mrs. Kennedy. I hope you enjoy your visit to Dallas."

She smiled at them as the elevator door closed again. Deb was hoping and praying throughout that day that she didn't lose her husband today.

en checked them out of the Texas Hotel, and they boarded a bus to the last stop in Fort Worth, in a neighborhood near the edge of the suburbs. They then hiked back into the forested area surrounding Benbrook Lake. They used the compass that Kim had brought to locate the machine that was well under coverage of trees and branches they had placed around it. Joe and Ken began setting the machine up for the return trip while Deb and Kim kept watch for anyone in the area. Deb was wondering what was going on in Dallas right now as the parade should start soon from Loves Airport where the President was arriving in Dallas.

After about thirty minutes, Joe announced they were ready to go. Deb and Kim loaded all the gear into the machine and they all got harnessed in for the trip. Joe started up the machine, and they again experienced the wind noise and the feeling of spinning. The bright light appeared and then, in a flash, they were coming to a stop, or what seemed like a stop from all the noise.

During the time Ken, Joe, Deb and Kim were gone, Mr. Brewster sat with Mary and Ryan at the big worktable. He announced they had some letters and went to retrieve them from his house. He handed a letter to each of them and held on to the letter Joe had written to him. Mr. Brewster explained that Ken and Deb had written them with the express instructions they be given out after they left.

Mary asked tentatively, "Are we supposed to open these now or if something happens later?"

"The kids didn't give me any other instructions. I don't know what you should do. I think I am going to wait to open mine from Joe."

"Then I will wait too."

They waited all day. Mr. Brewster tried to reassure Mary as the day wore on, because she was getting very agitated about Ken not being back yet. She kept asking Mr. Brewster if he had been gone this long, and was more concerned when Mr. Brewster explained that when he arrived back in the barn, only about twenty-five minutes had passed, even though he had been back in time for nearly four hours. Mr. Brewster tried to explain that the time travel made time here and there appear to pass at different rates, and that even though Joe might have set the date and time for just after they left for their return, they may not return at that exact time. Mr. Brewster had been working on a theory that while you were gone in the time machine, you could not come back to the minute you left. You would have to come back some amount of time later. He was trying to come up with the correct math formula to prove this out, but had been unsuccessful yet.

Ryan was very quiet all day, not really taking part in the conversations, and not willing to discuss his distress over the time Deb and her siblings had been gone. He reasoned they went three days before the date they needed to be there, and that would mean they would be gone far longer than Mr. Brewster had. However, Ryan was anxious about what was happening wherever Deb was located right now. He was still struggling with how to label or even think about the fact that Deb existed in another time, and that this machine of theirs could still access the past. He was also very worried he would lose Deb and was trying hard to concentrate on their time together, thinking that if he could still go over their time and dates and gifts and discussions, time would not alter for them.

Mr. Brewster and Mary made sandwiches for lunch and later made chicken for dinner. As it approached nine in the evening, Ryan said they had to get back to campus. They agreed that Mary and Ryan would return right after church services in the morning and Mr. Brewster agreed that if the kids returned, he would make sure that Ken left Ryan a message to receive as soon as he came down to go to church.

After Ryan got to his dorm room, he opened the letter from Deb. In it, she explained she was writing to be sure he knew what she remembered and to help him remember her if something happened. She detailed her thoughts about the day they met in the library, the movies, the calls when she was in the Hamptons and in New York, the skating and all her feelings leading up to the trip in the machine. She told him she loved him, and their hearts would find a way back to each other even if the time travel made him not remember her. He laid in bed and remembered all the things they had said to one another and did together again. He thought to himself there was no way he could forget her, but he was suddenly afraid to go to sleep, afraid he might not remember her.

Meanwhile, in the girls' dorm, Mary was reading her letter from Ken. Ken had also detailed what he remembered of Mary and how he felt about her and how he wanted to plan his future around her. Mary cried herself to sleep that night, worried for Ken's safety and the safety of his siblings, and afraid she might lose him. Over in the barn, Mr. Brewster read the letter from Joe. In this letter, Joe asked that Mr. Brewster release the information about the math and their tests of the machine only if Joe didn't come back, or if he couldn't finish what they started. He thanked Mr. Brewster for helping him sort out the calculations, finding the machine, and mostly for helping him through a hard time. Mr. Brewster laid down that night thinking that he if and his wife had ever had children, he would have wanted them to be like Joe. He prayed his wife would find a way to protect Joe and bring him back.

The next day, Ryan awoke and realized he had slept, but remembered all the time he spent with Deb. He remembered all of their dates, the spring dance, the winter formal, taking Deb with his family for a trip to North Carolina over the summer, the jerseys she gave him, the chain and necklace and charm bracelet he gave her. He walked over to the girls' dorm and met Mary, and they walked to church services together and then went over to the barn. The two of them did not discuss their memories of Deb and Ken except to ask one another if they still remembered they were dating. Mr. Brewster was tinkering with an old car in the barn's corner when they arrived. Ryan asked him what he was doing, and Mr. Brewster said it was helpful for him to stay busy while this was going on. Mary sat at the table and worked on homework while Ryan assisted Mr. Brewster with the car restoration. Just after the three of them had finished lunch, it got very windy in the barn and Mary's papers blew all over. Then the noise started and then a dazzling light flashed in the center of the barn where the machine had been on Saturday morning. Suddenly the noise and light and wind stopped, and the machine was there.

Mr. Brewster immediately tried to communicate with Joe inside the machine. Before he could establish the connection, the door swung open and Joe, Ken, Deb and Kim climbed out of the machine. Ryan rushed at Deb and pulled her into his arms and included Kim in a big hug. Ken walked up to Mary, who seemed a little shaken up and wrapped his arms around her, and Mr. Brewster grabbed Joe into a great bear hug.

Ken was the first to speak. "So what time is it?"

Mary responded, "It's Sunday afternoon, about two."

"Sunday? Are you sure?"

"We waited all day yesterday and last night for you to get back. Ryan and I came over today after church and I was getting so worried."

"I'm so sorry, Mary. We really did not know how long it would seem here for you all."

"I've been trying to calculate the time passage based on my trip, but this trip will probably provide us much more information toward that calculation," Mr. Brewster offered to help calm Mary down.

Kim pulled out of Ryan's hug. "Do you think we're still students here?"

"I know you are. This morning as we went into the church, your friend Rebecca asked me when you were all getting back to campus today."

"So, we fixed nothing," Joe said, looking down at the floor.

"Well, listen, we cannot presume simply because you are students here that you changed nothing until we look at all the information."

"The first big question, was President Kennedy assassinated on November 22, 1963?"

Mary pulled out her history book at that point, from a pile of papers on the table, "No silly, President Kennedy was assassinated in Austin, Texas on December 4, 1963. What are you talking about?"

"Well, clearly, we stopped the assassination in Dallas, but it happened anyway two weeks later. That might explain why we're still students here."

"I have an idea. Let's try to call our house in Cambridge. If one of our parents' answers, we'll know, won't we?"

"As always, Kim, you are the insightful one."

Mr. Brewster took Deb inside his kitchen for her to dial the number that had been their home number in Cambridge. When they came into the barn, Deb told them she had reached a home in Cambridge, but it was not their home. The person who answered said they had the number for over a year.

Ryan then looked at Deb a little funny and said, "That makes perfect sense to me since you all arrived here at Choate in January 1974."

Deb looked at Ken, and they both seemed very surprised. Deb thought for a minute and then said, "Ryan, we came in October nineteen seventy-four, in the middle of the fall term last year. Remember the first day I saw you in history class, you said to a friend of yours that finally some good-looking chicks were coming to Choate. You had on a blue vest under your uniform jacket."

"Deb, that all happened in January on the first day of the second term of our sophomore year."

"Not according to us, from the time we left here."

"I'm not sure what you mean."

"Listen Ryan, when we left here yesterday morning in the time machine, we had come to Choate in October. You and I started dating just before the winter formal. And more importantly, President Kennedy had been assassinated by Lee Harvey Oswald in Dallas on November 22, 1963. We went back to change that, since that is when my father met Mr. Davis and they started talking. The tragedy of that assassination, and then the assassination of Martin Luther King Jr. is what set my father on the course to business partners with Mr. Davis and the eventual air plane crash in late September, nineteen seventy-four. So clearly, if what you all know was common knowledge that President Kennedy was shot in Austin on December 4, then we changed things in Dallas, but did not totally prevent his death. That might be why it appears our parents might still have died."

"This is terrible. We did all that, changed history and did not change the course of our parents' death. In fact, it appears we may have sped it up by doing this," Joe lamented at their failure.

"I need to get to the library and do some research in the microfilm newspapers to see if I can find our parent's death information. Also, I think I might actually call Aunt Alicia and see how she's doing."

Mary held up her hand. "Wait a minute. You think you arrived here at Choate in October, but Ryan and I both remember you getting here the first day of second semester of the school year before you remember. Does that mean, Ken, you remember nothing that happened between us before October? Do you even remember asking me out or your birthday party or anything?"

Ken came back and wrapped his arms around Mary to reassure her, "Mary, remember I came to you as soon as I got out of the machine. I remember all the things we said and did together, but I only remember last fall forward. We can go over all this, but remember, my feelings for you have not changed."

"I guess if we're still students here, I need to finish some homework. I didn't do it on Friday cause I was planning on being back with Mom and Dad by tonight."

"Kim, don't get upset. We'll figure this all out."

"I'm going to stay here and gather up the information and data from the machine with Mr. Brewster and see what we can make of the time passage issue."

"Ok, Joe, but make sure you get back by dinner time, ok?"

"Yeah, I'll meet you all at the dining hall at six."

So, Ryan and Deb left for the library and Mary, Ken and Kim drove Ken's car back to campus and to the girls' dorm. At least Ken still had the Trans am from Mr. Reynolds, he thought, as Kim went to do homework, Mary and Ken went for a walk to discuss what they thought of things now.

"I don't know what to make of the fact that we now have different memories of when I arrived here and how things went down. Would you tell me what your understanding is? Hey, did you open my letter?" Ken asked Mary after they got Kim situated.

"Sure, Ken. I'm really confused about all of this. First, I remember meeting you in January on the first day of second term classes. You were fresh off of the football championships back in Cambridge and everyone knew your parents had died and you were going to miss senior year at your high school back home. We met when we had to work on a group project for religious studies. Remember, we were on a team with Kate and Brian? We became friends, as you were trying to keep things going with a girl you were dating back in Cambridge. That fell apart right at the end of the term and just as you were leaving to spend the summer at the Hamptons, we went out on our first date. You took me to town, and we had dinner at the Italian place and then had ice cream. We talked all summer and sent letters back and forth, and then sometime during this past fall term you told me that Joe had discovered a math formula that would make time travel possible and that you had tested it by sending Mr. Brewster back to meet his father who died in Normandy during World War two. You all wanted to go back in time to change something that would make your parents not end up in the skiing accident. You left yesterday morning and got back this afternoon. I did open your letter last night, and I don't remember it not making sense last night, but today when I read it over, the dates and things made little sense and that was why I was so worried about you all day today."

"Ok, this is really strange. First of all, my parents died in a plane crash in September, not in a skiing accident. Did we ever talk about Aunt Alicia or my going to the lawyer's office and finding out about the will and the trust and letters from my parents? Did we meet in New York during this past Christmas break? Did we go to winter formal? Did you give me a watch for my birthday? Did we have that great last night, Friday night, where I told you I loved you?"

They stopped and sat down on a bench.

"I'm certain you told me your parents died in a skiing accident. They were in Colorado with your dad's business partner and that guy's wife, and they were travelling from one ski resort to another, and there was some avalanche or something and it killed your parents. Yes, I know about your aunt. She has custody of Deb, Kim and Joe now that you are eighteen. Yes, you told me about going to the lawyer's office just after you turned eighteen, and how upset you were with your aunt for not telling you about the will and letters, and during Christmas we met up in New York after you set up a bank account. I fixed your grandfather's watch for you on your birthday. Do you still have it?"

Ken reached into his pants pocket and pulled out the watch. It had the same engraving on it. Ken was relieved. That meant most of what he remembered from their dating, she likely remembered. She just had nine more months of memories than he did.

"I wasn't dating anyone by the time I got here, in my understanding of how we got here. But if you remember meeting me in January, that would make sense as I broke up with Jennifer back home a little after Christmas that year. She was mad at me for not spending enough time with her, and not getting her a romantic enough gift, and we had a big fight, and I said I didn't want to deal with her nonsense anymore. It seems like you and I have different timelines until the fall term, but after that, they are the same."

"Yes, it sure does. I'm glad, though, that we end up in the same place. I was so worried that you would get back here and not remember me."

"Mary, I was worried about the exact same thing."

"So, what I do not have any memory of is what you were trying to change. I tried all day today to remember what you were going to do, and I was afraid to ask Ryan or Mr. Brewster."

"We went to Dallas, 1963, and stopped President Kennedy from being assassinated there. In my history, Lee Harvey Oswald shot him in Dealey Plaza on November 22, 1963, from the sixth floor of a book depository building. We went back there and Deb wrote letters to a reporter for the Dallas newspaper, and one that we slipped under a door of a room the secret service were using, and it resulted in the buildings on Dealey Plaza being shut down and Mr. Oswald being investigated by the police. I even talked to him. It was the weirdest thing."

"You talked to the man that was supposed to shoot the President? What did you say to him?"

"I pretended to be from a firm that represented a gun manufacturer and said they messed the firing pins up, and we were offering to replace them. See, in my history, we know all about the gun he used, how he mail ordered it, and I just said we needed to fix it. He said he was ex-military and would probably know if it was bad, but he got real nervous because he used an alias to buy the gun and I knew that, but called him by his real name and found him at work. This made him not come into work the day of the shooting and anyway, by then the police and secret service were clearing all the buildings."

"Ken, that sounds really risky. What if you had been caught or something?"

"I did kind of get caught. We went back to the plaza the next day while the secret service was scrambling, and the police walked up to me, cause Joe and I also talked to some managers at the book depository, and one of them came out of the building with the police and saw me across the street in the park."

"Oh my gosh, what if you'd been arrested and been stuck in nineteen sixty-three?"

"Don't worry, I used a trick my father taught me when I started high school. He said if you talk with authority, people presume you know what you're talking about, and they believe you. Of course, my name is likely in a police report from nineteen sixty-three. If they wanted to follow up, they would not have found Fitzgerald and Davis, a company out of Boston, or Ken Fitzgerald working there."

Mary rolled her eyes and jokingly punched Ken in the arm. "Don't do anything like that again, ok?"

"It'll be ok Mary, I'm fine."

"In the history books, there is mention of an assassination plot that was stopped in Dallas, but there are no real details other than the plot was stopped because of a note sent to the press," Mary said, remembering some information from history class.

"That was Deb. What ended up happening then?"

"Well, President Kennedy was to do a political speech and campaign stop in Austin in December of that same year. He was driving from one of those to the other, and a sniper shot him and Mrs. Kennedy as they were driving down the street. There was secret service in the car, and in cars in front of and behind them, but only the two of them were hit."

"So, we stopped it in Dallas, only to have it happen in Austin."

"Ken, remember how we talked before you left? You can't really change God's plan? Isn't this clear evidence of that?"

"I don't know Mary, I don't know."

"Let's walk over to the library and see if Ryan and Deb are still there and what they found out."

"Yeah, good idea."

Mary and Ken walked over to the library and found Deb pouring over microfilm of newspaper articles. Ryan was sitting next to her, trying to keep up as she scrolled through the information.

"What did you find, Deb?"

Deb looked up from the screen as Ken and Mary came to where she and Ryan were sitting.

"We found several articles from when Mom and Dad died. This time, it was a retreat that he and Mr. Davis and their wives went on to discuss a new line of business. They were headed from one ski resort to another to do some more skiing, and went through a mountain pass, and an avalanche hit their car. Mr. Davis and his wife were about ten minutes behind them and could stop before they got caught in it. Mom and Dad died instantly. It was just after Christmas in nineteen seventy-three. We were with Grandpa and Grandma at their house in Maine."

"How could this have happened?"

"Well, one article in Time magazine gives more details about the business planning that was going on. See, when I was corresponding with Mr. Davis, he said that they had started the business manufacturing medical devices like artificial hearts. They did this after witnessing firsthand the assassinations of Kennedy and Martin Luther King that they wanted to save people. Later, they also got into modular homes for low-income people to continue some part of the vision of President Kennedy. So, I thought if we stopped the Kennedy assassination, we would stop their correspondence and their plans for this track of the business just enough so that we would alter their timeline. Time magazine reports that their first invention was Kevlar, you know the fiber that is used in vests to make them bullet-proof, which took them down a different business path, but eventually, after all the money and association with the military and police departments, they went back into the medical devices. The ski trip was where they were looking into technology innovations. They have a lot more money, and I mean a lot."

"Who cares about that? Were they in the habit of going on this kind of retreat trip whenever they were planning a new innovation?"

"I think so. I'm writing some questions to ask Mr. Davis."

"Does the Time article tell anything more about how the business started?"

"Yes, it's much more detailed than anything that was in print before our trip. I think that must be because in this alternative history, they're so much more renowned because of the Kevlar invention. Anyway, they met in the bar in Dallas, but they were celebrating and didn't start communicating until after the assassination in Austin. Then they both were in Memphis when Martin Luther King was appearing, but in town, not near the hotel where it happened. They met again in a bar and started planning. They talked all night and eventually tried inventing something that would prevent shooting assassinations. d came up with the formula that created Kevlar."

"So, we kept them from talking for a short time and sent them down another path that resulted in our parent's death nine months before it had been. What do you make of that? Are we supposed to believe that their death is inevitable and anything we do will not stop it? And it seems we stopped the assassination in Dallas, but Kennedy died a few weeks later in another city in another assassination plot. It sure would look like we can't really change history."

"I'm not sure, Ken," Deb said, looking back at the screen.

At this point, Mary spoke up. "Perhaps that is the case. Maybe we should learn from this and not try to change anything anymore."

"If we stop now, Joe will not be happy and also, what's his discovery and work for if we find out it cannot help anyone?" Deb said, not looking up.

"Did you learn anything else?"

"Yes, there is mention in newspapers about the anonymous notes sent to the reporter in Dallas and left for the secret service, and the effort to stop an assassination attempt on President Kennedy in Dallas. Lee Harvey Oswald was arrested. Jack Ruby did not shoot him and he spent time in jail. They released him just last year from prison and he is now living outside of New Orleans. After that Dallas trip, the President went back to Washington and two weeks later planned another trip to Texas, where he was stopping in Austin and San Antonio. There was confusion between the Austin police and the secret service, and there was a period of time when the President was travelling without adequate coverage, but not in an open automobile, and a sniper shot him. There was an extensive investigation, and they suspected that Lyndon Johnson was involved, but the investigation couldn't prove it. The person convicted was someone that LBJ knew, and had been associated with, in Texas. He's still in prison for the assassination."

"Do you think Oswald was a front for a bigger plot?" Ken asked.

"I think it's very possible, but our actions changed that. Oswald was interviewed in prison and he admitted to knowing the person who ended up being convicted for assassinating the President, but no one could connect Johnson to the crime."

"That's amazing."

"Yeah."

Ryan looked over at Mary and Ken, who were holding hands and asked, "Is everything ok with you two from all the events of the past day and a half?"

"We talked about it. Clearly, you and Mary have a different understanding of our history over the last year or so than Deb and I do, but I think the important thing is that we are still together. Are you and my sister ok with the difference in your history?"

"We've been talking about that, too. We don't understand how this could be the case, but after a certain time, our understanding and your understanding seem to get in sync, and I know I want to be with Deb, so we have decided to just let the history difference go."

"We have pretty much decided the same thing."

"Deb, I suggest we all meet after class tomorrow to go over what we have learned and hash out how we are going to figure out more from Mr. Davis and what to do now."

"I agree, but we should include Mary and Ryan, I think."

"I want to be there, but I have a paper to finish. When and how long do you think we will be?" Mary asked.

"I think it would be best to meet at the barn at four and then we can all come back and go to dinner and then, Mary, you can work on your paper after dinner. Is that ok?" Ken offered.

"Yeah, that will work."

Deb cleaned up all the paper she had copied, and Ryan went to return the microfilm they had checked out. Then the four of them walked back to the dorms. When Ken and Ryan got to the boys' dorm, they found Joe, who had just returned and told him they wanted to all meet tomorrow. Joe said he would let Mr. Brewster know. Joe asked Ken what Deb found and Ken gave Joe the quick version and said that Deb could fill in all the details tomorrow. They all walked on to the girls' dorm and found Kim. The guys waited in the receiving room of the girls' dorm while Deb went and called Aunt Alicia.

Aunt Alicia was a little surprised to hear from Deb, she said, but glad. She asked how they all were doing and if Ken had heard from Harvard and how Deb had done on the SAT test. After Deb answered all of her questions, she asked Aunt Alicia how she was doing, how work was going, and asked about Mr. Reynolds. Aunt Alicia was very animated in her responses about work and the social scene in New York that she was enjoying with Mr. Reynolds. Deb learned nothing new from her conversation, but Aunt Alicia seemed to remember all the recent visits, so that made Deb feel somewhat reassured.

Deb relayed the conversation as they wall walked over to the dining hall for dinner that night. After dinner, they all went back to their respective rooms. It seemed they all needed some alone time to sort out what had happened and how they felt about everything.

13

The next afternoon, as they all sat around the large work table in Mr. Brewster's barn, no one spoke for quite a while. They all just sat there with the copies of pages that Deb and Ryan had brought from the library and the printouts of the logs from the machine. Ken and Mary had returned the costumes to the theater department with no incident on the way, but still no one spoke for a long a time.

Finally, Deb said, "I told Ken and Mary last night, but it appears from the history books, newspaper articles and everything we read last night that we did in fact change history by preventing the assassination of President Kennedy in Dallas. Unfortunately, we did not completely stop his assassination, as it occurred three weeks later in Austin. Not only that, but the person convicted of the sniper shooting was a known associate of Lyndon Johnson, who became President after they shot Kennedy. Johnson was implicated but never charged. It apparently plagued his presidency, and he did not execute the civil rights act. Richard Nixon signed it after he became President. Johnson was disgraced."

"I remember this in the news. The FBI found evidence that someone in the government did in fact create the confusion between the Austin police department and the secret service. This confusion caused far less coverage of the motorcade path from the airport to the place where Kennedy was supposed to be speaking in Austin. The sniper was positioned in a window of a building on the route and shot Kennedy inside the car. He also killed the driver of the car and it ran off the road, onto the sidewalk and into a building. Mrs. Kennedy was in the hospital for several weeks. When she got out, her things had been summarily removed from the White House, and that was reported on as much as the assassination was. People were very upset about how the Johnsons treated Mrs. Kennedy. Then when he was implicated in the investigation, people were calling for his impeachment, but I think he convinced enough of congress not to do it," Ryan relayed.

"That's amazing, Ryan," Joe said, shaking his head.

"We also appeared to have changed history for Dad and Mr. Davis as well. They met in Dallas after the parade, and instead of commiserating over the assassination, they celebrated seeing him. They didn't start communicating, however, until after Martin Luther King was assassinated. Again, they were both in town for the rally that they both felt strongly about. They met up again in a bar there and remembered each other and started talking about how they needed to figure a way to protect dignitaries from assassination attempts. The discussion eventually led to a material that could be worn as a vest or shirt or jacket that was impervious to bullets. Dad went back to Harvard and worked on a formula that became Kevlar. They made millions of dollars and worked with the military and police departments all over the world. Later, they got into medical devices because of gun violence they saw and ways to respond to seriously damaged organs. They were going on a retreat to discuss new innovations in machinery, specifically an idea that our dad got from his son, Joseph, for computer advancements. They were travelling in two different cars between one ski resort and another when an avalanche covered the road and the car where Mom and Dad were. Mr. Davis and his wife were in a car fifteen or twenty minutes behind and were not killed."

"So, I caused his death by talking to him about computers?" Joe asked, looking down at his notes.

"Joe, that was not the cause. In the Time article, Mr. Davis said that every time they were starting a new business line, they would go off like this somewhere and vacation and then talk the ideas over, and at the end of the four days, they would come out of the little retreat with a new business line. He said it was their 'bar' method that had been successful since Memphis."

"Still, if I hadn't talked to Dad about this great idea of mine, they wouldn't have been on this retreat."

"Listen Joe, you cannot allow yourself to think this. Dad completely supported your idea on computers. It was in the letter he wrote you that was with the will, remember? He might have done all of this anyway because of their own interest in computers, or into something else. So don't beat yourself up over this," Ken said, trying to keep Joe from heading down this path.

"Ken, we can make excuses about this all we want, and try to rationalize this. If they were off talking about computer business, because I brought it to his attention, then I'm responsible."

With that, Joe got up and walked over to the machine. He hit it, then rubbed his knuckles.

"Right now, I wish I'd never made this crazy machine. Now I know I caused all this."

"Joseph James Fitzgerald!" Deb cried.

"You think calling me by my full name like Mom used to do is going to get my attention?"

"Joseph, you will not do this. You will not take all the blame for this. First of all, Mom and Dad died originally because of a vacation trip, not your computer idea. Second, we all sat at this table and agreed that we would do this. We all understood we were going to try something and would have no way of knowing how it would turn out until we got back here. Finally, if anyone is going to take any blame here, it's me, because I had this crazy plan to stop this assassination and thought that alone would make a dramatic change in the course of our parents' lives," Deb stood to declare.

"Might I say something?"

"Of course, Mary, you have as much right as any of us to comment on things. It clearly impacts all of us now."

"Remember before you left, we talked about whether this was a good idea, because perhaps we should not meddle with the plan that God has for us all? Do you all remember the discussion where you debated whether this was the right thing to do? Maybe this is all proof that you shouldn't be doing this."

"What is the machine for if not to go back and help people, not just our parents, but others, like Mr. and Mrs. Kennedy? I met her. She's a nice lady. I'm glad that we did what we did to help them. If we could go back again, I would be sure to put in the letter we snuck into the secret service room that there was a plot from inside the government. That might have protected him completely, and kept Mrs. Kennedy out of the hospital," Kim said.

They all sat a bit dumbfounded, looking at Kim after she finished her little speech.

"As I said, you are the insightful one amongst us, Kim."

"Yes, she is insightful, but Deb, isn't this the heart of the matter? The big question. Do you meddle with the fabric of the higher plans or take steps to help others and try to save your parents? If we've learned anything from this one trip, it's that this question is the primary one that must be answered before another trip happens," Ryan offered.

"Well stated Ryan. Why don't we move on from that monumental question to what Joe and I have learned about the machine, passaging time while someone is travelling?" Mr. Brewster finally interceded.

Mr. Brewster spread out the printouts and the sheets of the calculations that he and Joe were working on. They all looked over the printouts and notes, but no one understood, so they all as one looked up to Joe and Mr. Brewster to explain what they were looking at.

"The machine appears to have functioned exactly as expected. There were no error messages and nothing unusual in any of the logs. That's great news," Joe started.

"The time, the passage issue was a bit harder to solve. With only two trips on the machine, one for only four hours, and the other one for three full days, we had to speculate a bit to come up with the calculation. What we think is that time moves slower the longer you have travelled in time. The first trip, the four-hour trip, time passed at a rate of one hour for the traveler to approximately ten minutes for those here. The elapsed time seemed to slow down so that an hour for the traveler meant approximately five minutes here. That is as close as we can come to estimating with only the two trips, but we know that on this last trip, you were gone for three full days, and here only thirty-two hours passed," Mr. Brewster explained.

"So, what do we do now?" Kim asked.

"I don't know. There is a nagging concern that we might be missing something in what we did. I'm going to go back to the library again after dinner and see if I can locate anything else that might help me. I'm also going to go over my letter to Mr. Davis and get it ready to mail," Deb said, thinking that the research would provide her with an answer to the question of what to do now.

"Ok, we should probably head back to campus for dinner anyway, and Mary has some work to do," Ken said.

"Mr. Brewster, thank you so much for everything you have done for us. We really appreciate it."

"Deborah, you don't have to thank me for anything. It has been a genuine pleasure having you all here, and I certainly hope we're not finished yet."

"We are not finished; remember, we committed to four trips. And I want to document the trips and details and the evaluations we have done on the time passage differential as well, Mr. Brewster, so we're definitely not done," Joe vehemently said.

"I think, Joe, we need to do some serious thinking and talking about this before we make the next move."

With that, the six of them got up from the table and walked back to campus. They all went to the dining hall and all of their friends asked about their weekend. Ken told his friends that they had gone to the city with Mr. Reynolds and it was great, so that was the story they all stuck with. After dinner, Mary went to finish her paper. Kim sat in the main hall with her friends with Joe and Ken, while Deb and Ryan went back to the library, where Ryan worked on some homework, and Deb tried to locate more information.

After determining there was nothing further that she could learn at the library, Deb made some adjustments to her letter to Mr. Davis and put it in the mailbox outside of the girls' dorm.

For the next few days, everyone was busy with schoolwork, classes, and commitments with their friends. All except for Joe, who seemed to spend all of his free time with Mr. Brewster documenting the trip they made and compiling all of their notes. Joe seemed very quiet whenever Deb saw him, and she was anxious by Thursday afternoon. She went in search of Ken after class to discuss it and found him in the main hall with Mary, working on projects. Deb walked up and asked if she could interrupt for a few minutes. They agreed.

"So, I'm worried about Joe. He's very quiet, doesn't talk at meals, doesn't appear to be doing much classwork this week, and spends all his time over at Mr. Brewster's house."

"I'm seeing it too."

"I'm worried that he's so focused on getting our parents back and blaming himself for the change in our history that he's not paying attention to his classwork, and that it's making it so much harder for him to move on. The first issue I think we can fix, but I'm not sure what to do about his grieving and emotional state."

"So, let's do this: we'll tell him and Kim that we want to study together all we can for this last month of school before I graduate. We'll meet every afternoon here and study together, and if one of us needs to be in the library for something, we'll book a study room. That way, he'll be forced to spend time with us, and we can be sure he finishes the year with good grades."

"That's a great idea, Kenny!"

"I'll talk to Mary and spend more time with Joe. I'll come up with some excuse. The graduating thing is going to come in handy, I think, and maybe I can get him to talk."

"Do you think that will be a problem? I mean, Mary had seemed kind of mad at me when you first told her about what we were doing with the machine. She got angry with me, kind of," Deb worried.

"It will be fine. She sometimes seems jealous of my spending time with you guys, but she's just going to have to figure this out. I'm your brother and I'm going to spend time with you."

"Ok, but how can we figure out what's going on with Joe and confirm if he's driven or it's something else?" Deb asked, "One thing I didn't think of," she continued, "he's actually talking with a girl; I hear from the gossip in the bathroom. Her name is Becky. I think she's in his math class and kind of a math Brainiac too. I'm going to get to know her and have her sit with us at lunch. Let's make sure Joe joins me at lunchtime. I will come up with some excuse. Maybe I'll tell him I'm struggling with math and might need his help at lunch to ask some questions, since I have math right after lunch."

"Good idea. This way, we have a few chances to get him to open up, or to just get out of this bad mood. Are you going to tell Ryan our plan?"

"Yeah, he might have some other ideas, too."

"I'll see about including him on a weekend thing every Sunday. That might be the ticket to keep Joe from wallowing in this."

"Thanks, Kenny. I'll see you at dinner."

That night at dinner Ken made a big production about realizing he graduates in a month and wanting to spend more time with his siblings and suggesting that they all study together each afternoon so they all finish strong and get to hang out before he heads off to college. Kim was very excited about it, but mentioned that they had Girl Scout things each Friday that she was already committed to. Deb suggested the studying be just Monday through Thursday, since no one would want to study on Friday, anyway. After dinner, Ken pulled Ryan aside and told him he was going to suggest things for Sunday with the guys for the same reason, just no girls allowed, and Ryan said he would be glad to help. They enlisted a few of their friends and asked two of Joe's friends to join them. Ryan suggested movies, baseball games, the bowling alley and some other things, and Ken thought they were all great ideas. The lunch idea didn't go over as well. Deb pressed Joe on the way to lunch on Friday to sit with her since she was struggling a little with math and he could help her as she prepared for tests and things. Joe agreed to help her, but didn't see the need to sit with Deb every day, as she would not be having a test every day of the week. She settled for a few days and hoped that he would decide to just sit with her all the time.

They all went bowling on Saturday because it was raining and had been since Friday afternoon. Mary's parents gave her a brand-new Oldsmobile for her sixteenth birthday that had occurred earlier in the year and told her she could have it on campus for the last month of school. The thing was a boat, according to Ken, but all six of them would fit in this car, so they took it to the bowling alley. Joe seemed very sullen, but he managed to laugh at Ryan's attempts to throw the bowling ball, and the crazy shoes that Kim had to wear because of the small size of her feet. When they took a break from bowling to grab some food, Mary asked Deb if they could talk. They went over to the spectator area and sat down.

"What's up, Mary?"

"I know you all are kind of taking it easy from the trip in the machine, and not talking about it or any plans for another trip, but I'm really worried about this. Ken doesn't seem to want to talk about it at all, so I'm going to try with you."

"Ok"

"You know I spend Sunday afternoon once a month helping with the Sunday school class at the church, right?"

"Yeah."

"I have to spend another Sunday afternoon each month going over the plans for the other days with the staff and other teachers and helpers. Reverend Patrick is there at each meeting. The Sunday you got back in the machine was supposed to be that meeting and Reverend Patrick called me to make sure I was ok since I missed it. I asked if I could go over to see him and I went yesterday after class."

"You didn't tell him what we did with the machine, did you?"

"No, no, I wouldn't tell anyone about that. I promised Ken I would keep your secret. But I wanted to talk to someone about the idea of changing history, changing God's plan for each of us. This has been a big issue for me ever since you all told me about the machine and brought me into this. I know Ken and Joe brought up good arguments about having free will and how that conflicts with the idea of a plan for each of us. I just wanted to talk to someone not involved in this and sort out my questions. Joe raises a good point. If you have free will, and there is a plan for each of us, what is the point of the predestined plan? So, I talked to Reverend Patrick about this. He explained it pretty well. He said that everyone is born with a plan or path from God. This plan is what God wants for us. The choices we make and free will guides us along this path and there are many forks in the road. But they will determine the final route we take in life. When I asked how people get so far off the path, Reverend Patrick explained that sometimes, the choices and forks we take lead us farther and farther from the path God planned, and we sometimes end up so far off that it's hard to get back to God, and some never find their way back."

"That makes sense to me."

"I asked about death, too. I used you four as my example to ask about why certain people die when they do and talked about you four that lost your parents. In the context of the plan discussion, I wondered why it was you four children's plan to live without your parents. Reverend Patrick said this was the hardest part of faith. Knowing that your lives would be easier with your parents here, why would God take them away? Faith is the answer. Faith that God knows what he is doing, and even though you miss your parents and grieve the loss, your path was always intended to include the four of you only. The faith is trusting that God knows what He is doing and you will all be stronger, better people because of this event in your life."

"Mary, I know that's the point. Faith that God knows what he is doing and not questioning that. But what if His plan was always that we would find this machine and do these trips and bring our parents back? What if this was the test? Can we stretch our intellect and our imagination and pick this fork in the road?"

"I put that to Reverend Patrick, too. Not by telling him what you are trying to do with the machine, but supposing that we had the power somehow to magically go back and change something as profound as a choice someone makes that keeps them from dying in some accident."

"What did he say to that?"

"Reverend Patrick said that he believes, and, his faith dictates, that the only part of our path that we cannot change is when we are called back to God. We may twist and turn throughout our life and make choices and exercise our free will, but we cannot change when God calls us."

"But he didn't say that was supposed to be everyone's belief, did he?"

"No, he was clear that this was his faith, and how he reasoned out things like children losing their parents; that his questions led him to this conclusion that you can't mess with God's plan on when he calls you to heaven. You have to have faith that He knows what he is doing, and that moment when you lose someone you love is the test of that faith. If you can let go and know that it's in God's hands."

They sat there silently for a long time. Mary wanted to give Deb time to let that sink in, and Deb wasn't sure what to say. Finally, Mary said, "Deb, do you want to go talk to Reverend Patrick? I'm sure he would sit with you and let you sort this all out for yourself."

"I don't know. Let me think about it a little. Did you tell Ken about this meeting with the Reverend?"

"Yeah, he brushed it off some, said he wasn't ready to hear this and didn't believe that God's plan would include losing his parents. He said his question was deeper than the plan part. If God was supposed to be good, how could he cause so much pain for you all by taking your parents away?"

"Yeah, I can see him saying that. When we were kids and went to Sunday school, the teacher always included some message about God being good and wanting to help us make good choices and be good people in every lesson. I think Ken really connected with that message. If God is good and wants us to be good and happy, then why would he take our parents while we were still kids? That would be Ken's question."

Just then, Kim ran up and said they were ready for another game and for them to hurry. Mary and Deb got up and returned to the alley.

"What were you two huddled over there talking about?"

"I'll tell you later Ryan, let's play. I have to beat Joe at least once today."

"No way, Deb, you will not take me. I am the bowling champion in this family!"

They all laughed and got down to serious competition. It was a great afternoon and on the way home, Ken treated everyone to burgers and shakes. At the diner, Kim teased Ryan because she actually had a higher score in the last game, and of course, Joe lorded over all of them. He had won every game they played, so he was the family champion. It aggravated Deb she couldn't beat Joe, but thrilled that he seemed happy and was having a good time. Then they all piled into Mary's car and headed back to campus. While they were driving back, Joe commented they should all try to get into the trunk when they got back because this car claimed it could fit six bodies in the trunk. Ryan and Ken asked how in the world Joe knew that was some sort of classification of cars once Joe convinced them it was a real measurement. Joe said one of his friends was really into cars and showed him a magazine shortly after Ken got the Trans am from Mr. Reynolds. In it was an article about the history of judging cars by the trunk space and how they started measuring it with bodies in the thirties and forties during the prohibition era. Kim thought it was hysterical that they would actually try to fit bodies in a trunk and advertise that, so of course, when they got back to campus, they all tried to crawl into the trunk. Other kids gathered around and some mother returning kids to campus that day rushed toward the car and exclaimed they would all get hurt or worse if they didn't stop it right now. Joe laughed after she walked away and asked what would be worse than getting hurt. Someone standing there watching commented that dying would be worse, and Deb wanted to scream. That immediately put Joe back into the sullen mood and he walked off, saying he had some things to do.

Ryan suggested they go play ping-pong and pool, and the others agreed. Ken took off to locate Joe to join them. He couldn't find Joe anywhere and presumed he went off to Mr. Brewster's. When Ken found the others in the main hall and told them what he suspected, Deb suggested they go get Joe, but Ken said to let him go for now. He had spent the whole day with them and maybe he needed a break.

Kim went off to watch the movie playing with her friends and so Ken and Mary and Ryan and Deb played pool and ping-pong. Later that evening, when Ryan was walking Deb and Kim back to the girls' dorm, he asked Deb what she had been talking to Mary about. Deb related the conversation and Ryan agreed with Deb. It was a personal question about faith, and the points from Joe and Ken were valid. They got back to the dorm before Deb could ask Ryan what he thought about it. She went to bed that evening with what felt like a heavy weight.

The next day, after church, Deb found Reverend Patrick and asked if she could schedule a meeting with him. She told him she was the friend that Mary spoke of that lost her parents and the Reverend immediately understood what Deb needed. He asked when she would like to sit down and she asked if he had time right then. He did, and they went to his office.

"So, Deborah, I believe, based on how you approached me, that Mary revealed her conversation with me. Is that true?"

"Yes, Reverend Patrick, she told me. I believe she was trying to help me and my brothers and sister when she came to you, as well as getting some of her own feelings sorted out."

"We all reach a point where we question the lessons of our childhood, I think. Your situation is a bit different, however."

"Reverend Patrick, my family went to church every Sunday, and I went to Sunday school, and when I was growing up, we learned God was good, and didn't punish us, but always wanted us to be good and happy. If that's the case, then how come my parents had to die in that accident?"

"It's hard when someone we love dies. It doesn't matter the circumstances. The problem for us humans is when someone dies, we want to know why. It's a big question. When a person dies because of a crime being committed or in a house fire, we know why. But when it's because they got sick, or had an accident, we wonder about the why part. I also think, when the death seems senseless, when the person or people that die were such good people and young, we even might search for something or someone to blame. That becomes very dangerous territory, doesn't it?"

"Yes, because if there doesn't seem to be something or someone to blame, some answer to the why, we eventually get to the answer that is must be God, who is responsible. Isn't that right?"

"Yes. If God is good, and wants us to be good and happy, why would he take your parents away?"

"I'm afraid that my brothers and my sister and I cannot move on from this loss until we can answer that question, Reverend Patrick."

"As I explained to Mary, we each have to arrive at our beliefs and faith in our own way and in our own time. At the heart of faith, the very center of faith, is the idea that you can believe all answers come from God, and that His grace will guide you and keep you, and He knows what he is doing. Even if we can't see it, even if we have no proof that God is there. That's faith."

"I thought I had faith, so what does it mean that I'm questioning God's plan? Does it mean my faith is gone?"

"Not gone, Deborah, it is just being tested by you."

He paused and then said, "Let me switch gears a bit and ask you how your life has changed since you lost your parents."

"Well, we go to Choate now. We spend school holidays with our aunt and her boyfriend. The visit to New York and see where my aunt works was a lot of fun. I met a young man at school here. He really means a lot to me. There are so many new friends that I've met, when I thought I could never. There's a closeness with my brothers than I ever expected to have. Of course, I miss my old friends, and my house, and neighborhood. I miss sitting in my father's office and reading on Sunday afternoon, and I miss visiting my mother's office at Harvard. I miss Christmas with my grandparents."

"Do you not see your grandparents anymore?"

"They died shortly before my parents died. First my grandmother and then my grandfather a month later. They were happy and in love, and I think my grandfather just missed her because there was nothing really wrong with him. He just went to sleep one night and never woke up."

"What is the difference between their deaths and your parents?"

"They were old and had lived their lives. They both died peacefully."

"You don't question the why because they were old and died peacefully?"

"I see what you're saying. Death is death."

"What about the other things you talked about that changed? You seem to have a lot of positives on the list. You have met some new people, made friends, and what about the last thing on the list? How close you have become to your brothers? Why do you think that would not have happened if not for your parents' accident?"

"We were all so busy back then with our own lives and our own interests. I don't think we paid any attention to what each other was doing most of the time. I doubt that would have changed. Ken would have probably gone either to a college to play football or to the Marines. Joe and I had nothing really in common, or so it seemed, and Kim is much younger than me. I would have gone off to college and we would have seen each other only on holidays, like my mother and her sister. Now, we need each other, we confide in each other, and our differences don't seem to matter anymore. I tell Ken things I would never have dreamed of telling him. I think he feels the same way."

"Perhaps that was always God's plan for the four of you. Perhaps you were supposed to join your paths more closely, and this was the only way."

"Maybe. Reverend Patrick, if you have the ability to change things, maybe go back somehow and warn someone you loved not to go on a trip or not to be in a place so they wouldn't die, would you do it?"

"No. I leave that in God's hands to decide."

"What if you knew you could help others, maybe you knew about some terrible event, like a flood and you could go back and warn people so they would get out of the way of the terrible event and save lives, would you then?"

"I would say, leave it in God's hands. He knows what he is doing. Just like you and your siblings getting closer, perhaps there is a greater plan that requires that terrible event to put it in motion."

"You seem so very sure. I wish I could speak about this with that much certainty."

"As I said, we each have to get there at our own pace. I would like to suggest some reading and some reflection. Would you be interested?"

"Yes, please."

Reverend Patrick went to his bookcase and pulled out two books. He handed them to Deb and told her she could come and speak to him any time. Deb thanked him for his time and his help and she walked back to campus alone, thinking about what they had discussed. She was very troubled and diverted her path and went over to Mr. Brewster's house. He was in the barn with Joe. Deb asked if she could talk to Mr. Brewster for a minute, and he suggested they go into his kitchen and prepare some sandwiches. While Deb helped Mr. Brewster, she asked him about his faith and why he didn't want to go back and prevent his wife's accident or stop his father going into war when he went back and just meet his father. Mr. Brewster thought for a long time before he answered. He pulled out a chair for Deb to sit in and then he sat down opposite her at the table.

"Deb, I didn't go back to save my wife or stop my father because I think we have to let the past be the past. I know you and your sister and your brothers are dealing with your parents being gone. Lord knows I had a hard time after I lost Bev, but at some point, you have to decide to keep putting one foot in front of the other."

"Why did you help us go back and try to stop our parents' accident, then?"

"I knew you all needed to try. I also knew that Joe needed to see it work for himself before he would be ready to give the ideas and notes and machine to the public."

"I talked to the Reverend at the church today. He says that faith means you have to trust God's plan, know that He's here even if you can't see Him, and that some very positive things have happened because of our parents' death, and maybe the accident had to happen in order for these positive things to happen."

"I know you're younger, but I also know you're all very intelligent and very thoughtful. So, I know you can hear this and have an open mind. You have to experience loss to really experience happiness, and you sometimes have to take what God has given you and turn it into something better."

"Without going into a time machine, you mean?"

They both laughed and got up and took the sandwiches to the barn. Deb asked Joe to show her all his notes and documentation of the trips, and they talked for a bit. Mr. Brewster then said he had to take care of some things, so Deb and Joe walked back to the dorms. They found Ken and Mary and Ryan in the receiving room of the girls' dorm waiting for Deb because she didn't return with them and was not at lunch. Ryan was really worried and was trying to convince Ken and Mary to go look for her as they walked into the room.

"Where have you been?"

"Ken, I told you I wanted to talk to Reverend Patrick after the service today, and he said he had time, so we were in his office. Then I wanted to talk to Mr. Brewster and found Joe there. We talked, had sandwiches and now we're here. Don't have a heart attack."

"Deb, we were all worried."

"Sorry Ryan, I didn't mean to worry any of you. So, what's up this afternoon?"

"Kim is with her friends. Mary and I were headed to the library and not sure about the two of you."

"I don't have any homework to finish today. I did it all Friday," Deb said.

"I have a test tomorrow, so I'm going back to my room," Joe said, getting up.

"Joe, I will pick you up for dinner then on my way from the library, ok?"

"Sounds good Ken."

Joe left, and Mary and Ken got up to go to the library. Deb turned to Ryan and asked if he had homework. He confirmed he didn't either, and they were deciding to go for a walk when one of the girls came in and said Deb had a call.

When Deb returned from the call, Ken and Mary were still there, waiting to hear who called. When Ken raised his eyebrows at Deb, she replied, "It was Aunt Alicia. She was checking to see how we all were and confirming the date of your graduation ceremony. She got some notices in the mail and had received tickets. We're apparently going to the Hamptons for the summer and will sometimes be in New York. She asked me to check with you, Ken, to see if you had other plans for the summer and what you would need to prepare to go to Harvard in the fall."

"Tickets, is she bringing Mr. Reynolds to graduation?"

"Apparently, he insisted on attending. You will probably hear from him because Aunt Alicia asked if you were around as he wanted to call you. I told her you were going to be at the library all afternoon, so he should try after dinner tonight."

"Are you ok with this plan?" Ken asked.

"It's not like I or Joe or Kim have a choice. The beach will be fun, but I'll miss my friends and you, Ryan."

"Well, I'm sure we can arrange some visiting back and forth. My mother already asked if you would like to go with us to North Carolina for July fourth week. We go every year to see my grandparents and you came with us last year."

"And I would love it if you could come up to Boston for a week this summer, Deb," Mary said.

"That would be great."

"Let's talk about this at dinner because we need to include Kim and Joe in the planning. Maybe I can suggest some things to Mr. Reynolds so we can see our friends this summer and have fun before I go off to college."

"Sounds good Ken."

Ken and Mary left for the library, and Deb and Ryan went out for a walk. They went into town since it had finally stopped raining and was nice out. They didn't get very far before Ryan asked Deb what happened today.

"Ryan, I really am sorry I worried you. When Reverend Patrick said he had time, I didn't even think. I just went to talk to him."

"That's ok. I know something has been troubling you since yesterday when you sat off with Mary and talked. Are you ready to tell me?"

Deb nodded yes and recounted her talks with Mary, the Reverend and Mr. Brewster. By the time she was finished, they were at the ice cream parlor, so they went in and ordered some ice cream. While they ate, Ryan thought about everything Deb had told him. As they left the ice cream place, he said, "So what are you thinking now, after all these discussions?"

"Well, Ryan, I was kind of hoping to get your take on all of this, maybe before I go into how I'm feeling now."

"Ok, I know I've said this before, but I have no way of understanding how I would feel if my parents were gone. But I can say that I believe you should not go messing with history again, and I think the machine should be retired. I'm uncertain if that is because of faith or something else. I just don't think it's going to help anyone, least of all Joe, which is why you said you were going along with the time travel in the beginning."

"If it's not faith, what makes you so sure we shouldn't do it again?"

"Well, from a purely scientific approach, which I think will make sense to Joe, your trip proved without a doubt that you can't really change history. You stopped one assassination, but Kennedy was still assassinated. Your parents still died, and in fact died sooner because of your efforts. I'm afraid you try this again and it will get worse, not better."

"But what do you think about the questions I asked Reverend Patrick and what Mary said?"

"I don't know, sweetheart. Don't get angry with me. I just am not sure I believe the whole God's plan idea. I'm way more on the side of Ken and Joe than this. How can there be free will and a greater plan at the same time?"

"I don't know, but Reverend Patrick explained the choices and path and twist and turns pretty well."

"Well, it's definitely easier for me to put in the purely scientific form for now, I guess. I'm also scared that the next time something more serious is going to happen to all of us. Remember Deb, what you did changed what happened in Dallas, but then there was a sniper in Austin, and it almost took both President and Mrs. Kennedy. You almost did to their kids what was done to you. Are you sure you want that on your conscience? And you won't know until you get out of the machine what you did. It will be too late then."

"That's not something I thought of at all. My changing one thing had a domino effect on the Kennedy's and you're right, I wouldn't want to think I hurt someone else trying to save my parents."

They sat on a bench for a long time, not speaking as each thought about what the other had said. Finally, Ryan said, "Listen, Deb, if this is a spiritual issue for you, I'll do what I can to help you sort that out. For me, it's more factual. Something bad could happen. To you, to me, to Mary, to Ken or Joe or Kim. What if you hopped out of that machine next time to find that Mr. Brewster never became a groundskeeper here? Or what if you found out something you did made Mary's parents not have Mary? That's what is important to me."

"Now that you bring that up, that's important to me, too. I'm just thinking about in a context you're not."

"So, have you talked to Ken about any of this?"

"Mary tried, and he really is stuck on the primary questions. I haven't had time to talk to him or Joe yet."

"What do you want to do?"

"Today in the barn I saw that Joe and Mr. Brewster have really polished the notes and put together quite a paper on what they did, learned, and everything. It could be taken public really soon, I think."

"Is that what you're thinking? Take it public and not have the four of you trying any more trips?"

"I don't know, maybe."

"Well, I think you should go into a discussion with Ken and Joe, confident about what you believe and where you stand. Anything less and they will talk you out of it. I think you should include Mary and me as well, as she appears to have some strong opinions and so do I. I like you all, not just you, and I don't want anything happening to any of you."

"Ok, I think I will do some reading and maybe talk to Reverend Patrick again before I am ready to bring this up in the group. And, Ryan, I would want you there. You're very important to me."

Ryan took Deb's hand and smiled. "You're pretty important to me, too."

14

At dinner that night, they all started talking about summer plans. It became apparent pretty quickly that their friends wanted to see Kim, Deb, Joe and Ken during the summer, so they plotted out a calendar. Ken was going to speak to Mr. Reynolds about what they wanted to do, and see if he would agree to some friends coming to the Hamptons, and for the four of them to be off visiting friends sometimes.

Deb was rather quiet for the next day or so while she read and thought about the conversations she had. They all kept planning their summer trips as Mr. Reynolds thought it was a brilliant plan and said he was fine with kids visiting there. By the end of the week, Deb thought she was ready to talk to Reverend Patrick and called to make arrangements to meet him after church on Sunday while the boys all went to a movie.

"Reverend Patrick, I read the books you gave me and they really helped me sort out the questions of how to overcome the testing of faith. I feel much calmer now than I did last weekend. But how do I help my brothers?"

"Well, they have to sort it out for themselves as well. What conclusions have you drawn? Perhaps your journey can be the guide to help your brothers."

"I read in one book about finding the peace of believing. Finding within yourself the peace of knowing God is with you. That led me to several passages in the bible and helped me to find a new perspective. Some of the passages really touched me about the gift of grace, the comfort of knowing God hears you."

"I'm so glad you have found some guidance from the materials and have been able to reflect over the past week. I would caution you that this is a journey, not something that you will find is over this week or even this year. It will come back up for you, just as it comes back up for each of us throughout our lives."

"I suppose, but I can see how losing my parents is somehow required for me to grow and become who I'm supposed to be. I just need help to help my brothers see that."

"Share the books with them, share your story with them, and then listen to them. That is the only way to help."

"Did you want the books back?"

"No, those are for you. Share them or keep them. You might need them in the future."

"Don't you need them?"

"I have copies, many copies. I find those two books very helpful in my counseling. They helped me many years ago, and now I use them to help others."

"Thank you, Reverend Patrick. I really appreciate it."

"You are most welcome Deborah. Come back anytime."

Deb went back to campus and talked everything over with Mary, and the two of them sat with Kim and did the last of their homework while the boys had their "no girls allowed" afternoon. Deb also spoke to Aunt Alicia, and confirmed all the plans for graduation, a big dinner she had planned in New York after graduation, and different dates of all their coming and going to visit friends. Kim was going to spend two weeks just after graduation with her friend Kathy in Philadelphia, Joe was going to spend the fourth of July in Atlanta with his friend, and Deb was going to spend the fourth of July with Ryan. Mary was coming to the Hamptons for the fourth of July with Ken and Kim, and Deb was going to Boston with her after she returned from North Carolina. Ken and Deb were going to be in New York during Joe and Kim's travels and through the rest of June. It was going to be a busy but fun summer.

Later that week, Deb asked everyone to meet in the barn on Thursday afternoon instead of the study session to talk over some things she had been thinking about and to give Joe and Mr. Brewster a chance to showcase their efforts to summarize everything into a paper. They all met in the barn and Deb asked Joe to go over his notes. Joe seemed very proud of what they had accomplished to document and presenting the material. Everyone cheered when he wrapped up.

"So, Joe, are you wanting to go public with this information now?" Ken asked.

"I thought we were going to wait until we had made the four trips? I still want to firm up the time passage formula, and I think that will sort itself out over the next three trips."

"Well, before we talk about any more trips, I want to go over some things I've been thinking about and give you all a chance to respond and say what you're thinking."

Deb waited and when no one objected, she continued, "So, I think there are two tracks here. First, what did we accomplish, and what were the effects of the first trip? What did it prove? And there is the more subjective track of should we continue. I know we agreed to four trips, but I think we owe it not just to the scientific research, but to ourselves, to evaluate that now, and probably after any future trips."

"I agree Deb, so continue."

"Thanks Ken."

"So, what did we accomplish? We built the machine, and it works. We travelled through time. Through our efforts, we foiled an assassination attempt against the President in Dallas. What were the effects? We changed events in Dallas, but we did not stop the President from being assassinated. In fact, by what we did, we nearly caused both the President and Mrs. Kennedy to be killed in Austin."

"Deb, that was not our fault. Simply stopping things in Dallas did not directly cause the events in Austin," Joe said, getting agitated by where he thought Deb was going.

"Joe, we changed history. We have to be ready to admit that through our actions, we started the chain of events that led to that sniper in Austin shooting into that vehicle and killing the President and the driver and nearly killing Mrs. Kennedy," Deb countered.

"She was a very nice lady. We met her. I wouldn't want anything bad to happen to her. And didn't they have kids too? We almost made them lose their parents in a car accident, just like we did," Kim added.

"Insightful, Kim," Ken said, smiling at his little sister.

"I don't think that matters," Joe said sullenly.

"Joe, how can that not matter? If you do not go into the machine thinking, we could cause some harm to someone, you're not acting responsibly. Furthermore, you can't work to change events that benefit you without also being ready to accept responsibility for changing events for someone else," Ryan said, a little frustrated with Joe's tunnel vision.

"Ryan, you're just on Deb's side, and she clearly doesn't want to make any more trips."

"No, Joe, that's not what I am saying. I'm just trying to evaluate the situation. Isn't that the scientific process? Isn't that what we should do with this discovery?" Deb said, trying to be patient.

"And, yes, I'm on Deb's side in this. Question everything. Isn't that what the science teacher tells us in class? Experiment, question, and draw conclusions, report. You have experimented. Now it is time to question." Ryan tried another approach to reach Joe.

Joe looked down, but said nothing more.

Deb continued, "Any other thoughts on the scientific approach other than Kim's insight?"

"I hadn't thought about the possibility we would harm others in this. That worries me," Kim added.

"What about what might happen to the four of you while you are doing this? This trip you stopped an assassination plan, and changed your father's business, maybe for the better as he's now wealthier than you said he was before, but you caused your parents to have an accident months before they did in your timeline. That is harmful, isn't it? What if next trip you change something and your parents decide to stop at three kids and you get back here and Kim is gone?" Mary said emotionally.

"Would that really happen? Would I be there on the trip and then just disappear when we got out of the machine?" Kim asked, somewhat panicked.

Mr. Brewster replied first, "I doubt that's what would happen. It's more likely if something like that occurred, where you changed history to where one of you wasn't born, you would still be here when the machine came back, you just would have no history with anyone and no one but us would know you. I think that's what you proved with your first trip. You still have full memory of your original timeline, but Ryan and Mary, and I have a different understanding. I think that would hold true in a literal sense like this."

"That's certainly good to know."

"Actually, Mr. Brewster, I don't know about Deb, but I'm starting to lose the sense of our old timeline. Especially with regard to my time with Mary. The new timeline feels so much more real and the old timeline is very fuzzy," Ken said.

"I noticed it too, but the next morning after we got back. It's like the old timeline is disappearing. I only talk about it because we wrote it down and I know in my mind it has to be there, but it's fuzzy for me too," Deb said.

"However, that would mean that if something you did made a change and say, me, not be born, you would get back here and I wouldn't be here," Ryan said.

"Ryan, don't talk like that," Deb said, with a shocked look on her face.

"That Deb, is the risk you take every time you all step into that machine, and your first trip proved it, even in this small way of our different understanding of the timeline."

"This is a real risk we would have to understand and be ready to accept if we decide to make another trip. Deb, you have an even bigger point to make, don't you?" Ken worked to circle them back.

"Yes Kenny, I do. If the risk isn't big enough yet, what about us not bringing our parents back, we in fact, moved up their deaths? Is messing with history, messing with peoples' lives and death not something we should do? Should we leave the bigger plan to a higher power?"

"We've gone over this, haven't we? What about free will? We have free will to choose how we want to act and what we want to do. Deb, are you telling me you don't want our parents back?" Joe exclaimed, now very agitated.

"Joe, I used to think, back when we first got here, that I wanted nothing more than to have our parents back, to be back in our home and for things to go back to the way they were. Now I'm not so sure." Deb tried to explain her dilemma between missing her parents and starting to be happy with their new life.

"You don't want them back? That's what you are saying?" Joe said again.

"Joe, Deb is just saying she's not sure if she wants to go back. Maybe she's saying she wants to go forward," Ken tried another way to explain for Deb and calm Joe down.

"Ken, I am not a small child! Don't talk to me like that. I'm the one that figured out the mathematical theory that allowed all this to happen, remember?"

"Joe, of course I remember it's your genius that got us here. All I'm saying is that I think Deb has a point. We need to move forward, not always looking back and trying to get back there. If we keep all this focus on going back to stop our parents from being in an accident, how can we ever expect the loss to get any easier to deal with?" Ken said.

"So, I see what you're saying. Stop going back and stop trying to save our parents and it won't hurt anymore," Joe said somewhat sarcastically.

Mr. Brewster cut in again. "Joe, remember what we talked about, that your brother and sisters are dealing with the loss too, and that each of you has to deal with it in your own way and at your own pace. At the end of that journey, you each have to find a way to move forward in whatever way you intend."

"Mr. Brewster, I want to move forward by returning my parents to the land of living and have them with us. I don't want to forget them and just go on," Joe said, trying to not cry.

"No one is saying you forget them, Joe. I think what Ken and Deb are trying to say is that focusing on going back to stop your parents' accident is trapping you from dealing with your feelings and this loss," Mary added.

"Now you're ganging up too, Mary? Like you understand at all, either you or Ryan. Both of your parents are going to be here to pick you up at the end of this school year."

"Joe, look at me," Deb said quietly.

Joe looked straight at Deb.

"Joe, you don't need to lash out at any of us, least of all Mary and Ryan. They don't understand how it feels to lose parents. You're right about that, but let me ask you this. Do you think Mom or Dad would want you to be this upset, this angry, and act this way toward others that we all know you care about?"

"I just want them back, Deb. I miss them so much, and I just want them back."

Joe looked down, and Kim started crying. She climbed out of her chair and went to Joe. She tried to hug him, and he finally pulled her into his lap. Ryan got up and went to join, then Ken, then Deb, then Mary and Mr. Brewster. They were all in a big hug together and they stayed that way for a long time.

"I can hardly breathe in here."

"Nice way to break it up, Joe," Ken said, smiling.

They all laughed and separated back to their seats.

"So, from all of that, we have this question. Should we meddle again? Should we go into the machine and try to stop our parents from having an accident? Is it right for us to change their history?"

"I thought this was going to be a question of whether we believed in God," Ken said. "I thought that's what you were leading to."

"Ken, it isn't about believing in God, it is about believing that He knows what he is doing."

"What do you mean?"

"Well, I know you all think there cannot be a higher plan, a higher power and free will at the same time, but what if the free will guides you along a path and provides forks in the road? I think the plan is more like a hope from God about how you will stay with Him and choose Him. What if the free will allows you to choose which fork to take, which turn to take? What if you have the means to get so far off the original plan that it doesn't look like the same plan anymore, but it doesn't change the fact that the plan exists?"

"She's got you there, Ken," Ryan said.

"Ok, maybe I can see it, you can have free will and higher plan at the same time. That allows for our parents making the choice to have this planning meeting and getting caught in an avalanche or getting on an airplane to meet clients and having an accident. It allows us to get to Choate, have Joe discover the math and create the means for time travel that might be his choice of careers or might not," Ken said, starting to see.

"If the plan wasn't in place, and the choices not made, we would not be together like this," Kim said.

"That is my insightful little sister, that I could no longer live without, and would never have the opportunity to know if not for all of this," Ken said, reaching for her hand across the corner of the table.

"You really believe you would not be close to Kim if our parents hadn't died?" Joe asked.

"Joe, be honest, you would not have spent time with Kim if we hadn't all ended up here. And if not now, when? After you graduated from college and had this booming career in computers or time travel?"

"We would meet a couple of times a year like Mom and Aunt Alicia did," Kim said sullenly.

"So, you all want to scrap any future trips in the machine, don't you?" Joe asked.

"I'm not sure, Joe, but I think we all need to think about what we talked about here. Maybe you and Ken need to do some serious soul searching about your feelings, about losing Mom and Dad, about how God can do this to you, and how to make sense of it all. I think only then can we decide whether we get back into the machine."

"You aren't going to answer all of this today, and if you don't all get back to campus, you will miss dinner," Mr. Brewster said, looking at his watch.

"How about we each do some more thinking and if one of us needs a group discussion, they will bring that up to the others and we'll meet back here? Otherwise, maybe we can decide next week when to check in."

"Sounds like a plan. Thanks again, Mr. Brewster, for letting us use your barn as our base of operations and place to sort things out," Joe said.

"Joseph, I hope you all know that you are welcome here anytime. You have all become very precious to me, and I'm always going to be there for the six of you."

With that, they all walked back to campus and headed to the dining hall for dinner. The next day was Friday, and it was the last school-planned free night because there were only two weeks left of the year. A week of classes, then finals, and then it was summer. So, they all stayed on campus and enjoy the activities with their friends that weekend. Kim left Saturday morning with the Girl Scouts for the last camp out of the year, and Joe was busy with his friend Todd, who had received a model airplane for his birthday that they were deep in the building. Ryan and Deb and Mary and Ken spent Saturday in town and saw a movie and got something to eat. On Sunday, the boys went to the field and played baseball. The next week flew by, and everyone was busy finishing up school work. Deb asked, but no one was ready for further discussion, so they didn't meet at the barn that weekend.

Then it was finals week and everyone was getting ready to leave for the summer. Ken was absolutely jubilant when Thursday evening arrived because all seniors were done with tests that day. Friday was graduation practice and Friday night was awards night. Saturday was graduation and Sunday everyone was leaving campus. The ceremony was long, but everyone was happy because Ken was graduating. After the ceremony, everyone was mingling on the field in front of the main hall. People were taking pictures and celebrating. At some point in the afternoon, Deb realized Joe wasn't around. She located Ken, who was joking with his friends. Ken hadn't seen him since Mr. Reynolds took pictures. Deb found Mr. Reynolds talking with some of the other parents and Aunt Alicia was with Kim and a bunch of Kim's friends, as Kim had told everyone that her aunt was a famous fashion reporter. Aunt Alicia was regaling the girls with stories about models and fashion, and in her element. Deb finally broke down and went to the dorms and called Mr. Brewster. There was no answer, so she told Ken she was going to run over there and see if Joe was in the barn. Ryan went with Deb, and they found Mr. Brewster asleep in his living room. When they went to the barn, they were shocked. Joe had been there, because he left a note that he was doing what he felt he had to. The machine was not in the barn.

Deb and Ryan practically ran back to the field and found Ken. When they finished telling what they had found, Ken was boiling mad.

"First, we have to make an excuse to Aunt Alicia and Mr. Reynolds about why Joe isn't around. Mr. Brewster said he would wait in the barn all night if he had to, and would come and get one of us when Joe got back," Deb said.

"I know. I will find Todd and ask him to cover for us. He's going to dinner with his parents and then not leaving until tomorrow. I will tell him Joe is pretty upset and wanted to be off by himself, and see if he will do this for us," Ryan thought.

"Great idea, Ryan. Deb and I should probably wait here. Once we know we have a cover, we can go find Mr. Reynolds and Aunt Alicia. It's about time for us to leave for dinner, anyway."

"Are you sure we should leave campus with Joe out there somewhere?" Deb asked.

"There isn't anything we can do at this point, so we don't want to alarm or alert Aunt Alicia and Mr. Reynolds. We would have no way to explain this," Ken said, shaking his head.

Ryan left and talked to Todd, who agreed to cover for them. He knew Joe was struggling with missing his parents, so he was happy to help. Ryan told Deb and Ken and they went to find Kim and Aunt Alicia. They all met in the driveway and Aunt Alicia asked where Joe was.

"Joe was asked to go to dinner with a friend and he came to me a little bit ago and asked if it was ok with me if he skipped this dinner since he's spending the summer with me. I told him it was ok cause this is a friend he won't see until next fall."

"Well, Ken, if you're ok with it, I don't see the harm in it," Mr. Reynolds said, to keep Aunt Alicia from getting upset.

"Thanks, Mr. Reynolds."

"Now wait a minute. I planned this as a family dinner to celebrate the graduation. I do not see why Joe ducked out of it," Aunt Alicia said, getting upset despite Mr. Reynolds' efforts.

"Alicia, he's fifteen and wants to spend more time with his friends before he leaves for the summer. I think we should be very glad the kids have made such good friends here at school."

"Oh fine, then let's go."

15

They all left for dinner, and Ryan and Mary joined them. Dinner was a formal, but good, time. Aunt Alicia gave Ken a very nice watch and a briefcase for graduation. Mr. Reynolds gave Ken a set of luggage. They drove back to campus and Ken indicated he had some friends to meet up with tomorrow morning, and Mr. Reynolds agreed to pick them up early in the afternoon. Aunt Alicia and Mr. Reynolds went to their hotel, and the kids acted like they were going to the dorms. They all circled back and headed directly for the barn. Mr. Brewster was there and said he had not seen anything, but had found some notes about the date and navigation Joe had selected. They realized when they looked it up that Joe was going close to home about a year before their parents' accident. After a couple of hours, Ken suggested they all get some sleep and get packed up. They agreed to meet at breakfast, the last one Ken would have at Choate, and then head back to the barn. Mr. Brewster agreed to call Ken if Joe came back.

They walked back rather slowly, talking about how they might discover what Joe was up to, since no one recognized the date as anything significant for their family. Mary was very worried about the possibility Joe would meet himself since she remembered that being something they all thought would be terrible. When they got back to the dorms, Mary and Deb helped Kim pack up and get ready for bed. Deb and Mary then went to Deb's room to talk.

"So, what do you think he is doing?"

"All I know is he is trying to do something to bring our parents back. He's sure we won't want to go back in the machine, and he's taking this on himself. I'm just so worried something bad will happen, and we'll wake up tomorrow and have no memory of him or the machine or something."

"Is there any way you can figure out what he might do?"

"I don't know of anything unusual that happened on that day. It was a Saturday during football season, so he probably went with my mother to Harvard while Ken was at practice. I was probably at the library or forced to watch Kim while my dad did some things. It wasn't anyone's birthday, no big game that I can remember."

"What if he doesn't get back before your aunt shows up tomorrow?"

"I don't know."

The girls finished packing Deb up and then went and finished packing Mary up. Then they went to their separate rooms to sleep. Deb didn't really sleep at all. She paced back and forth in her room, hoping to remember something about the date Joe picked that might help them figure this out. Around three in the morning, Deb stopped and realized there might be a clue in the letters she had gotten from her parents from the will. She pulled them out of the box they were in from earlier in the day packing and opened her mother's letter. She read it over again and there it was. Something she didn't remember reading before, but now seemed to all make sense. Her mother said that Joe had a strange day recently where he said he was going to be in the lab, but made it back home and tried to convince his father not to go on any trips after Thanksgiving. She said Joe was talking a mile a minute to his father about discovering something and being able to travel through time. Of course, said her mother's letter. They thought perhaps he was just fixating on something he had been researching or a dream or something. The letter asked Deb to keep a close eye on Joe, and make sure he was ok if something happened because of this, and not to blame their father for the issues it caused in their family.

Deb sat there reading the letter and realized that was why she was so troubled about the time travel. Vaguely, she remembered this not being in the letter before. She got dressed and ran to the boys' dorm. She tried to get Ken's and then Ryan's attention by throwing tennis balls that were all over the yard in front of the dorm. After what seemed like a hundred tries, she got Ken's attention. He came downstairs and out into the yard.

"What are you doing, Deb?"

"I have the letter you gave me from Mom. I know I asked you to read it before. Quick, tell me if you remember anything in the letter about Joe sneaking home from Harvard on a Saturday during football season and trying to talk Dad out of going on any trips after that fall?"

"No, I don't remember that."

"Read this."

Deb handed Ken the letter, and they walked back closer to the door so Ken could read by the door light. He looked up at Deb when he got to the part about what Deb had described.

"Now this makes sense, why you were so worried about the machine. You now have full memory of this letter, don't you?"

"I can vaguely remember, or maybe I just feel like it wasn't there before."

"What do we do now?" Ken pondered.

"Well, if he only went back for that Saturday, he should be back here in the morning. Let's grab Ryan and Mary and Kim and go back to the barn first thing, and skip breakfast or grab something and get out of there as quick as we can."

"First, when you get back to your room, write everything you remember right now about how Mom and Dad died and what we have done. Not a paper or anything, just some bullet notes. I will do the same and bring them in the morning."

"Ok."

The next morning, Deb grabbed Mary in the bathroom and told her what happened and then got Kim and they headed to the dining hall. They all grabbed some cereal and some fruit and took off for the barn. Deb had her notes, but as agreed, they waited until they got to the barn to look at them.

Deb looked at her notes and wondered why they said some things they said. She could vaguely remember some of it, but it did not seem like her memory of some events at all. Ken said the same thing, but they kept the notes to themselves.

They waited until about ten thirty.

"What are we going to do if he doesn't return before we are supposed to meet Aunt Alicia and Mr. Reynolds to leave campus today?"

"I don't know Deb."

"I'm going to have to leave to meet my parent, Ken. They will be at the dorm in about twenty minutes," Mary said.

"I will walk you back, Mary. My parents are going to be here soon too," Ryan offered.

Deb and Ken went outside the barn to say goodbye to Mary and Ryan and promised to call later with word on what happened.

When they walked back into the barn, Mr. Brewster was talking with Kim, who had become very agitated. He explained he would call their aunt and say that he asked the kids to stop over, after becoming so close to them this year, to say goodbye and kept them longer. He was going to drive them back to campus to leave. That seemed to calm Kim down, and Ken agreed that was a plan. Mr. Brewster was walking toward the door to go make the call to the hotel where their Aunt Alicia and Mr. Reynolds were staying when suddenly the wind picked up in the barn and papers blew all over. The noise started and then the machine was back. They waited, not attempting to establish communication with Joe. Finally, he opened the door and saw them all standing there. He looked expectantly at Deb first, then at Ken.

Then Deb said, "Joe, what did you do?"

"Why is your face all messed up?" Kim asked.

16 ▌

Authors Notes

Although this is a work of fiction, several aspects of the story of the Fitzgerald kids are based on actual places and events.

Choate Rosemary Hall is an actual boarding preparatory school located in Wallingford, Connecticut. It was founded as Rosemary Hall for girls in 1890 by Mary Atwater Choate. Later, a boys' school was added, the girls' school moved and then returned to the original location. It became a Co-Ed School in the 1970s. President John F. Kennedy, and many other famous people attended throughout its history. Several of the buildings named here are actual buildings at Choate. However, the inclusion of younger children Kim's age and various aspects of the schedule, buildings and activities there are my creation. You can learn more about this wonderful school at: www.choate.edu.

President John F. Kennedy was, in fact, assassinated in Dallas, Texas, on November 22, 1963, while traveling in a motorcade through Dealey Plaza. It is a historical fact that he and Mrs. Kennedy stayed at the Texas Hotel in Fort Worth, Texas on November 21 and then flew to Dallas on the morning of November 22 after President Kennedy gave a speech in the hotel parking lot. Lee Harvey Oswald is known as the single assassin. He did mail order a rifle under the assumed name of A. Hidell from an advertisement in a magazine and did work at the book depository. The other details of the hotel, plaza, newspapers and secret service activity that day were created here for the story. Any references here to the later assassination in Austin, Texas and those involved are my creation.

Vogue magazine has been in production since 1892. It became the premier fashion magazine later in the 1960s. Grace Mirabella was, in fact, the editor of Vogue during the time period of this story. Several of the people and places mentioned related to Vogue are factual. However, Aunt Alicia being employed there and her activities are created here for the story.

References to Eileen Ford as a force in the fashion industry in the 1970s is based on fact. She was an important figure in the New York fashion industry and invitations to her events were highly sought after. However, the association with Aunt Alicia is my creation.

"Little House on the Prairie" is a book written by Laura Ingalls Wilder. It is one of a series of books chronicling Ms. Wilder's and her family's life in the 1800s. This series was a favorite of mine growing up, so I had to include it here.

Other details mentioned here are based on events and trending stories of the time period of this story. "Star Wars", "The Godfather" and "Benji" movies all, in fact, premiered, in the early 1970s. Kevlar was, in fact, invented in the 1970s, but not by Mr. Fitzgerald.

Although it may seem hard to believe, the Trans Am and Oldsmobile Cutless were very popular automobiles during the time when Ken and Mary would have been driving. You, the reader, might find comparable desired autos in the Lamborghini and Lexus models of today.

Of course, there is the time travel. There have been many theories proposed regarding the ability to travel through time, as well as many novels describing the fantastical aspects and putting forth the paradox of not meeting yourself in another time. All of this is theory at best. However, recently several scientists have postulated new theories, based on the ideas of relativity and power and magnetic fields that are quite interesting. My placing these ideas into the 1970s is purely for fictional benefit.

JB Yanni was raised in a boisterous family with three other siblings in a quiet suburban town outside of Chicago. As a child she was always writing, drawing or reading. Oh, and climbing trees! Over time, this creativity focused on writing. After raising three children, and discovering all readers are not the same, JB wanted to tell a story that meant as much to readers as her childhood favorites meant and had some appeal to many different kinds of readers. This is where the time travel story began.

The Time Benders series follows the Fitzgerald siblings as they face trauma, life changes, and challenges. They begin time travel to try to bring their parents back, and begin to learn both about the pitfalls of time travel and about themselves. Each book shows how they face these challenges, and use time travel to answer questions, help others and discover not just history, but all they can accomplish together.

JB has also written a very personal story about her mother, Lee, who was diagnosed with Alzheimer's. It speaks to everyone of family, legacy and the fact that while our lives may be ordinary, there is a little extraordinary in us all.

When JB isn't writing, or reading, you will find her at the beach. In fact, if she could find a way to plug in her laptop, she would be there every day!